STORM RISING

STORM RISING

LINDA KAY SILVA

RISING
TIDE
PRESS

Rising Tide Press
3831 North Oracle Road
Tucson, AZ 85705
(520) 888-1140

Printed in the United States on acid-free paper.

Publisher's note:
All characters, places and situations in this book are fictitious
and any resemblance to persons (living or dead) is purely
coincidental.

Publisher's Acknowledgement:
The publisher is grateful to Eric Tobin for technical assistance
provided.

First printing April, 2000
10 9 8 7 6 5 4 3 2 1

Edited by Merryl Sloan
Book cover art: Lori Lieber graphic design, inc.

Silva, Linda Kay 1960-
        Storm Rising/ Linda Kay Silva
        p.cm
ISBN 1-883061-27-X
Library of Congress Control Number : pending

DEDICATION

This is for the three most important women in my life: my mother, who epitomizes unconditional love; my friend Delta, who constantly nourishes my creative soul; and for you, who know the value and importance of total acceptance. You love me just the way I am, flaws and all. If ever someone were truly appreciated for who they are, that would be me. Thank you all for that special and rare gift.

As Delta, Connie and Megan's lives change dramatically in this book, so does mine, and I'd like to thank the following individuals for supporting (and often contributing to) those changes.

Jo and Bill-for your love and friendship...does Billy know how lucky he is to have you?

Donna-through it all, we survived...and doesn't that just burn them all up? Good for us!

Ginny-your enthusiastic support has always made sharing with you so much fun!

Ernest-for showing the way. I'll always be grateful.

And finally...
Kelly and Sunnie-for loving your Mom enough to accept us... and for being the daughters I never thought I'd have. You're goofy, but I love you.

ONE

It was like coming out of anesthesia: blurry vision, voices drifting in and out like a radio signal losing frequency. Something moved above Delta's head, but she couldn't focus enough to see what it was. Her body was numb, and this strange, groggy feeling plagued her. Closing her bleary eyes, Delta tried to lick her dry, cracked lips, but even that simple gesture took more energy than she possessed. Opening her eyes once more, she noticed a hazy figure before her, like some cosmic ghost hovering between worlds.

When the misty figure dribbled water between Delta's parched lips, most of it ran down the sides of her face. Her parched mouth wasn't cooperating. Sighing heavily, Delta closed her eyes and tried to clear the cobwebs from her head. Her whole being felt on fire.

As the fever raged through her body, Delta floated. Sometimes she saw visions. Frequently, sleep gave a temporary peace from the nightmarish flashbacks she endured these last few...hours? days? How long had it been? Fever made everything impossible to decipher. What was real? What was a figment of the flames roaring through her body? Time both stood still and raced past.

Then the vision changed. Something happened when she jumped for the leg of the helicopter, but she didn't know what. All she knew was that darkness, like a moonless night, engulfed her entire being. It was so black and so cold; it was as if she'd been swallowed in the vacuum of outer space. Then, someone pulled her out of the Caribbean water in which she plunged.

Someone had saved her life, and in that moment, Delta knew she lived. Beyond that one memory, Delta's dreams were filled with blurry visions of the jungle, of Delta having to shoot a man in a warehouse, and of her lover, Megan Osbourne. Delta tossed her head and sighed, falling deeper into a sleep that knew only nightmares.

Megan stood at the large bay window of the Gran Hotel staring at the street below, her long blonde hair tied neatly in a ponytail. Remembering the last time Delta had run her hands through Megan's hair brought a rare smile to Megan's face. She loved it when Delta touched her anywhere. She had the most incredible touch, it was electrifying.

"Where are you?" Megan murmured, her eyes searching faces in the crowd. It had been three days since Delta had disappeared among the foaming waves of the blue Caribbean. Three long, grueling days of searching, of phone calls, of praying. Three days, and not one shred, not one sign that Delta Stevens had even been to Costa Rica. Three days of this living, breathing nightmare was beginning to take its toll on her.

Megan had thought that nothing in the world could match the horror of being kept a sexual slave for Colombians who had infiltrated Costa Rica's rain forest in search of gold unearthed after the 1991 earthquake. She didn't think there was anything worse that could happen to her than to be forced to have sex with a man again in order to stay alive. She couldn't have imagined a fate worse than scurrying through the dark rain forest, fleeing a band of soldiers who were all too eager to perform sexual atrocities on her again if they found her alive.

She had been wrong.

The greatest horror in her life was watching helplessly as the woman she loved plummeted hundreds of feet into the water after being shot twice by the pursuing Colombians. That horror multiplied as each day yielded no clues. Had she survived the fall? Had she drowned? Had she swum to shore, only to be recaptured by her pursuers? The questions taunted Megan.

Three days were an eternity when one did not know if one's lover was dead or alive. Three days of not knowing whether or not Delta was being brutalized or tortured was hell on earth for Megan, who would have surely changed places with her lover. Three days of trying not to think about a life without Delta was far worse than anything General Zahn had made her do. He could have skinned her alive, and the pain would have been nothing compared to the heart-wrenching anguish she had felt when Delta slipped from her grasp. A part of Megan was torn from her when Delta plummeted into the Caribbean.

Watching an old woman shuffle down the pot-holed street, Megan fought back the tears that so often threatened to roll down her cheeks. These moments of sorrow, these flashes of grief increased with every hour Delta remained missing.

Delta had to be alive. After almost three years together, and countless adventures, Megan believed with all her heart that she would feel it if Delta were dead. She had no doubt about the strength of the ties that bound them together. They were each other's heart and soul. They had suffered the loss of a dear friend, and they had seen their own circle of friends grow. Together, they had brought down cop killers, and taken care of Connie and Gina when a psychopath threatened their lives. Delta had supported Megan as she left the "oldest profession" in order to get her business degree. Their lives were so deeply intertwined, Megan did not know where she ended and Delta began.

But there was another whose bond with Delta Stevens was equally as unbreakable. There beat another heart, which, most assuredly, would know the moment Storm's spirit ceased to exist. Another woman in Delta Stevens life existed in this living hell with Megan, suffering the ache of losing Delta in that water. That woman was Connie Rivera, Delta's best friend and colleague. If anyone would know the moment Delta's courageous heart stopped beating, it would be Connie.

Turning from the window, Megan studied the diminutive Latina who had not slept for more than two of the last seventy-two hours. Like some whirling dervish, Connie had set into motion a myriad of agencies to ensure that anything and everything that could be done to find Delta would be done.

One phone call after another, Connie had asked, yelled, and sometimes pleaded for people's help. The American embassy was useless. After all, who really believed that drug runners from Colombia were mining for gold in the heart of Costa Rica's largest rain forest and using kidnapped women from all over the world? It was that disbelief creating the void of assistance Connie was seeking.

The American Embassy had told them to wait until the Drug Enforcement Agency arrived to take their statements. It was all Connie could do to keep from laughing. The DEA(she believed) was owned by the cartels! Who did they think they were kidding? She wasn't about to wait around to step into a body bag. The run-around she had received was a joke, and Connie had left the embassy realizing just how on their own they were. But then, she should have known this.

When their helicopter landed in Panama hours after Delta plunged into the sea, the Panamanians merely shook their heads and looked away, so scared were they that the individuals Megan spoke of were part of one of the most powerful cartels.

They had received absolutely no help from the Panamanian government, and, much to their surprised, were asked when they would be leaving. All the Panamanians did for them was patch up their wounds and send them back to Costa Rica.

Connie had even contacted a friend in Washington, DC, who sadly explained to her that relations between Latin American countries and the US were tenuous at best since the banana embargo had stirred up anti-American sentiments. Even her own government had failed to offer assistance, and, since then, Connie had sought help from any place possible. She didn't care if she had to hire convicts to scour the rain forest and sea floor for Delta; she wasn't leaving Latin America without her best friend. Period.

Even now, she was pacing back and forth with a phone in her right hand and a clipboard in the other, speaking in the clipped Spanish Megan had become accustomed to hearing from her. In a word, Consuela Maria Dolores Rivera was amazing. Fluent in five languages and possessing a black belt in karate, there appeared to be no limit to what she could do.

Until now.

Now, not even Connie's genius-level IQ could locate Delta, and that was beginning to wear down her normally persistent tenacity. In the three years they'd known each other, Megan had never seen Connie so close to panic, and it was beginning to frighten Megan. Connie was usually so calm under pressure, but this void of answers drove her closer to the brink of terror. Staring at her friend now, Megan wondered how much time they had before Connie hit the wall.

"Gracias," Connie said, hanging up and immediately dialing again. Holding the phone against her ear with her shoulder, Connie's eyes met Megan's. Try as she might, there was no hiding the fear and desperation in Connie's eyes.

"Gotta call Gina again," she said, tearing her gaze from Megan's.

Sighing, Megan nodded slightly, still watching Connie as she paced across the floor. Connie was more than Delta's best friend; so much more. Together, those two women had shared a part of life no one would ever truly understand. More than soul mates, Delta Stevens and Connie Rivera were almost one and the same. They shared a connection that Megan could never fully comprehend, but that did not prevent her from appreciating it. They were two equal halves of something mystical, something magical, and Megan feared what might happen to Connie if Delta really were...really were...Megan shuddered at the word hanging on the edge of her mind.

"I love you. Be careful," Connie said, hanging up the phone. Tying her waist-long black hair into a knot behind her, she turned to Megan, her face a mask of anxiety.

"Don't tell me," Megan said, stepping up to Connie. At six feet, Megan towered over every woman she knew.

"I couldn't talk her out of it," Connie said, shaking her head. "She has a flight coming in tomorrow."

Megan's eyebrows rose in question. "I thought you both agreed she should stay home."

Releasing a pained sigh, Connie shrugged. The dark circles under her eyes and the weariness of her countenance explained why Gina was on her way. Connie tried to sound okay on the phone, but her voice sounded as exhausted as she looked.

"Couldn't fool her tonight," Connie said, lying down on the bed and rubbing her face. "She heard right through me. You don't stay together as long as we have and not know each other's voices. She wouldn't take no for an answer."

"And the baby? Isn't flying dangerous for a fetus seven months along?"

Connie shook her head. "The baby will be fine. I just wish Gina had listened to reason. She shouldn't come here. There isn't anything she can do except..."

"Except hold you together, my friend. You're starting to come apart at the seams. That's what she's hearing. You won't admit it, Con, but you need her here."

"She should still listen to reason. There's the baby to consider."

Megan sat on the bed and held Connie's hand. "Since when have any of us been reasonable? You're the most important person in her life, even more so than your baby. If the positions were reversed, could she stop you from coming?"

Connie shook her head sadly. "Not a chance." Connie barely smiled. "She made a good point that we could use someone as our home base. But she's not, and I repeat, not going into that jungle. I don't care what she says. Going into that goddamned jungle is out of the question for her."

Megan squeezed Connie's hand. "And are we?"

Connie's eyes narrowed as she looked up at Megan. "Are we what? Going back?"

"Uh huh."

Looking up at the ceiling, Connie shrugged, heaving another pained sigh. "I don't see any other choice, do you?" Locking eyes with Megan, Connie reached out and squeezed her hand in return. "It's been three days, Megan, and we haven't turned up a damn thing. She's out there somewhere. I know it."

The rain forest, on a postcard, or from a plane, it looks like the Garden of Eden, with its multitude of greens and the vibrancy of life. The rain forest is something the primary school kids back home are learning about protecting. They are shown beautiful tropical pictures and azure-blue waterfalls. To many, the rain forest is paradise.

It needs protection from logging, and its wildlife ecosystems need protection from pollution. But in reality, when poachers are hunting endangered species, when drug runners use it to hide out, and when your lover is lost in it, it is anything but paradise.

"I'll go to hell and battle Satan himself if it means finding Delta."

Connie nodded. "Knowing what you know of General Zahn, that's exactly what we might have to do."

Megan stared into Connie's coffee-brown eyes and knew that, for all her apparent bravado, Connie Rivera was scared to death.

"You don't think he has her, do you?"

Connie shook her head. "If he does, she's dead."

Megan visibly recoiled. In the three days since Delta had fallen, no one had used Delta's name and that final word in a sentence together. Pulling her hand away, Megan straightened up and walked back to the window. She had not asked Connie what her heart told her; for fear that she wasn't prepared for the answer. But now, now that they had decided to go back into the forest, she had to ask. She had to know. Turning from the window, Megan gritted her teeth and asked the question she knew they had all been asking inside themselves. "Is she?"

Connie slowly rose to one elbow, not taking her eyes from Megan's. She had wondered when Megan was going to ask; wondered if Megan had the same sense that she had about Delta's spirit. Part Native American, Connie believed in the powers of the spirit, and she believed that her spirit would know, unequivocally, if and when Delta Stevens ceased to exist. It was part of the incredible bond they shared, and Connie would bet her life on it. She would know the instant the light no longer shone in Delta's eyes.

Shaking her head, Connie's sigh matched Megan's. "No, Meg, I don't think she is. I'd know if she was. Delta's alive out there somewhere, and it's up to us to find her."

"You think she made it out of the water?"

Connie grinned for the first time in three days. "I'm sure she's washed up on some shore somewhere, giving the natives grief."

⊕

Again, Delta forced her eyes open as foreign words splashed her ears like the tide on a beach.

"Mayor. Oh." The voice sounded like it had seen the better part of a century.

"Si. Fiebe abajo."

A soft pair of hands lifted Delta's heavy head and gently spooned some lime-tasting medicine into her mouth. It had that medicinal after-taste of a syrup her mother had once forced down her throat when she had pneumonia. That medicine had given her horrendous hallucinations of breathing walls and purple monkeys. To this day, those visions were as real to Delta as any memory. She could only hope such visions could not locate her here. Wherever here was.

Prying open one eye, Delta tried, unsuccessfully, to focus on the owner of the softer, younger voice on the other end of the spoon. At least two women appeared to be caring for her, that much she knew. But...what was wrong with her? Delta could not bring forth any clear memories. The visions visited her often, and the effort she expended to understand them was exhausting her.

Fatigued by the effort and aided by the medicine, Delta closed her eyes and floated away again before succumbing to the cloudy inner filmstrip of her memory bank.

She saw herself running to Megan, who was yelling, but Delta couldn't hear her. The whirling sound of the helicopter blades was like white noise. In her fevered visions Delta pushed to reach the helicopter, but something prevented her. Rolling to her side, Delta's breath came in ragged bursts.

One year, while playing softball in college, Delta was attempting to steal second base. Half way there her hamstring snapped and rolled up the back of her leg like a window shade. She had crumpled to the ground, incapable of standing. That was sort of how her leg felt as she leaped for the leg of the helicopter as it took off. She managed to grab the leg as the copter whirled off, but then something happened. Megan reached for her, and just as their hands touched, Megan let go. Delta rolled back over and stretched her arms, her fingers clawing at the sheet.

No. Megan would never have let Delta fall. One minute, she was being pulled up into the helicopter, and the next...Delta fought the fog and haze drifting in and out of her mind. Something had caused her to let go of Megan's hand.

"I was shot," Delta muttered, remembering now the painful impact as the bullet ripped through her shoulder. She hadn't been stung at all, and it wasn't a torn hamstring, either. She'd been shot twice, once in the leg and once in the shoulder, which had forced her to release Megan's hand. Megan hadn't let go. Delta had released her grasp to keep from pulling Megan over with her. No wonder she was feverish. Two bullet wounds and near drowning were wreaking havoc on her body. Trying to force her heavy eyelids open, Delta felt a pair of hands gently press on her shoulders.

"Dormir," the soft voice implored, as fingertips lightly fluttered across Delta's eyelids and down her cheeks. "Dormir."

Closing her eyes, Delta murmured, "Sleep. Can't...sleep. Gotta...go...back." But the medicine was stronger than she, and Delta settled her heavy head back into the pillow. When sleep mercifully carried her away, Delta dreamed of a thatched hut, a medicine man, and making love with Megan.

"Go...back," Connie mumbled in her sleep.

"Shh," Megan whispered, leaning over and brushing some stray hair from Connie's sleepy face. Fear and caffeine had been fueling Connie's empty tank, and Megan worried that Connie would work herself into the ground if she didn't slow down and get some rest. For three days they had been searching the coastlines of Costa Rica and Panama, combing nearby towns and port villages. They had sent their good friend, Josh, to check out hospitals and police stations all along the coast, but not one person remembered seeing a 5'9" brunette with green eyes and two bullet holes. Still, it was inconceivable to Megan that Delta had simply drowned in the sea. Her body, or at least some clothing would have washed ashore by now. There would be something offering itself up as a piece of evidence. Three days had yielded nothing. She had simply disappeared. Maybe Connie was right. Maybe it was time to go back into that jungle and look for her.

Maybe they were the only people who could help her. Closing her eyes, Megan released a fractured sigh. She could not believe how desperately her heart missed Delta.

Delta had come to Costa Rica to find Megan, who had been abducted by General Zahn and used for slave labor in gold mines that had been discovered after several large earthquakes hit the tiny rain forest country. It was no surprise to Megan that Delta had dropped everything to come find her in an environment that was as foreign to Delta as the bottom of the ocean. It was also no surprise that Delta brought Connie, Josh, and Sal with her. Delta was nothing if not resourceful, and she had utilized everyone and everything at her disposal to get Megan out of the rain forest.

And now, Delta was lost. The irony tore at Megan's heart until her eyes filled with more tears, and a sigh slid jerkily from her, prompting Connie to stir.

Connie's eyes slowly opened, and she stretched, yawned, and sat up. "What time is it? Damn, you shouldn't have let me..."

"We have to go back, Con."

Getting off the bed, Connie strode over to a large topographical map of Costa Rica pinned to the wall and studied it for a long, quiet moment. Delta had fallen over an area marked by blue pins. Gold pins marked where they suspected Zahn and his mining operation were. There was a third color, a green grouping of pins that Connie pointed to. She knew there was only one way to find out if Delta was still alive. One way, that is, if you believed.

"The Bribri," Megan murmured, nodding. "That's what I'm thinking."

Connie nodded back. "She's one of them now. If anyone can find her in the jungle, they can." Connie studied the map closely. "You know, the Native Americans have always known the power of the spirit. It's part of our culture that even the Europeans couldn't drive out. I believe the Bri can help us find Delta, but do you? Are you willing to believe in something outside your frame of reference?"

Megan looked from Connie to the map and back again. She'd seen, firsthand, what believing could do. She had believed in Delta; believed that she would come for her.

Believing that the Bri might somehow know Delta's whereabouts was easier than she thought. "At this point, Con, I'm so desperate, I'd believe in Santa Claus if it meant finding Delta."

Connie released a deep breath. "That's it then. We've tried every conventional means at our disposal. I suppose it's time to do what we do best: make up our own rules."

"It's been pretty successful so far."

Connie barely grinned as she picked up her clipboard and studied the names and numbers on it. "We'll pick Sal up from the hospital, get Gina from the airport, tell Josh what we're going to need and then..."

"We're going back into that goddamned rain forest."

Stepping through the hospital room door, Connie quickly approached the tiny woman wearing green army fatigues with a matching baseball cap. Sweeping Sal off her feet, Connie hugging her tightly. "Hey there, slugger. How are you feeling today?"

"I feel like kicking some Colombian ass," Sal said, grinning and forcing a deeply embedded dimple to show in her right cheek.

Connie held the small woman close to her. "You look better than you did yesterday. You feeling better?"

"Much better," Sal said, hugging Connie back. "My butt only hurts when I sit on it wrong. Wanna see the wound?" Sal grabbed at her pants and was beginning to lower them when Connie and Megan looked at each other and grimaced.

"No, thanks. Maybe some other time," Connie answered, winking at Megan.

Sal shrugged. "Suit yourselves, but it's really a cool thing. Look." Sal reached down and grabbed her father's dog tags, which she'd worn since his death in Viet Nam. Attached to the chain, hanging next to the dog tags was a compressed bullet. "Guess where this came from?"

Megan shook her head. "Gross. You had them save the bullet?"

Sal nodded proudly, and when she did, her short, reddish hair bobbed beneath her army cap. Sal was the only woman Megan knew who looked at home in regulation army fatigues.

"You bet! Think of all the conversations I can start by showing people my scar and the bullet that made it."

Connie shook her head. "Megan's right. You're gross."

"Maybe, but I'm alive to tell about it." Sal peered toward the door. "Where's the big guy? He hasn't been in to see me this morning to bring me my ration of real food. If you thought hospital food in American hospitals was bad...sheesh."

"He's bringing the car around and signing you out."

"Is he packing?"

Connie shrugged. "I don't think so. The weapons he's getting..."

"Not weapons, goofus! Food! Is he carrying any real food?"

Connie couldn't help but grin at the small woman who had risked her life to come help Delta find Megan. It wasn't the first time, either. Sal and Josh had come into their lives during a caper when they needed Sal's impressive electronics abilities. No one could have predicted that they would have to kill two men in order to save Delta's life, but they did. In cold blood. Josh had spent time in the forests of Viet Nam and his jungle expertise had already proved invaluable here in Latin America. With their help, Connie and Delta had managed to find Megan, but as they were escaping the Colombians, Sal was shot; an experience Sal intended to share with the rest of the known world.

"I've seen that look on your face before, Con," Sal said, suddenly perking up. "What's the plan? Man, laying around has made me stir crazy."

Megan put her arms around Sal's shoulders, towering over the would-be soldier. "Crazy enough to go back into the jungle?"

Suddenly the door was flung open, and a big, bearded man filled the entire doorway. "Did I just hear you say we're going back into the jungle?"

"Josh!" Sal released Megan and threw her arms around the large man's neck and hugged him. He, too, was wearing green army fatigues. In his left hand, he carried a plain brown bag.

"How you feeling today, Salamander?" Josh asked, handing the bag to Sal, who ripped it open and stared down at the contents.

"Donuts! All right!"

Josh grinned, as Sal tore into a glazed donut, his love and adoration evident in his eyes.

Sal's father had saved Josh's life, as well as the lives of four other young men, before being killed by the Viet Cong. The Cong not only killed Sal's father, but they had cut his head off and rammed it on a pole to parade around. The men whose lives he'd saved swore to watch out for the little girl whose daddy would never return.

They managed to keep their promise, making sure Sal wanted for nothing. While Josh lived with Sal and made sure she finished high school, the other men started a college fund for her. When she graduated from college with a degree in electrical engineering, they all bought her car. Sal may have lost a father, but she had gained four big brothers who took care of her every need. Josh and Sal were each other's family; a family that eventually extended to Delta, Connie, and Megan.

"I'm feeling good enough to go back after Delta, if that's the question."

Megan stepped up to Josh and quietly asked, "No luck on the water?'

Josh shook his head sadly. He had managed to commandeer a boat from a local fisherman and had spent from morning to dusk on the sea, hoping to spot any sign of Delta. Each day, he had returned exhausted, darkened by the constant sun, and with no news.

"I suppose no news is good news, eh?" Josh asked softly.

Megan barely nodded. "We want to go back to the Bri village. Con and I think they might be able to help."

Josh looked confused. "But she went down in the water. It only makes sense..."

"Nothing makes much sense where Delta Stevens is concerned," Connie said, and she, more than the others, would know. For seven years, she and Delta had been best friends. They were partners in crime in the River Valley Police Department, and one didn't move without the other knowing which direction. While Delta was a beat cop, Connie was an informations expert whose job was to track down evidence in a more technological fashion. Both had different strengths and varied weaknesses, yet their relationship bordered on the paranormal. Connie was the thinker, the contemplator, and the brains.

She looked before she leaped. Delta, on the other hand, was the doer, the hero, and the champion of those less fortunate than she. Delta leaped before she looked.

Delta was the warrior, the physical one who had killed two men, escaped a fiery death as she saved children, and pushed herself through the unfamiliar terrain of a rain forest in order to save the woman she loved.

Touching Josh's shoulder, Connie said, "Delta became part of the Bri in a ritual that made her a Bribri warrior. Megan and I are of the opinion that Shaman may be able to tell us where she is."

Sal took her hat off and scratched her head. Sal was as secular and as pragmatic as they came, and she had a hard time believing anything that wasn't right in front of her face. "We're that desperate?"

Connie and Megan nodded. "I don't know where else to turn," Connie said, her voice betraying emotions she was trying desperately to hide. "They know the jungle better than anyone. If Delta is anywhere near it, they'll know where to look."

"Besides," Megan added, "Delta's not the only one who needs our help."

Sal groaned. "Oh, don't tell me..."

Megan nodded. "I made a promise to Siobhan that if I got free, I would bring help back. With or without Delta, I don't intend to break that promise."

"Tell me we're taking some of the Panamanian army with us," Josh said, knowing full well the impossibility of that. The Panamanians had made their position crystal clear. They wanted nothing to do with Colombians, gold, or crazy Americans in search of their friend.

Connie shook her head. "I wish we could, Josh, but General Zahn is well known here. It would be a mistake to trust anyone who might be on his payroll."

"And that list most likely covers ambassadors, cops, judges, you name it." Megan watched Sal stuff a donut in her mouth. "People who underestimate the power of the cartel wind up as fish food."

Sal glanced over at Josh as she wiped her mouth. Unspoken words traveled between the two. Though there had never been anything sexual between them, Josh and Sal were as much mates as any married couple, and they knew what each was thinking. "So, what you're telling us is we're going back into the jungle. Alone. Again."

Nodding, Connie pulled a map out and spread it on the bed. It was another topographical map of the terrain of La Amistad Park, a large rain forest area in Costa Rica and Panama. La Amistad, which meant Friendship Park, had been anything but friendly.

"Where'd you get that?" Josh asked, impressed.

"Connie hasn't slowed down since she landed that helicopter." Megan rested her hand on Connie's shoulder. It was a rock beneath her fingers. She and that damned computer are miracle workers."

Flattening the map, Connie pointed to some green marks. "As best as I could get from the locals, the Bri's village is in this vicinity. Considering where we started in Rivas, and where we ended up, I'd say this was where the Colombians were when we left them."

Everyone studied the map as Connie moved her finger over it. "Delta fell in here. See these lines? They show the natural current. If the current carried her, she could have ended up over in this area."

"But I've been through there a dozen times," Josh said. "And we didn't see anything. There ain't a town, a village, not even a dock. Nada."

"It's possible she could have made her way to shore and gone back to the jungle where she knew she could get help. If I were Delta, that's what I'd do."

"And risk being killed by the Colombians?" Josh asked, reaching for the bag in Sal's hands. Sal slapped at his hand before reaching in and handing him one of the donuts she didn't want.

Connie nodded. "She's hurt. She needs help, and she knows the authorities could very well be on Zahn's payroll. If Delta is going to turn to someone, it's going to be the Bri."

Josh studied Connie a moment as silence hung in the stale hospital air. "You know her better than anyone. If you think that's where she is, then I say it's a go."

Sal pulled another donut from the bag she kept out of Josh's reach. "So, you want to find the Bri and then what?"

"See if they have Delta. If they do, that's one less thing we have to worry about."

Sal's eyebrows raised. " One less?"

Megan stepped up and nodded. "I made a promise to get those people help, Sal. Once we know that Delta is alive and safe, then I have a promise to keep."

"That promise could be suicide, Megan. Those men have high-powered weapons, scopes, and communication. What have we got?" Sal bit hard into the donut.

Megan looked over at Josh. "Josh, what have we got?"

Josh cleared his throat. "I got my hands on a couple of M16s, a Beretta sniper, and a few HKs. Oh, yeah. I also got a Ruger Mark II with a silencer. He sort of threw it into the bargain. We went with rifles for accuracy and sniping. A handgun won't do shit in the jungle."

Connie nodded. "Anything else?"

A slow grin spread on Josh's face. "Two really nifty pairs of night goggles. I ain't about to go back in there in the dark again."

"Night goggles?" Sal piped in. "Can we afford those?"

Josh shrugged. "They're on loan."

Sal stared slack-jawed at Josh. "And just how in the hell did you get your big oven mitts on those type of weapons?"

Josh swiped the bag of donuts and grinned. "Gotta few buddies down here who, well, let's say they make a killing selling rifles to the highest bidders."

"A killing, eh? How come you never told me about them?".

Josh shrugged. "These aren't the kind of guys you talk about and live, Salamander. They mean business."

Connie nodded. "And so do we. I really appreciate you going to bat for us, Josh."

Josh studied the donut he was holding. "I pulled Smelly's fat outta the fire once. Guys from Nam never forget. It's just how things are with us."

All three women repeated, "Smelly?"

"Long, gross story. Anyway, Smelly can line us up with a boat, too. That little old fisherman's boat is just too damn slow. If we're going back in, we're gonna need a boat that's got some guts to her. Just give me the word, Meg."

Everyone turned to Megan, who stared down at the map. For a long, silent moment, she said nothing. Then, she looked up from the map and made eye contact with each of them.

"I know it's a long shot, but I believe in my heart that Delta's alive. I'll understand if you don't want to take any more risks. After all..."

"After all, what's another piece of lead in my cute bum?"

Megan grinned at Sal and Josh. "You guys are the best."

Sal put her arm around Josh and hugged him. "Yes, we are. And that's exactly why we're going to bring your gal home."

Home. Delta tried to remember the last time she was there. Who was feeding her cat? And how in the hell was...what was his name? That guy that took Miles' place as her partner? Carducci. Yeah, that was it. Delta wondered how he was doing all by himself, as she forced her eyelids open and woke completely up. It took a moment to focus, but she managed to clear her vision enough to see an old woman hunched over her. Long, white hair hung loosely over her shoulders, framing deep wrinkles and caramel-colored skin. She was the oldest woman Delta had ever seen.

Trying to orient herself, Delta looked slowly around, her eyes aching from the fever. There was a bamboo fan rotating fitfully overhead, and a glassless window on one wall. The old woman was speaking Spanish in a low, gravelly voice, and Delta wasn't coherent enough to make out any of the words. She was awake enough to know she was, indeed, alive. And if she really was alive, and this was no fevered vision, then Connie would also know she was alive.

Connie. The image of her swam before Delta, making her smile for the first time in forever. Surely Connie would be calculating this very minute how to find Delta. She would be planning and scheming, bossing everyone around in an effort to locate her best friend, and Connie would not rest until she did. On that, Delta would bet her life. The thought of Connie frantically racing to and fro erased the grin, and warm tears ran down the sides of Delta's face.

The old woman bent over to look in Delta's eyes.

"Buena," Delta said, in a voice that didn't sound like her own.

The old woman smiled a near-toothless grin. "Flora!" she shouted, as she turned and hobbled from the room.

Slowly sitting up, Delta felt a surge of pain in her shoulder. "Shit," she cried, lying back down. From outside the wooden structure, Delta heard the rapid voices of the old woman and someone else. When she heard the door open, Delta looked up and saw one of the most beautiful women she'd ever seen. With waist-length shimmering black hair and smooth, bronze skin, she looked exactly like what Delta thought Pocahontas might have looked like, only more mature.

"Buenos," Delta said, wishing she knew more words than the dozen or so in her repertoire.

Pocahontas smiled and sat next to the bed. This was the woman Delta had seen earlier, when she was swimming in the fever. She could tell, not by her appearance, but by her energy. There was something different about her.

"Feel better?" Pocahontas asked with a Spanish accent.

Delta's eyebrows shot up. "You speak English?"

Pocahontas held her thumb and index finger an inch apart. "Poquito. It is a long time since I say it."

Delta nodded. "You speak it just fine."

Pocahontas blushed. "Gracias."

Slowly sitting up, Delta ignored the throb of her shoulder and the ache in her head. "Where am I?"

"A small island name Sura."

Delta looked around the barren shack. The only things in this room were a bed and the fan.

The walls and floor were wooden, and a small light bulb hung nakedly from one wall. She had been in a Costa Rican, or Tico home before, yet none had been quite as sparsely decorated as this place.

Pocahontas grinned at Delta. "My father has boat. See you fall, pick you up. Simple."

Delta grinned. In her life, nothing had ever been simple. "Your father has a boat?"

"Si.."

"He wouldn't have a telephone, would he?"

Pocahontas shook her head. "No. Well, we did..."

"But?"

Her eyes glazed over with fear. "The Colombians," she said in a tiny voice that Delta had to strain to hear.

Just the word brought Delta completely upright, a flash of pain igniting in her shoulder. The Colombians? In an instant, so many images fast-forwarded through her memory. They were why she was here! They were the ones who shot her; shot her as she was running. The memories were still fuzzy, but Delta knew from previous experiences with concussions that they would clear up soon enough. "The Colombians? Tell me about them."

Pocahontas glanced at the door, as if she were afraid they might walk in any minute. "They come. Tell Papa to pick bags each four days."

"Your father has to pick bags up from the Colombians every four days?" Delta's head was now throbbing in unison with her shoulder as she struggled to clear her memory.

"Si.. Then a boat come and take bags from Papa. "

"And they ruined your phone."

"Si.. Very mean. Scare me and Papa."

Delta nodded, suddenly seeing Megan on a rock in the middle of a lake. Then, that image turned into a crocodile that had saved Delta's life. And that crocodile transformed into a tall, sturdy-looking man named General Zahn. The rest of the memories flooded back like a dam had been breached, and Delta remembered exactly why she was there and how she had come to be in that warm Caribbean water.

"They're pretty scary folks." Delta could see fear in the woman's eyes, and they reminded her of the fear she'd seen in Megan's. The memories of what Zahn and the Colombians did to Megan made her sick to her stomach. With the fever subsiding, her thoughts became sharper, and Delta was beginning to differentiate between memories and visions. Neither of them was very appealing.

"They are bad. Muy malo." Pocahontas's eyes grew larger.

"Did your father say what happened after I fell?" Delta was remembering plunging into the water and resurfacing in a whirl of waves created by the helicopter. She'd inhaled countless pints of salt water trying to rise above the waves, but it was no use. She had been weakened by the second shot and the fight in her was all but gone.

"Si.. The heli...heli..."

"Helicopter."

"Si.. The helicopter fly away."

"If you are so afraid of the Colombians, why did your papa help me?"

"Papa no like Colombians. Helicopter is Colombian, but you no Colombian. Entiende ?"

Delta nodded. "Entiendo. When was this?"

"Three days."

Delta nearly fell out of the bed. "Three days ago?" Her voice rose so loud, she scared herself. "I've been here for three fucking days?"

Pocahontas's eyes grew wider, and Delta realized she'd scared her as well. "I'm sorry," Delta said softly, reaching out to touch Pocahontas's hand. "It's just...I just can't believe..."

Pocahontas nodded. "Caliente fever. Mi abuela..." Pocahontas struggled to find the English equivalent. When she did, her eyes lit up. "My grandmother take two...uh, two..."

"Bullets?"

"Si. Here and here." Pocahontas pointed to Delta's shoulder and leg.

Delta remembered. As she had made her way to the helicopter, something had bitten her in the leg, and she had stumbled.

She'd been shot, and when she had jumped for the helicopter, she'd been hit again, lost her grip, and plummeted into the blue abyss below.

"And your grandmother took them out?"

"Si. Then, you get fever."

Delta looked into the warm, brown eyes searching her face. "You took care of me."

"Si."

Delta extended her hand to the young woman who, quite possibly, had saved her life. "My name is Delta."

"Flora." Flora took her hand and gave it a slight squeeze.

"It's a beautiful name. Thank you, Flora, for taking care of me."

Flora bowed her head in a sincere, humble gesture. "Papa say you bring good fortune."

Slowly lowering her feet to the floor, Delta suddenly realized she was completely naked. "Good fortune?" she asked, covering her exposed breasts and feeling silly for doing so. The blue body paint Shaman had painted on her during her initiation would forever be a part of her body, and she saw Flora staring at it in awe.

Delta had been shot and left in the Caribbean to die and Flora's father considered her lucky? Her head felt like someone was pounding it with a drum...or was that like a drum? It didn't matter which. She ached from stem to stern, and there was only one thing on her mind: She had to get word to Connie and Megan that she was alive. Suddenly, a huge ball of fear found its way to Delta's throat.

"The helicopter. Did it make it?"

Flora cocked her head. "Make it?"

Delta nodded vehemently. "Yes, yes, did it get free?"

Flora nodded. "Si. Papa say it fly away, smoking."

Delta heaved a sigh of relief. Then they had made it. Maybe they were the lucky ones. "Why does your Papa think I am good fortune? I wound up in the sea."

Flora rose, stepped from the room, and returned with Delta's clothes, blood free, and cleaner than when she'd worn them last. She handed the clothes to Delta. "He see this." Flora reached out and fingered the jaguar tooth necklace hanging around Delta's neck.

"This? I don't understand." Delta looked at the tooth and sighed. "So much had happened to her since she'd left River Valley.

"Papa save Bri warrior," she said, pointing to Delta. "Bring good fortune."

Delta touched the necklace. The tooth was cool and smooth. The Bribri tribe had managed to reunite Delta and Megan and, in the process, made Delta's spirit a member of their tribe. Shaman had said she had a warrior spirit that would bring strength to their diminishing people. The ceremony had been one of the highlights in Delta's distinguished life, at least, what she could recall of it. There had been an odd mixture of realism and visions that night, and Delta hadn't even begun to sort through it all.

What she did know was that she was now, and would always remain, a Bri warrior, whether she was in the rain forest or back at the River Valley Police Department.

Delta nodded in understanding. It appeared Shaman had still been watching over her when she had fallen, for how else could she explain Flora's father being there in time to pull Delta's ass out of the water before she drowned or bled to death? "Where is your father now?"

Flora pointed. "Fix boat. Hit a rock bring you in."

Good fortune, eh?

"Maybe I can help." Delta started to rise but felt dizzy and quickly sat back down. "Maybe not."

Flora nodded, holding Delta's shirt out for her to put on. "Still healing."

Nodding, Delta closed her eyes for a minute to think as she struggled into her shirt. She felt Flora's soft hand touch her cheeks as she buttoned up the bullet-holed shirt. Opening her eyes, she found Flora gazing admiringly at her.

"Never before meet a woman warrior," Flora said shyly.

Delta smiled softly. She sure didn't feel like much of a warrior. All she had managed to do was get shot, fall in the drink, and wind up on some tiny island who knew where? If she truly was a warrior, she had to start thinking like one and get herself off the island and back into the game. For surely, Connie, Megan, Sal and Josh were worried sick wondering what had happened to her. Delta had known that feeling when she received that horrible call that Megan was missing all those days ago. Had it only been days? It felt like months.

"When will your father return for the gold?"

"Manana."

"I must go with him. I have to get to the mainland. Those men must be stopped."

Flora nodded and patted Delta's good shoulder. "I tell him. Where you go then?"

Delta thought for a moment, her head slowly becoming accustomed to throbbing. Where would she go? She needed to make sure that the Colombians were finally, irrevocably stopped. She needed to get help. There was only one place to go. "Where else? Back to the Bri."

"The Bri are the only ones we can trust," Connie explained to Gina as they drove back to the hotel from the airport. Gina reached over and took Connie's hand before trying to adjust her weight to a more comfortable position.

"So, you go back in there to find them, even though the Colombians may still be there."

Connie looked at Gina's pregnant body and nodded. While it was wonderful to see her, their reunion was bittersweet, as Connie replayed the last three days of hunting for Delta. "There isn't another choice, hon."

"There's always another choice, Connie." Gina was in private practice as a psychologist, and consistently tried to get Connie and Delta to see that there were always other choices in a crisis. Gina had expressed her fears to Connie that one day, Delta would make the wrong choice, and it would mean the end of her life or someone else's. Connie had retorted that people made those decisions every day, whether they were cops or not. Still, Gina always tried to be the voice of reason whenever Delta pulled Connie into one of her schemes.

"There are more people who need our help, Gene," Megan offered softly from the back seat. "We're going back for Delta. We're going back after everyone. It's what she would want. It's what she would do. It's what's right."

Gina shook her head. "I understand that, but don't you think the odds of finding one person in a jungle that size seems a little...impossible?"

Connie squeezed Gina's hand. "Normally, I'd agree. But we managed to find Megan, and with the help of the Bri, we should have no problem finding Zahn again."

"Then, you're going to their village first?"

Connie nodded. "That's the plan."

Gina cocked her head. "You call that a plan?"

Connie nodded again. "It's the best we can do."

Gina brought Connie's hand to her lips and kissed the back of it. "You're going in search of a tribe of people that even the Costa Ricans have a hard time finding? Why doesn't that make me feel better?"

Connie sighed as she pulled in front of the Gran Hotel. "Finding the Bri will enable us to find both Delta and the Colombians in one fell swoop. It really is our best hope." Connie watched Josh amble up to the car. The Costa Ricans on the street were constantly staring at him because of his enormous size.

Opening the car door, Connie hopped out. Josh had showered and his hair was slicked back. "How's Sal doing, really?"

Josh opened the trunk of the car and shrugged. "Honestly? I think her leg hurts like hell, but she's not about to let a little pain keep her from helping you guys. She's mighty fond of Delta, and, well, to be honest, there's a certain Colombian she'd like to see pushin' up daisies. I wouldn't worry too much about Sal. She's a fighter." As Josh hefted Gina's luggage from the trunk, he grunted under its weight. "What in the hell you got in here?"

"Eddie and some other equipment, "Gina replied.

"Eddie?" Josh queried, raising a bushy eyebrow.

"My laptop computer," Connie answered. "With this baby, we'll be able to retrieve information and track down data without making the Panamanians, Costa Ricans, Colombians or anyone else suspicious."

Josh gently set the luggage down. "Good thinking. Who knows how many government officials this bastard Zahn owns. Rumor has it that the cartels even have a number of our own government representatives in their back pocket."

Once they got back to their room, Connie flipped open the luggage and unpacked Eddie. "Now, we don't need anybody to help us get info. With Eddie, I can get in and out of places to retrieve information, and no one will be the wiser." Megan peered over Connie's shoulder as the computer clicked and whirred. "Isn't technology incredible these days?"

Connie nodded and then turned to Josh. "Smelly get us a boat?"

Josh nodded and joined Megan in looking over Connie's shoulder. "Taken care of."

"And no one can trace it or the weapons to us?"

Josh shook his head. "Not without a fucking crystal ball."

Placing a pillow under her back and trying to get comfortable after the nine-hour flight, Gina let out a loud sigh. "Why would that matter, honey?"

Not taking her eyes off the screen, Connie started typing." The less anyone knows of our existence down here, the better. It's unfortunate the Panamanians had to know we're here, but that couldn't be avoided. Zahn could have people looking for us, or someone could get wind of what we're doing and try to stop us."

Josh nodded. "Things don't work down here the way they do in the States. The less we're seen or heard from, the better."

Connie continued typing away. "Okay, so we have weapons, a boat, and Eddie. Now, Megan saw a phone in General Zahn's trailer. That phone could be his undoing."

Megan winced at the unwanted and very painful memory of General Zahn's trailer; one of the many places he had forced her to have sex. During one of those horrid sessions, she had noticed a phone and a laptop on his desk, with a generator nearby. "It was there, all right. His is not some amateurish operation. He came fully equipped for a long stay in the jungle."

Connie nodded and turned from the computer to Gina. Her lover's belly showed the bulge of a baby they had waited years to create, and she was unsure of how she felt about Gina being there. On one hand, they needed someone to stay at a home base, and on the other...Well, what did it matter? She was here, and that was that.

"The idea I've been thinking about, hon, is for Eddie to locate as closely as possible either the Bri village, or Zahn's encampment. With these great topo maps, satellites, and my buddies on the Internet, we should be able to come within a half mile or so of their exact locations."

Gina looked up at the map on the wall. "And then?"

"Then, we go kick ass," Sal said, appearing from the adjoining room, toweling her hair dry. "Good to see you again, Gina."

Gina grinned. "Con tells me you took one in the shorts."

Sal nodded, limping slightly over to the bed. "The docs are surprised at how well the wound looks. When I tried to explain that Delta rubbed some kind of herb on it, they just started ramblin' in Spanish before laughing at me. Whatever it was, I tell you, was some kind of miracle drug."

Gina nodded. "Miracle and Delta are often used in the same sentence, eh?" To Connie, Gina asked, " So, you go back into the rain forest, rescue those poor people, take them through the jungle again, and then what?"

Josh turned from the computer and lumbered over to the empty chair. "That's what the boat's for. There are miles of coastline and any number of places to hide a boat. Once we get everybody to the boat, we should be home free. I have friends in El Salvador who have a plane and will fly us home if everything goes according to plan."

Gina sighed loudly. "That's a big if, guys."

"It's all we got." Connie turned to Gina, her eyes burning with intensity. "You'll be on board the boat waiting to pick us up on the coast. We'll make the boat home base."

"How will I know where to go?"

"Smelly or Logan will be on the boat with you, making sure you and the boat are safe," Josh replied. "It goes against everything I know to take you along, but Connie said she doubted we had a choice."

"Damn right, cowboy," Gina said, pushing her weight forward so she could sit up.

"Delta is my friend, too, and if there is anything I can do to help, then I'll do it. This isn't River Valley, you know. We're going to need all the help we can get to help her out of this one. Look, I know you're all worried about this life inside me, but to be honest, I know what the loss of Delta will mean to the lives outside of me. And it's not a pretty picture."

Everyone in the room knew exactly how Gina felt, and it was that loyalty, that sense of family that had brought all of them down here in the first place. "We know what you mean," Sal said softly. "Delta has that effect on people."

Connie returned her attention to the computer screen and typed in several numbers. "A friend of mine is an eco-botanist and she came down here to study with the indigenous peoples of Panama. She's been out of the office for the last three days, but I know she checks her email every few hours. If anyone can give us the longitude and latitude of the Bri with pinpoint accuracy, it's Cassidy Sheldon."

"Cassidy's down here now?" Gina asked.

Connie nodded. "Came down to study the migration of some nocturnal wasp or something."

"Wasps? The world is going to hell in a hand basket, and she's studying wasps?" Sal asked, tossing her towel in the other room. She may have showered, but her change of clothes had been yet another pair of fatigues.

"I've left her a message and an email."

"What else were you doing on-line, Con?" Gina asked, knowing full well that Connie, who could type a blistering ninety words per minute, had not taken that long to send a quick note to Cassidy.

Connie grinned and jotted something down on the pad next to her laptop. "Oh, just cruising down the old information super-highway."

Connie closed the laptop, but kept the computer on. "Once we get a bead on the Bri, we'll send Gina and the boat back to the cliff where Delta fell and have her wait there. The rest of us will enter where we entered before, near the town of Rivas."

"You don't think a boat off the coast will warn him?" Gina asked.

Sal chuckled. "The boat looks like one of those smelly old fishing boats. He'd never imagine it's our getaway vehicle."

Connie nodded. "The important thing will be to not come to shore until you see us or the signal flare."

Gina sighed. "It's going to seem an eternity before we see each other again and waiting for a flare while bobbing up and down in the Caribbean will give me gray hair."

Connie leaned over and kissed the top of Gina's head. "As long as you're around to enjoy every one of those gray hairs with our child, this will just be another adventure in the lives of Delta Stevens and company."

Gina grinned warmly at her lover. "Another adventure? My love, when did you become the mistress of understatement?"

Connie shrugged. "What can I say? I have faith that she's alive, that we can get to her, and that we're going to save those people from General Zahn. All we have to do is follow our plan. It's that simple."

⊕

Delta wondered if her plan was too simple. She was missing something. She dreaded making a grave error in judgment by thinking Connie and Megan would know that she was going back into the jungle, back to the Bri, after Zahn. She may have underestimated his greed. She thought he would surely pull his men out after they had escaped his clutches.

Delta had made several mistakes; one had been misreading the fire burning in Megan's eyes when Megan told her that she was going back after her friend Siobhan and the others that Zahn had captured. After finding Megan in the Bri village, Delta had been content to go home with her lover and finally stop feeling like she needed to save the world. But, to Delta's surprise, Megan had said she was going back to Zhan's camp with or without Delta.

That was a turning point in their relationship, one that would allow both women to see inside each other's hearts and finally come to an understanding about the roles they both played. Delta was sure that Megan had meant it; that she would, indeed, go back after those hostages, because that was exactly what Delta would be doing right this minute.

"We get you to beach tomorrow evening," Flora said, after speaking with her father, a smallish man with large, cracked hands and slicked-back black hair. Delta had managed to stand and pace back and forth to test her leg, surprised by how good it felt. Whatever the old woman had been putting on it had seemed to do the trick. Looking down at the back of her thigh, where the first bullet went in, Delta realized that the wound had been sewn shut.

"Fish wire," Flora said, smiling.

Delta nodded. It seemed that the lack of technology didn't hurt people as much as sociologists and other researchers assumed.

"Papa say no good to go jungle at night."

"I know, but my friends, my family, do not know I am alive." The words pained her just to say them.

Flora nodded in understanding. "Papa can no go but to get bags and back. Entiende?"

Delta nodded. Flora's father's boat commandeered by Zahn was probably being closely watched. If he attempted to take Delta to the authorities, it would mean trouble, or worse, for him and his family. It was a risk she wasn't willing to take.

"I understand. But you see, I must go when it's dark so they cannot see me."

Flora sighed. "Back into jungle?"

Delta grinned at the beautiful woman. She looked like she had just stepped off a postcard. "Yes. Back into the jungle. My friends will be expecting me there. But until then, is there anything I can do here to help?"

Flora thought for a moment before nodding. "Grandmother make medicines for you. Need herbs. You okay to go with me?"

Delta tested her leg once more. The old woman sure knew her herbs. She also knew how to stitch as well as any doctor. "I can't think of anything I'd like better than to go herb hunting with a beautiful woman."

Flora frowned, "Huh?"

Grinning, Delta extended her hand. "Okay to go with you."

Taking Delta's hand, Flora walked slowly to the door. "You dream much."

Delta nodded, thinking of the nightmarish visions she'd had during her fever. "Yes, I did."

Flora nodded. "Tell me about you. About North America. Tell me things."

Delta looked over at her while pushing the ugly thoughts about the United States in the back of her mind. Delta could acknowledge that her view of American society was somewhat screwed, but she didn't feel as though this was the time to break a young girl's dreams.

"What would you like to know?"

A huge sigh escaped Flora's lips. "Tell me about colleges."

Delta stopped and turned to look at her. "Colleges?"

"Si. Entiende?"

"Entiendo."

"Entiendo," Connie said, jotting a number down before hanging up the phone. Everyone else except Gina had left on a variety of errands. This time, they would be prepared when they entered the bowels of La Amistad. Before, they'd gone off half-cocked, unaware of the very human dangers lurking there.

They had plunged into unfamiliar territory without regard for their safety, and barely made it out alive. This time, they would be prepared with the right weapons, compasses, first aid, filled canteens, and accurate maps. The jungle would not best them, as it had before. They were prepared: not only for the rain forest but also for that bastard, General Zahn. This time, he would be the hunted, not the hunter. His own arrogance and machismo would have prevented him from returning to Colombia and leaving the second vein of gold. He would never be expecting them to come back for him. That pomposity would be his downfall.

Megan had told them there was a second vein the general had plans to mine. And while it would be difficult tracking him down, Connie was sure the second vein must be near the first. After a quick seismological check on one of the web pages on the Internet, Connie concluded the second vein was possibly within a mile of the first. If it were, Zahn would be there, a handful of hostages already doing his bidding.

If they could find Delta, if they could get her to the boat and to a hospital before her wounds killed her, they would return to the general and attempt to rescue the others Megan had left behind. If...if...if...

"You okay?" Gina came up behind Connie and rubbed her shoulders. Any other time, under any other circumstances, Connie would have melted beneath her lover's touch. But not now. Like a cobra coiled and ready to strike, Connie's muscles were tensed, ready to spring into action when the time came. She would not rest, would not relax until she had Delta back.

Connie released a sigh that could have cut glass. "I'm scared to death." Connie's voice came out weak and small. Turning around, she knelt down and buried her face in Gina's growing belly. They had a child on the way, god damn it, and Delta was the godmother. She couldn't be dead. A life without Delta was unthinkable, unimaginable. The rest of forever would be bleak without Delta Stevens. Connie couldn't raise a child in a world that didn't have her Storm in it.

Storm. It was the perfect nickname for a woman who stormed into any situation before thinking.

Delta was Connie's Storm, and had been ever since they met when Delta was a just a rookie. It was odd to think of a time when Delta wasn't the consummate professional she was now.

Back then; Delta drew action to her like nothing Connie had ever seen. She seemed to get out of one mess and then immediately stepped in another. It appeared some things would never change.

"What if we don't ever find her?" Connie asked quietly, allowing tears to run down her face.

Gina held Connie tightly against her. "What does your spirit guide tell you?"

Connie pulled away and wiped her face. Gina seldom mentioned Connie's spirit guide, as it was a part of Connie's heritage that she kept private. But she had, indeed, consulted her spirit-guide, and she knew that Delta lived. "That she's alive. I've searched every corner of my heart to see if I am simply clinging to false hope, but she's still there. Delta's still alive."

"Then, hold onto that. You know Delta. She'll find some way of letting you know where she is. Just keep believing in her,. that's what she needs from you right now."

Connie nodded, sighing deeply. "You, more than anyone, know that I'll feel it the moment her spirit is no longer of this earth. But, oh god, honey, I don't know if I can handle that."

Gina stroked Connie's hair with one hand and pressed her head deeper into her large belly with the other. "Hopefully, you won't have to. I know how much it scares you to think you might have to, but you can't think that way. You must believe like you always have."

Connie slowly rose and wiped her face. "I need her to be the godmother of our child. I need her to listen to my stories, to laugh with me, to think I am as insane as she is."

Gina gently wiped Connie's cheeks. "You need her, sweetheart. It's as simple as that."

Connie walked over to the window. It was a three-quarter moon, and she wondered if Delta was looking up at it as well. "Yes, I need Storm. It's odd to think that I need someone as reckless, as crazy, as hopelessly idealistic as she is."

Gina stood beside Connie and took her hand. "You're both pieces of some strange, cosmic puzzle, babe. If anyone can find her, it's you."

The tears continued their descent, and Connie was afraid that once she really started crying, she would never stop. "I'm going to give it everything I have."

"As she would expect you to." Gina walked over and drank some water from a glass on the small wooden nightstand. "If she is out there, sweetheart, she's expecting you. You need to think like Delta thinks."

Connie chuckled and wiped her eyes. "God, now there's a scary thought. No one thinks like Delta Stevens."

"Maybe not, but you can. You must."

"I know. I'm trying."

"What about Megan? How is she holding up? She seems so different than when she left."

Connie turned to Gina. Everything seemed so different now. "The Megan we used to know would have folded before now. But that hooker is long gone, and has been replaced by a stronger, tougher woman who is more likely to kick ass than give up. Don't underestimate her or the power of her love for Delta. She's not kidding about going back after those people, Gene. She is more like Delta than I would have ever thought possible."

"I can't even imagine it. She has changed so."

"Wait and see. Megan is ready to do business with this General Zahn. There's a fiery vengeance in her eyes that, quite frankly, frightens me a little. But, he underestimated her before. If he does so again, it may very well cost him his life."

Gina nodded. "Revenge is a dish best served cold. You don't think she'll endanger us in her effort for retribution?"

Connie shook her head. "You know, I've asked myself that question a dozen times, and I just don't know. I don't know the new Megan as well as I did the old. If she thinks Zahn is responsible for Delta's...you know...I honestly believe Megan will kill him or die trying."

Gina reached up and lightly stroked Connie's face. "You two keep each other safe, you hear me? I'm not going to raise this baby by myself."

Connie kissed Gina's open palm. "I'm so glad you came. It was against my better judgment, but I think I was wrong."

Gina pretended to be surprised. "What? Did I hear you correctly? Did you say wr..."

"Shh,. as long as Delta isn't around to hear me say it. Yes, I was wrong. I guess I'm just as bad as any man who acts like his pregnant wife is incapacitated, huh?"

Gina grinned. "You have been a bit overbearing, sweetheart, but I think it's cute. You just love me, that's all."

Connie kissed Gina tenderly on the lips. How this woman had put up with her and Delta's shenanigans for so long was beyond Connie. Gina's life had even been threatened by a crackpot named Elson Zuckerman, who had stalked Connie in a deadly computer game. Only Delta's involvement had kept them all safe and alive. Gina Tarabini was the salt of the earth, and Connie loved her more every day.

"I do so love you, you know."

Gina kissed Connie's nose. "You are my knight in shining armor, and I have no doubt that you'll find Delta and rescue those other women."

Connie placed her hand on Gina's belly and rubbed it counter clockwise. "Did you decide which name you wanted?"

They had had several name discussions since conception, but only two were acceptable to them both. When Connie had left for Costa Rica, they had yet to decide on a name.

"I like either Cheyenne or Dakota, babe. It's so sixties. So retro."

Connie grinned. Delta had given her a bad time about being a Navajo and naming her baby after another tribe, but Connie didn't care. They were cool names that couldn't really be shortened into some silly nickname, and they had a strength to them that many names did not possess. "Retro? What have I told you about watching too much MTV?" Wrapping her arms around Gina, Connie hugged her tightly as she stared at the moon. Yes, she was glad Gina had come down. She needed her strength, her foresight, and, most of all, her grip on reality.

And that was important to a woman who felt frighteningly on the edge of it.

Turning to face the 3/4 moon, Delta closed her eyes. She wanted Connie to hear her thoughts, to know she was alive. By now, Connie would be a nervous wreck, and Delta knew she would reach deep in her Native beliefs to see if Delta was still alive. Delta wanted her to know it, beyond any doubts.

After the Bri ceremony, Delta also believed that Connie could, and would, discover that Delta still lived. And she would come after her. Connie would convince everyone that Delta was still alive, and she would search every corner of her heart to see if she could ascertain which direction Delta would head.

Delta had gone over her choices a thousand times and each time, she arrived at the same conclusions. Connie and Megan would scour the water, the coast, and every hospital in a hundred mile radius. After finding nothing, they would come to the only possible solution: the Bri. Connie had been there with her, when she had become a Bri warrior. Somehow, Connie had projected her spirit into the middle of Delta's drug-induced vision to let her know she wasn't alone. If Connie Rivera had the power to do that, she certainly had the ability to find the Bri again. They had united Delta and Megan once before, and they could surely do so again. They were the only ones Delta felt she could turn to, and she was confident that Connie would know that.

Connie seemed to know more than anyone Delta had ever met. And it wasn't just that she was a genius, it was that she could see inside of people. Maybe it was her Native American roots or maybe she was just perceptive. Whatever it was, it gave Connie a greater command of the world around her than the average person. And right now, Delta was counting on her to be well above average. It would take every bit of Connie's vast abilities to do what Delta needed her to do. First, she needed Connie to know that she was alive. Then, she needed Connie to remember how Delta thought, to go with whatever her instincts told her Delta would do. The options were limited. Delta could not trust any of the authorities that, by now, had probably been forewarned about the tall American woman who might show up in a hospital. Zahn's influence must extend far and wide for him to have the kind of operation he was running in the middle of the jungle. Connie needed to remember these things. She needed to get inside Delta's head and heart and figure that Delta would return to the only place she felt was safe.

Turning from the moon, Delta rolled over and looked at the wound on the back of her leg.

Flora's grandmother had done an incredible job of sewing her up, and Delta had managed to keep up for most of the afternoon, until she tired and had to come back with Flora.

The day had been an interesting one. After she and Flora found and harvested various plants, her grandmother, who looked older than dirt, explained to Flora what each did and what she needed to mix with it in order to achieve the desired results. Delta had asked Flora if she didn't already know all this, and Flora explained that her grandmother could not read or write, so all her knowledge had to be passed down orally. Even if Flora had already learned what her grandmother had told her, she said it would be rude to say as much to an elder. So, Flora listened quietly and then translated as best she could for Delta, who found the entire process fascinating.

Her thoughts about the day made her grin. If someone had told her a month ago that she would actually find herbal medicines interesting, she would have laughed them off the planet.

Delta had been so pragmatic, so temporal in her thought processes that she would never have believed herself capable of sitting still long enough to garner the wisdom of an elderly woman. But her mind had opened since the Bri ritual. She began to look at the world through new eyes. She had never realized how limited her vision had become in the city. And though Delta knew she had always struggled with black and white, she was beginning to not only see, but also understand the grays. She was not the same, never would be, and she was so glad. She should care about the environment. She should have some connection to nature. It was unnatural not to. How had she managed so long without being tied to the earth? Delta only hoped that she lived through this so she could put all she had learned into practice.

After they returned, they made a dinner she recognized as Tipico, rice, beans, eggs, tortillas. Flora said it would give her strength for her journey.

Journey. That was an understatement. What she was attempting could only be called suicide. She was going back into the forest in search of a tribe few westerners knew existed. Last time, the Bri had found her, not vice versa, and who knew what would have happened if they hadn't?

Delta rolled back over and studied the moon and knew, in her heart, that Connie and Megan were looking at it also. It made her feel more connected to them, and she needed that now, more than anything.

"I'm coming, gals. Just hang in there a little longer, okay?" Turning from the moon, Delta was startled to find Flora standing by her bed.

"I didn't hear you," was all Delta could think to say.

"I walk quiet."

Delta grinned. "Yes, you do."

"Papa say boat ready tomorrow night."

"Good. Will you come with us?"

Flora nodded. "Soldiers want see us. Know we there."

"I see. How many soldiers are there when you pick up the bags?"

"Four, maybe five. Two ride back with Papa to help put on big boat."

"And they stay on big boat?"

Flora shrugged.

So there was another boat in the picture. These guys weren't taking any chances. If the old man were caught with the gold, little harm would come to him from the authorities. Hell, he'd probably become a national hero. Once the gold was out of her father's hands, Delta suspected it went to yet another boat, probably owned by the Colombians. They would handle the gold much like they handled drugs, and that was something she did know a thing or two about.

"Do they ever...bother you?"

Flora's brow wrinkled as if she didn't understand. "Bother?"

"Molest, bug."

"Oh, moleste. No. No moleste. Well...si...only one time."

Delta's cringed. "What happened?"

"He kiss me. That's all."

Delta imagined that wasn't "all" but let it go. The woman deserved her self-respect. Shaking her head, Delta wondered when Mother Earth was finally going to put an end to the destructive patriarchy ruining the planet. Camille Paglia had been right. Women would always be in sexual danger. Until, of course, the punishment for ill-placed penises was their immediate removal.

The thought made Delta grin.

Not that all men were bad, of course. Even Carducci had turned into an okay human being. But not, Delta noted, without a great deal of effort on her part. With a little work, she concluded, some brutes could be tamed.

"Delta?"

Shaken from her thoughts by Flora's soft voice, Delta looked at her. "Yeah?"

"You dream at night...of a...what is the word?" Flora wrinkled her forehead, searching her vocabulary. "Shaman?"

Delta nodded. He seemed to be orchestrating her dreams, not merely existing in them. "Yes, Flora, I do dream of a shaman."

"Por que? I mean, why?"

Delta studied Flora's face for a moment in the flicker of the small light bulb. She needed to explain to this young girl that her warrior spirit was joined to the Bri because of its strength and integrity. Flora was asking her to reveal the spiritual plane she had visited during her initiation celebration. Delta had faced swamps and crocodiles as she became more connected to nature and to her inner soul, and that had changed her life. It was so much more than Shaman giving her the tooth of the jaguar as a symbol of her courage and strength, so much more.

"Shaman is a friend of mine. He made me a Bri warrior."

"You have many friends?"

Delta grinned widely. "Yes. Yes, I do."

"They will come for you?"

Delta nodded as someone knocked on the door to her room. "Yes, Flora, I think they just might."

When Connie heard the loud knocking on her hotel room door, she looked at her watch. Everyone had been gone less than an hour, and she didn't think any of them could be back so soon. Connie opened the door a crack, and she couldn't have been more surprised if the man at the door was standing there naked with a feather boa around his neck.

"What in the hell?" Connie asked, staring at the large man in the doorway.

"My partner is missing, Connie. I thought maybe you could use some help."

Connie suddenly threw her arms around Delta's beat partner, Tony Carducci. He returned the hug with equal enthusiasm, his two-day-old beard growth scratching the side of her face.

"How did you know she was missing?"

Carducci grinned. "Josh called. Said you guys might be in need of a shooter. Took me a day to get all my comp time covered, but here I am. What do you need?"

Connie could hardly contain her joy, her surprise, or her tears. He had come to Delta as one of life's greater challenges. After one of Connie and Delta's "adventures," Delta was relegated to Training Patrol, a task few good officers were fond of. Carducci was her first, and only, student.

When he arrived, he was something out of a movie; brash, arrogant, inflexible, and oh-so macho. Tony Carducci got his ears pinned early by a cop who would always be his better. Like a pit bull pup that thinks he's the alpha dog, Carducci soon discovered that, as long as Delta Stevens was his partner, he would be the beta dog. Taking the blob of unformed human beta clay into her skilled hands, Delta had helped mold him into a fine young cop worthy of being her partner.

Now, it appeared, he had also transformed into a fine person as well.

"Come in, come in," Connie said, releasing his thick neck. With the exception of the time she kicked his ass, it was the first time the two had ever made physical contact.

Connie's eyes were welling up, but she willed them to stop. Now was not the time for silly sentimentalism. Now, they not only had another pair of hands but a marksman who could shoot the wings off a fly at a hundred yards. "Josh didn't say anything about contacting you."

Carducci shrugged. "I told him I didn't know if I could get my comp time covered, and that if I did, I'd see him within the next thirty-six hours."

"We could really use your help, Tony."

Carducci tossed his single bag on the floor and looked around the room. "HQ?"

Connie nodded. "We've just about lined up our ducks. There's a hell of a lot going on down here, once we get our bearings, things are going to heat up."

"Speaking of heat, I couldn't get a weapon through LAX, but I figured Josh could find something in my size."

Connie nodded. Carducci was one of the top candidates for the next SWAT opening, and he was a shoe-in. No one had the range marks to even come close to his scores. He had only to finish his field training with Delta before he became eligible.

Field training, Connie thought. How could that even compare to the "field" he was about to enter? It was funny how one's perspective could change. Not long ago, she thought Tony Carducci was a complete idiot. Now, when Delta needed him most, here he was, and she amended all of her earlier views of him. Leopards really could change their spots. "It was good of you to come, Tony." It was the first time she'd ever used his first name.

Carducci shrugged. "Hey, man, she's my partner. She'd do the same for me. I've learned a shitload from her, you know? Coming down here is the least, the very least I can do for her."

Connie couldn't help but grin at his youthful exuberance and fanatic loyalty to Delta. Yes, Delta would have done the same. The amazing thing was that Carducci knew Delta well enough to know she would. Delta had taught him well.

"We can use you more than you know."

Carduci's demeanor didn't change. "She's hurt, isn't she? Josh wouldn't elaborate. He just told me to get my ass down here. Said he was making other calls as well, I assume, to some of his Nam buddies."

Connie gestured to the empty chair. "You better sit down for this, Tony. It's a long one."

An hour later, when Josh and Sal strode through the door, Connie had just finished filling Carducci in.

"Jesus," he muttered, shaking his head. "Isn't anything simple in Delta's life? Ever?"

Connie shook her head. "You know better than that."

Carducci rose and shook Josh's hand. "Good to see you again."

Josh cut his eyes over to Connie as he shook Carducci's hand. "Glad you're here, man." To Connie, Josh said, "Sorry I didn't say anything, but I didn't want to get your hopes up."

Connie nodded. "No problem, Josh. Thank you for thinking about him. We could use the help. Tony said you called some of your Nam pals."

Josh nodded. "I've just lined up some help along the coast, should anything go sour on us. There's more help than you might realize, Connie. Carducci is just the first one to get here. I don't know if the others will get here before we leave, but at least we know help is in the neighborhood."

Sal walked over to Carducci and ran her hands across his chest in a way that could only be labeled sensual. "Hey handsome, want to see my bullet wound?"

"Sal!" Connie cried, tossing a pillow at her. "Down, girl."

Sal backed off and laughed. "Doesn't anybody want to see my bullet wound?"

Carducci cocked his head, realizing she wasn't kidding. "Sal, you were shot?"

"Right in the bum. Well, my upper thigh, but it's the same thing. Wanna see?"

Carducci looked over the top of her head to Connie, who merely rolled her eyes. "Uh, maybe later, okay?"

Connie turned to Josh, who was pulling boxes of ammunition from a bag. "Give him the best you've got."

Josh nodded and motioned for Carducci to follow him into the next room. When the two men were out of earshot, Sal looked hard at Connie, who shrugged and smiled. "What can I say? A lot of people care about Delta."

Sal jerked her head toward the adjoining room. "But him? I didn't think he had the depth."

Connie snickered. "Makes you change your whole impression about him, doesn't it?"

"I'll say. Who'da thunk it? The big guy has a heart after all."

"I didn't think it was his heart you were after."

Sal feigned hurt. "Ouch. You do me wrong, Con. I think the big lug is cute, that's all." Sal strode over to the computer and stared at the screen.

There was an email addressed to Connie from Cassidy. Although Connie was the genius of the group, nobody was better with electronic devices than Sal. "I see you've gotten a hold of your friend, Cassidy."

Connie rubbed her eyes, tired from viewing the small screen.

"Yep. She's faxing over a map she made showing the Bri's and other indigenous tribes locations. Before you know it, we'll be on our way."

"Our way where?" Carducci asked, walking back into the room.

"To the jungle, Tony," Sal answered lightly. "Where there's snakes the size of alligators and spiders the size of cats. Think you're ready?"

Carducci looked around the room at the other faces, searching for some sign that Sal was joking. "You're kidding, right?"

Connie stepped up to him and patted him on the shoulder, "Sal's just kidding. Actually, the spiders are more like the size of dogs."

Carducci grinned and laughed with the others. "I don't give a shit if they're the size of horses. Let's go get her and bring her home."

TWO

Looking at Flora's father as he prepared the boat, Delta wondered whether or not she was going to be able to pull this one off. She'd made the best plan she could think of, but even the best plans seemed to go awry in the jungle. For the first time in a very long time, Delta was unsure of herself.

"We walk," Flora said, taking Delta's arm and pulling her toward the beach.

"I don't need to walk," Delta grumbled, feeling angry with herself for being so grouchy. Her leg was feeling better, and she was antsy to get off the island.

"I watch you three days," Flora said, threading her arm through Delta's as they walked. "I see fighter. I see stubborn. I see woman want to live."

"And?"

Flora stopped and looked hard at Delta's face. For the first time, Delta realized they were almost the same height. "And now, I see fear."

Delta looked away. She was afraid. This nature hike had gone on long enough and it was time to get home, but to what? A part of her wanted to just give up. She wanted to get to San Jose, get on a plane with her friends and go home. She could just walk away and get back to living her own life. But surrounding herself with the dregs of society every night, only to see them back out in the street in less time than it took to book them wasn't what she wanted any more, and this surprised her. Everything about her surprised her now. Everything she thought she wanted, everything she thought she knew, had become altered forever. Her life held a different meaning for her now. The life she had been living seemed so senseless down here.

Putting the badge and gun on every night was a thankless job that, in the end, really didn't change anything except create a backlog in the already over flowing criminal court system, and for what?

Delta was afraid all right, but not of the task at hand, and not of the darkness of a place that would frighten even the bravest being. No, Delta was afraid she might not have the chance to change that life she'd left.

"I am afraid, Flora. I'm afraid I let my life get out of control. I'm out of control. I have been for a very long time, and I just want the chance to make things right."

Flora reached out and fingered Delta's necklace. "Bri warrior." It was not a question.

Delta nodded. Warring was what she'd spent the last three years of her life doing, and she was tired of it. Tired of fighting bad guys, tired of doing what was right when every inclination she had was to do whatever needed to be done. Delta was tired of putting her relationship second to a career that was sucking the life out of her. Delta was tired. If she was, indeed a warrior, she was becoming a reluctant one. All she wanted to do was curl up with Megan, watch movies and eat popcorn, and not give a damn whether or not the pusher she just arrested was out on bail. She just wanted to fall asleep in Megan's arms without worrying about the child molesters, wife beaters, and sociopaths running around her beat destroying lives. Delta wanted to just live a more peaceful life with the woman she loved.

"Do you believe?" Flora asked softly.

Delta touched the jaguar tooth, remembering the incredible ceremony where her spirit became one with the Bribri's tribe.

"Yes, Flora, I do."

"Then, pray."

Delta looked puzzled. "Pray?"

"Si. Find warrior inside." Flora tapped Delta's chest with one finger. Then, she kissed Delta's check before taking off toward the boat. "Pray, Delta. Believe."

Believe? Delta looked out at the rain forest in the distance on the mainland. Believing in herself was what had made her such a good cop.

Believing in her friends was what had made her such a good partner. Delta believed all right. Perhaps Flora's simple solution was the best. Perhaps it was time to pray. As Delta walked along the shore, she thought maybe Flora meant for her to look inside herself for the strength she needed to do this.

A little farther down the beach, Delta looked at the sea and admired the way the sun reflected off the waves as they danced in the water. Ever since the ceremony, life was so much more vivid, so exact. In the sea, she could pick out five, six different blues, and she saw several shades of yellow in the rays.

Before, she never would have noticed water or the way it moved. No amount of prodding would have enabled her to see the colorful and awesome world around her the way she did now. Shaman had spilled her blood on the earth, and she had become more aware of the life on it.

It was time for Delta to celebrate life, not the nightly death and sickness she experienced on her beat. Delta was a changed woman, and she liked how she felt. She loved the peaceful way of the warrior. It filled her heart and soul with a comfort she had never known.

Then why was she afraid?

Closing her eyes, Delta inhaled the sea breeze and tasted the salt air. She could understand how Megan had fallen in love with this place. It was as if you could see things more clearly here, as if all the life surrounding you opened your heart and soul to emotions and ways of being you only dreamed about.

Opening her eyes, Delta nodded to herself as she listened to a voice in her head she had never heard before. For the first time since she'd become a cop, Delta was looking at a problem from more than one side. Instead of just charging in after the general, crashing recklessly around the forest, she was letting herself express her fears of the situation. Maybe that's what being a warrior was all about: knowing oneself completely and being able to translate that knowledge into possibilities. Maybe her days of fearless flying and rash decision-making were over. Maybe Delta Stevens was finally ready to grow up. There was no doubt that leaving the hostages to whatever fate Zahn had in mind was irresponsible. Everything was becoming so much clearer to her now.

It was simple: she would follow-through with her plans to find the Bri. They would help her find her way back to Zahn's camp without running into the general's men. They would show her the way.

Sighing loudly, Delta turned from the surf and found Flora standing a few feet away.

"Find it?"

Delta grinned. "Yes, thank you. You're a smart woman, Flora. How'd you get so smart all the way out here?"

"American school. Papa say English important soon."

"So you were an exchange student and then you came home?"

"Si. Ten months I go school. Come home."

Delta wondered what future there was for a young woman on a tiny island in the Caribbean.

"Did you like the US?"

Flora's face brightened. "Oh, yes. So much to do!"

"What would you do if you could go back?"

"Go to college. Be phamacista."

Delta was taken aback by her answer, until she remembered watching Flora carefully pluck the various herbs, barks, leaves, and roots as her grandmother continued with her lesson. "I see. Think you'll ever make it back?"

Flora heaved a sigh and stared out at the surf. "I must belief. It is all I have."

Nodding, Delta took her hand and walked back to the boat. "Sometimes, sweetie, it's all any of us have."

"I believe, my love, that you have been hiding something in your sleeve." Gina flopped down on the bed and waited for Connie's response. "I've seen that look in your eyes, and I want to know what rabbit you are trying to pull out of the computer. Who are you trying to track down?"

Picking up the phone, Connie winked at her lover. "It's scary how well you know me." After dialing the phone, Connie waited for what seemed an eternity before making a connection.

She then spoke Spanish to a variety of people. Finally, the voice on the other end was the one Connie had been waiting for.

"Bueno?" came the voice.

"Hi. This is Connie Rivera, Delta's friend," Connie said, reverting back to English.

"How'd you get this number?" The voice didn't sound suspicious as much as it sounded curious.

"Not important. Delta's in trouble. Big trouble. We could use your...expertise."

The voice did not miss a beat. "I can be on the next plane out of Brazil and be there in thirteen or fourteen hours."

"Actually, we're in your neck of the woods. Central America."

"Then make it four. I'll get a private charter. How can I reach you?"

Connie gave the number where she could be reached, her email address, and the address of the hotel.

"Anything else?" the voice asked with concern.

"Bring your equipment. Have you ever been in the jungle?"

"I live in Brazil, Connie, what do you think? Of course I've been in the jungle."

"Well, be ready to go deeper into the jungle than just Club Med, because we have a feeling she may be trying to make her way back to a village."

"You think?" The voice asked. "Is she all right?"

"We don't know. Just hurry."

"Gotcha. Ciao."

Hanging up the phone, Connie pulled from her pocket a lavender card that she had snagged off Delta's desk moments before they headed to Costa Rica. The card had a picture of Mrs. Emma Peale from the 1960's show The Avengers on the front. However, it was the note on the inside that had made Connie pocket the card, call it a premonition, call it intuition. Whatever it was called, Connie had managed to track down the only person she knew who could get in and out of anywhere without detection.

"Who on earth was that?" Gina asked.

Connie smiled mysteriously. "Someone I had the feeling we would need someday."

Gina shook her head. "Is there no end to the connections you have?"

Connie grinned. "Suffice it to say, Delta...affected this woman to such a degree that I had no doubt she'd come running as soon as she received my SOS."

Gina's eyebrows rose. "Don't tell me you called her?"

Connie nodded. "I most certainly did."

"Did someone here send out an SOS?" asked a petite woman with a black punk haircut. She was wearing dark sunglasses and was draped in a beautiful, flowing peach-colored silk jumpsuit.

Connie opened wide the door of the hotel room. "You made great time."

"It sounded urgent."

Connie motioned for the woman to enter as Gina walked into the room from the bathroom. "It is very urgent." As the woman strode through the door, Connie shook her head. "Traded your leather jumpsuits in for silk, I see."

"The weather dictates my attire, Connie." The woman bowed elegantly before Connie. "I still owe you for that sweep kick, you know."

Connie laughed. "In your dreams, sweetpea."

For a moment, there was an awkward silence, broken the second Carducci walked into the room.

"You!" Carducci cried, stopping short.

"Hi, big boy. I've come to bail your partner out of yet another mess."

Carducci looked over at Connie, his face pleading for an explanation.

"We need someone skilled at getting in and out of high places undetected, Carducci. You and I both know Taylor is the best."

Taylor grinned over at Connie. "Thanks. I am retired as a jewel thief, Tony, but when Connie called and said Delta needed help; I dropped everything and flew up here. This time, we're on the same side."

Gina moved next to Connie. "So, this is the rabbit you pulled out of your hat?"

Connie shrugged. "Had to. If we're going to get Delta and the rest of us out of here alive, we're going to need the best of the best. Taylor has gotten into some of the most secure museums and private residences in the world without being detected, and she's amassed a fortune doing so. She has beaten every known surveillance system, from heat sensors to infrared lights. If anyone can get in and out of Zahn's camp, it's her."

Taylor shrugged. "Museum, house, jungle, hell, they're all the same to me. Point me to this Zahn's place, and we're as good as in."

Carducci looked at Connie and then put his hand out for Taylor. "Glad to have you on board, Taylor."

Taylor took Carducci's hand. "Anything for Delta, right?"

Carducci nodded. "Apparently."

Gina slid over to Connie and said softly, "Does Megan know?"

"Know what?"

"Does she know you called Taylor in?"

Connie shook her head. "Not yet."

"Oh, that's just great."

"What's great?" Megan asked, walking through the door with a bag full of groceries.

Everyone turned, but no one said a word, as Megan closed the door behind her and set the bag on the dresser. "Who are you?" she asked Taylor before cutting her eyes over to Connie.

"This is Taylor. I've called her in to help us get into Zahn's camp for the hostages, and to help us find Delta."

Megan nodded. "Help? That's great. What's your specialty?"

Taylor grinned. "I go where no woman has gone before. I'm a...I was a jewel thief in another life. I used to scale tall buildings in a single bounce. Connie thinks you could use my help."

Megan shot Connie a look of surprise before eyeing Taylor up and down. "You must be good, or Connie wouldn't have wasted the quarter."

Taylor grinned and shrugged. "Yeah. If my bank accounts mean anything, I'm pretty good."

Megan nodded. "Excellent. Welcome. I'm Megan, Delta's lover." Megan extended a hand to Taylor, who looked over at Connie before taking it firmly in her own and shaking it.

"Good to finally meet you," Taylor said. "Delta is sure crazy about you."

Megan's face was a question mark. "How is it you know Delta?"

Carducci coughed. "Taylor...uh...well, she sorta...well...bested us back home."

This made Megan chuckle. "You bested Delta? My, my, you must be good."

Taylor shrugged again. "Not good enough to get the gem I really wanted but maybe some other time."

"Oh? What gem was that?" Megan asked, but Connie stepped in between the two women. It served no purpose to explain to Megan that Taylor had a thing for Delta, and that it was this infatuation with Delta that had brought Taylor into their lives in the first place. The "gem" Taylor was referring to was Delta, and though Connie never felt like she had gotten the whole story from Delta about a certain late night visit Delta had received from the precocious jewel thief, she knew that now was not the time to deal with any of those issues.

"We can get to know Taylor more later. Right now, there's work to be done. I say we grab dinner and discuss where we need to be at this time tomorrow."

When everyone found that agreeable, they all trooped downstairs, except for Connie, who grabbed Taylor's arm as they started from the room.

"I really am glad you came. I appreciate it more than you can know."

Taylor grinned. "I wouldn't have missed it."

Connie nodded. "Look, I don't know what happened between you and Delta, but you're not just here because Delta's your friend, are you?"

Taylor's eyes narrowed. "Does it matter why I'm here, Connie?"

"It does to that blonde who is scared to death she may never see Delta again. I just don't want to add any more pain to her already scarred heart. She doesn't deserve that."

Taylor grinned and patted Connie's shoulder. "I'm here because the world needs Delta Stevens plain and simple. You said I was the best of the best, but you were wrong. Delta is. Do I have feelings for her? Frankly, that's none of your business. Don't worry. I have no intentions of adding insult to the injury to Megan's heart."

Connie inhaled slowly. "I'd appreciate that, Taylor. Really I would."

Taylor stepped closer to Connie and laid her hand on Connie's shoulder. "We all love her. Isn't that good enough?"

Nodding, Connie started down the stairs. "It sure the hell is for me. Thanks."

Taylor stopped at the third step before the lobby. "That's not to say that I wouldn't grab her if I had the chance, but you know as well as I do that Megan is all she sees, all she wants. I mean, Megan's why she's here in the first place, right?"

Connie nodded. "Yes. Megan is Delta's heart and soul, and I don't know that Delta could stand losing her."

Taylor looked at Connie hard and slowly shook her head. "Who are you trying to fool? Megan may be a lot of things to Delta, but heart and soul? Don't those positions belong to you?" Taylor held up her hand to stop Connie's response. "Don't answer. It was a rhetorical question. Come on. I'm starving."

Sitting around the dinner table, the seven people were chattering on about the endless possibilities they could run into and how to handle each when a small, dark-haired man approached the table with two governmental types on either side of him.

"Manny!" Connie cried when she looked up and saw him.

Manny nodded his curt reply. "This is not a pleasure call, I'm afraid."

Connie, Josh, and Sal exchanged looks. Manny had escorted Delta into the jungle, where he was eventually shot. Josh had carried him all the way back through the jungle and to a nearby hospital a week ago. They would have thought he'd be a little more pleasant upon seeing them again. They had, after all, saved his life.

"If not pleasure," Josh growled, "then this must mean business."

Manny pulled a chair over and addressed Connie even though it was Megan who was at the head of the table.

"There's no easy way to say this, Connie," Manny said, offering official identification. "I am an agent for the DEA."

"I knew it!" Sal cried, slamming her hand down on the table. Then, to Josh, "I told you his English got better as we went along."

"Aw, shit," Josh, muttered, shaking his head. "Like we fuckin' need this right now."

"What does that mean to us?" Connie asked, folding her arms across her chest.

Manny looked around and lowered his voice when he spoke. "We've suspected General Zahn of running drugs, kidnapping, and murder for quite some time. When Delta came to town looking for Megan, I never dreamed she would actually find her."

"Then, you knew where Megan was all along?" Connie's voice was cold and hard.

"Oh no," Manny answered quickly. "We suspected Zahn had gone underground. No one thought he'd actually engage in slave labor."

Sal snorted, "Oh, this guy's for real, here. Yeah, the guy is a butcher, a thief, and a drug czar, but boy were we surprised he would condone slavery! Get real."

Manny glared at Sal before returning his attention to Connie. "I'm afraid that's what I'm trying to do here. You see, I know you want to go after Delta..."

"And we are," Carducci interrupted, rising from the table. As he did, both government men went for their guns.

"There's no need for that, gentlemen," Manny said, stopping his men from drawing down on Carducci. "But, I'm afraid I can't let you do that."

"What do you mean, can't let?" Connie asked coldly. She gave Carducci a look that told him to take his seat, and he did so, never taking his eyes off the other two men. Several other patrons at the bar slid from their chairs and disappeared outside as the tension started building.

Manny leaned forward, his voice a hushed whisper. "I've seen what you people are capable of, Connie. Whatever your plans are, I'm sure you'll see them through, and I can't allow that to happen."

"So, the problem is what?" This was almost her worst nightmare come to pass. If the government guys got involved, they could ship them all out, or even send them to jail if they so desired. The rules were much different than those they played by in the states, and Connie realized Manny could stop them before they even got started.

"We don't want Zahn touched right now."

Connie's jaw dropped.

Megan's hands formed into fists.

Josh dove across the table and grabbed Manny by the front of his shirt and dragged him clear across the table, sending cups of coffee and dessert plates clattering to the floor.

"I saved your life, you little piece of shit. Don't come in here telling us what we can and cannot do, you son of a bitch. I should..."

This time, the two government men actually drew their weapons and pointed them at Josh's head. He never took his furious eyes off Manny.

"You got some kinda balls, little man, you know that?" Josh held his face to within inches of Manny's, ignoring the two automatics pointed at his face. "I dragged your sorry ass through that fuckin' jungle, and you think you're gonna just waltz in here and tell us to go home? You owe us!"

"Josh," Sal whispered, lightly touching his arm as she eyed the guns. "Please put him down."

"Oh, I'll put him down, all right, and then I'll mash him into the ground with the heel of my boot like the little cocksucker he is." Shoving Manny backwards, Josh also pushed both silver barrels out of his way as if they were toys. "It'd take better men than you two fuckers to whack me. Get outta my way before I kill you both."

The two men looked to Manny for direction, but retrained their weapons back on Josh. The remaining patrons scooted out the doors.

Manny straightened his shirt and tie. His face was tinted pink. Taylor leaned over to him and whispered, "Next time, think about a clip-on; they're safer."

Manny motioned for his men to holster their weapons. "I figured you would be difficult." Reaching into his inner blazer pocket, Manny withdrew a foot-long white envelope.

"Here are seven tickets to LAX. Either cooperate and fly out of here in the next three days, or I'll have you all thrown in jail. Ever seen a Central American jail?"

"Ever seen your blood all over the pavement?" Josh loomed closer, waiting to strike.

Connie held her hand up against his barrel chest. "No, we haven't, and no, we don't intend to."

"I didn't think so. Look, I'm not the bad guy here. I'm really sorry I have to come off like this, but you're getting into the middle of something much larger and more dangerous than you realize."

Megan stepped up to Manny. He was a good six inches shorter than she was, and she could smell an abundance of some kind of cheap cologne. "In our opinion, there is nothing larger or more dangerous than the hole left by Delta Stevens. Your operation and whatever gains you hope to make are nothing compared to the lives we're trying to save. Shouldn't you be trying to do the same?"

Manny inhaled slowly and sighed, running his hand through his short black hair. "The needs of the many outweigh the needs of the few. I'm afraid that's how these things are looked at."

"Then you can go to hell, Manny," Sal tossed out. "This few have no fucking intention of worrying about the needs of the many. God, I can't fucking believe this shit! We shoulda left you to die in there."

Manny blushed a deeper red. "I didn't expect you to understand. Look, we'll get Zahn, but there are other things to consider. You'll only wind up either getting in the way or getting hurt."

Everyone looked at Connie, who was glaring openly at him. "You're not leaving us much choice, are you?"

Manny shook his head. He wasn't enjoying this. "Just to make sure we understand each other, these two gentlemen will watch your doors. You Americans are far more resourceful than our intelligence would indicate."

"What we understand," Carducci said, leaning closer, "Is that you're putting us under house arrest."

"If that's what you'd prefer to call it, yes."

"For three days," Gina added.

Manny nodded, looking at her belly. "You people must be crazy to drag a pregnant woman through the rain forest. What is wrong with all of you?"

Josh gulped back his anger so loudly; everyone at the table heard it.

Taylor rose and faced Manny. "We have a saying in the states about riding a Harley Davidson. When people ask us why, we simply say, 'If we have to explain it to you, you wouldn't understand.'"

"What I 'understand' is that you're all loco. Going back in after Zahn would be the death of you. You caught him unaware once. You won't do so again."

Connie nodded and motioned for everyone else to rise. "Then we have three days to just hang around here and wonder if your people can pull their heads out of their asses in time to save a bunch of innocent people?"

Manny nodded. "Yes. With the striking airlines, three days is the soonest I could get you out of the country, otherwise you'd be in a taxi right now."

"What will prevent us from returning?" Gina asked. "After all, you have noticed how resourceful we Americans can be. What makes you think you can stop us?"

"Return, and I'll have you arrested."

Connie frowned as she studied Manny's facial expressions and gestures. Something wasn't right. "That is, if you catch us. You've sorely underestimated us if you think we're just going to pick up our jacks and go home."

"Do not underestimate us, Consuela. Ours is a poor country, but we do not take lightly to people ignoring our laws. Return and you'll wind up in a very primitive jail."

Connie stared at him a long time before replying. She didn't know if it was the way Manny was talking, or the cavalier attitude he had about leaving them free for three days, but her gut told her something was amiss. "Can we finish our meal in peace?"

Nodding, Manny spoke briskly in Spanish to his men. "Yes. But remember, three days from now, you'd better be boarding that plane." With that, Manny left, leaving his two guards standing at the doorway, and out of earshot.

The table erupted in indignation, until Connie raised her hands to silence everyone. "Look, we don't have much time, so listen up."

Everyone leaned closer as Connie spoke softly. The restaurant was empty now, save for a table of waiters who would look over and shake their heads. "Does anyone else think something is off here?"

Carducci and Josh raised their hands.

Connie smiled at them before turning to Taylor. "Taylor, was there an airline strike when you left Brazil, or when you came in this afternoon?"

Taylor shook her head. "Not that I saw."

"Tony?"

Carducci frowned and shook his head. "Nope. Shitty service is all, but that's not unusual."

"Honey, where are you going with this?" Gina asked.

Connie shot a glance at the two men standing guard. They were idly chatting to each other, not paying them the slightest heed. "First off, there isn't an airlines strike."

"So?"

"So, if Manny really wanted us out of here, he would have put us on a plane, any plane, today or tomorrow, or he would have had us jailed until then."

"But he didn't," Sal added, thoughtfully.

Connie shook her head. "No. He gave us three days. I don't think it was Manny's decision to stop us. I think he was following orders."

"Then, you think the little squirt was buying some time for us?" Josh asked.

Connie shrugged." Why else would they give us any time at all? If we were such a risk, wouldn't they jail us or keep us under something more serious than house arrest?"

Sal nodded. "He even admitted we were good. You're right, Con. This doesn't make any sense."

"So, what do we do now?"

Connie picked up the packet of tickets and tucked them in her back pocket. "I say we leave for Rivas two by two until we can get to our first coordinate. It'll be less suspicious if we travel in pairs, anyway."

"When should we take off?" Megan asked.

Connie looked at her watch. "Let's get some sleep. Josh and Sal can leave first thing in the morning. Megan and Taylor should shoot for late afternoon, and Tony and I'll follow separately soon after, while Gina flies to the coast. Sound okay?"

Everyone nodded.

"You really think something's not right, don't you?" Megan asked.

Connie nodded without hesitation. "It just doesn't add up. And whatever it is, I don't like it."

"Con's right," Sal added. "It feels like we're being played."

"Thank goodness he didn't stop us," Megan murmured. "To be stopped before we even began would have killed me."

Gina patted Megan's hand. "Have you taken a good look around you, hon? Does this little group appear to be one easily stopped?"

Megan grinned as she looked at each face around the table. It was true that you really know who your friends are when you have a crisis party and they show up. "I don't know how I can thank all of you for putting your lives on the line like this. Delta will be touched to know you all care so deeply for her. Thank you."

"If she's out there, Meg, we'll find her," Carducci offered, rising from the table.

"What do we do about Hansel and Gretel over there?" Gina asked.

Josh chuckled, "Leave them to me. Those boys don't look like they've seen the fighting end of a chicken, let alone a Viet Nam vet. They'll never know what hit 'em."

Carducci joined Josh. "Josh and I have a few items to go over before morning."

Everyone said their goodnights as the two headed upstairs.

"Good men," Taylor said, motioning for the waiter. "They give me hope in mankind."

Connie grinned. "Indeed."

"You know, hon, you're right. There's something about that Manny guy I just don't trust." Gina said contemplatively, her hand lying atop her big belly. "His eyes were all over the place, and he couldn't look at you very long. I can't quite put my finger on it."

Connie turned to fully face her lover. Gina was one of the best psychologists in River Valley and what she knew about the inner workings of people's minds was as vast as the knowledge Connie had about languages and computers. "What is it, hon?"

"If Zahn is such a wanted criminal, and we already know he's murdered at least two of the people he kidnapped, why aren't they blazing in there with guns drawn? Why would they let him rape their land for millions in gold, knowing that the money is going directly back to the cartel?"

Everyone looked around to see if anyone had an answer.

"I mean, whatever it is they're waiting for is..."

"Us."

All five women stared at Connie, who shook her head in anger. "He's setting us up."

No one said anything for a few moments, and then Megan muttered under her breath, "The sons of bitches."

"What?" Sal asked. "What are you two mumbling about?"

Connie deferred the explanation to Megan. "The Latin American governments are so afraid of the cartels and what sanctions might be imposed against their countries if the gold or major players are abducted, they're willing to let us do the job for them. That's what you're getting at, isn't it?"

Connie nodded. "He knew we'd move more quickly if he threatened jail or deportation. He's expecting us to go as soon as possible now. That's why he made up the strike excuse and the three day deal."

Taylor held her hands out. "Whoa! You telling me the combined Latin American governments are too scared to act against a dirtbag like this Zahn?"

Everyone nodded.

"Manny expects us to make a move. He actually wants us to go. So, we go charging in there, guns blazing, and when the smoke settles, no government will claim responsibility. They'll point the finger at a band of loco gringos and let the US take whatever consequences come along after that."

"I knew the Colombian cartels were powerful, but this?"

Connie sipped her coffee and sighed. "Colombia supplies 80 percent of the world's cocaine.

Eighty percent. Now, that's a fact every government is aware of, yet do you see boycotts, embargoes, or other economic sanctions imposed on Colombia?

Taylor shrugged. "I wouldn't really know. I've been out of the loop."

"Why our government, Europe, and Latin American don't squash Colombia economically is a mystery to many. But when you consider how much money that 80 percent brings in, you have to know there are many, many payoffs, payoffs to our own government officials as well. Otherwise, the US would be doing something to stop Colombian production of cocaine besides pitiful Just Say No slogans."

Megan nodded. "We have a growing drug problem in the US which leads to growth in crime, homelessness, unemployment. The US is crumbling under the weight of drugs, yet we still do business with Colombia. The cartels have their hands in everyone's pockets, and it's too lucrative, not to mention dangerous, not to do business with them."

"Shit," Taylor mumbled. "Sounds like we're going up against some big boys."

Setting a fresh cup of coffee cup down, Connie patted Taylor's hand. "No one will think less of you if you want to..."

"No way! Are you kidding? I live for challenges Connie, you know that. So this Manny guy throws a little wrench in the works. You know, my mentor taught me there are three kinds of people: winners, losers, and those who don't play. Well, the only way you can get in the first category is to play. So count me in."

"You could get hurt or worse."

Taylor chuckled. "Like scaling skyscrapers isn't hazardous?"

Connie grinned. She liked Taylor's spunk. "Point taken."

"So, how do we avoid being somebody's pawns?" Taylor asked. "I don't mind playing, but I abhor being used."

"We just do what Delta always does."

"And what's that?"

Grinning, Connie said, "We go for broke."

THREE

Delta watched Flora crafting arrows out of branches and feathers. Flora had restrung an old bow for Delta, and when they finished with the arrows, she showed Delta how to use it.

"Bring back to cheek, and... no, no look at...at..."

"The target."

"Si."

Delta pulled the bow taut with two fingers of her left hand and sent an arrow flying. It missed the target completely.

"Very good," Delta said, shaking her head. "Give me a barn and maybe I could hit it."

"Eh?"

"Nothing. Come on, let's just keep trying."

For the next two hours, Delta practiced until she felt fairly proficient. Her lone memory of archery in high school was when all of her basketball buddies thought it would be funny to shoot their arrows straight up in the air, not having brains enough to realize the things had to come back down. Delta had managed to make it to an awning just as the first arrow landed a few inches from where she had been standing. She hadn't picked up a bow since then.

"Bien," Flora said, when the final arrow nicked the target's center. "You ready."

Delta laughed. Ready? She had two healing bullet wounds, a bow and arrow for defense, and no idea where the hell she was going. If this was ready, she was in trouble.

"We leave tonight, then?"

"Si. You go with Papa. Go in water before shore."

Delta nodded. Flora had told her earlier that the Colombians always boarded the boat to make sure no one else was on it. Then, they weighed the gold right there prior to sending her Papa back to the island. A slip of paper with the weight and a stamp of some sort accompanied the gold until it was transported to the big ship.

The big ship.

Delta wondered how difficult it would be to get aboard that big ship and make her way to Mexico or Florida. There was a germ of an idea kicking around in her head, and she decided she'd just let it sit and ferment.

"My grandmother say you watch nature."

"Watch nature?"

Flora nodded. "Si. You Bri. Bri nature. Grandmother say they one. Watch nature."

Delta looked at Flora and smiled. Seemed everyone had some idea of the true nature of the Bribri. "I'll remember that, Flora. Thank you." Turning to the boat, Delta sighed.

Flora shook her head. "No entiende. You no understand. You Bribri. It not just name. Grandmother say you need to listen, to feel, and then you find your way back."

"Find my way back? To the Bri?"

Flora shook her head again. "To your heart. Corazon. Si?"

Delta nodded, thinking she understood what Flora was saying. Delta needed to remember that being Bri was a way of life, not a label, not some sort of club or group. It was a connection to the very place that had nearly taken Megan from her. It was a bond with a collective spirit that could very well help her find her way back.

And Delta was determined to get her life back. "You're right, Flora. My heart is out there, and I'm counting on her to find me."

⊕

"She's counting on us to find her, Con," Megan said, pulling a chair up next to Connie, who had been glued to her keyboard since dinner. "How will being on the Internet help us do that?"

Connie clicked a window on her screen and watched it change. "If we're being set up to clean this guy's operation up, it means we're considered disposable, to everyone. We can trust no one. Not even our own government. We're going to have to find a way back to Delta and Zahn's camp and still be able to get the hell out of there without any help from any cavalry."

Megan nodded. "Thank you," She whispered.

Connie turned from the monitor. "For what?"

"For not thinking I'm stupid for wanting to go back after the others."

Connie grinned, returning her attention to the computer. "Stupid? Hardly. You've been hanging around me and Delta too long, that's all. You know she'd go back to get them if the roles were reversed. With or without her, we have to help those people. It's what she'd want. It's what she'd do."

Megan sighed loudly. "This just got way more complicated, though, didn't it?"

"Governments and drugs are complicated issues, and we happen to have stepped on a live one that affects a lot of countries. Someone thinks they can use us to get Zahn, the gold, and probably a great deal of cocaine. And whoever they are, they have another thing coming." Turning from the computer, Connie locked eyes with Megan. "How are you holding up?"

Megan shrugged and dropped her head. "I'm just hanging on to hope as tightly as I can."

Connie patted her hand. "Good. You just keep hoping and praying."

Megan looked up with tears in her eyes. "You know what's so strange?"

Connie waited.

"I feel like I finally understand Delta, her motivations, her drive, and her integrity. For the first time since we've been together, I finally get what it means to walk in Delta Stevens' shoes. I understand what makes her do the things she does; the things I thought were a reflection of her love for me."

Connie cocked her head in question. "Reflection? How so?"

Megan shook her head. "It always felt like, no matter what, Delta wasn't picking me. She left me standing outside a restaurant when she chose to go in that burning house after those kids. She puts her life on the line, not thinking how losing that life would affect her lover. For the longest time, I felt that Delta never picked me, she never chose us. Just once, I wanted to be first."

"And now?"

Megan released a heavy sigh. "Now, I realize that her choices have absolutely nothing to do with either me or us. It's those choices that make Delta, Delta.

Those choices are the reasons we love her so deeply. I understand that now. It just doesn't seem fair to finally understand your lover only to lose her. Know what I mean?"

Connie nodded. "I don't know what I'd do if I ever lost Gina. She's as much my lifeline as food, water, or air."

"I'm glad she's here. You need her."

This made Connie grin. "Yes, I do. But I also need Storm." Connie looked down, trying to control the tears welling up in her eyes. "I'm not sure I ever realized just how true that is."

Megan rubbed Connie's back lightly. "We'll find her, Con."

"Yes, we will." Connie looked into Megan's face. There was more that needed to be said. "Something else is bothering you, isn't it?"

Looking away, Megan nodded.

"Want to talk about it?"

Turning back, Megan sighed again. She had not wanted to deal with this now, preferring, instead, to house the feelings someplace else until she was strong enough to handle them. But the truth was eating at her, and her dreams had become distorted visions of reality. "I killed a man, Connie. I put his head in the cross hairs of my rifle and I blew him away. I didn't even give it a second thought."

"Survival is a strong instinct, Megan. Don't beat yourself up for it."

"Oh, I'm not beating myself up for it, Con. As a matter of fact, it was much easier than I thought it would be. Perhaps that's what bothers me the most. I feel neither regret nor guilt. It was like taking out the trash; just something you had to do and no one else wanted to do it."

Connie frowned. This didn't sound like the Megan she knew.

"Pulling that trigger was like second nature. After seeing and experiencing the horrible atrocities these men are capable of, taking that fucker out actually felt good."

Connie suddenly felt her heart hurt. Kind, warm Megan would never be the same. "You need to understand the one demon Delta has been struggling with since she killed that asshole in the warehouse. Killing doesn't make you a killer, Meg. And just because you have no remorse doesn't mean you're a bad person."

Megan stared down at her hands. "I've changed a lot, Connie. While hope keeps me on my feet, revenge pushes me forward more than I'd like to admit."

"Revenge?" Connie's heart ached even more, and she knew, right then, what had changed in Megan. Even though Megan had been a prostitute, she had still possessed a softness about her, a genuine kindness in her heart. What Connie had been feeling since they'd returned from the jungle was a loss of innocence. Megan Osbourne wasn't just out to get Delta back. She was out to kill General Zahn. A sadness flooded over Connie she could not hide. "Meg..."

Megan shook her head. "Revenge, Connie. I want to see that man bleed. And not because the bastard made me suck his dick and do all sorts of disgusting things I used to get paid top dollar for. No, Connie, his men shot my lover in the back. Whether she's alive or not, I will not rest until he is dead and bleeding at my feet."

Connie stared into Megan's cold, blue eyes. This woman who stood before her was not the one who had left River Valley, and for the first time since they'd met, Connie was a little afraid of what had become of Megan. "Megan, you're not a killer. Zahn's not worth..."

"Jack shit. He's not worth the lowest of slugs in the rain forest, Connie, but if you think you can talk me out of this, you're wasting your breath. I want his blood on my hands. Period. End of story. And I'll go to the ends of the earth to see that it happens."

"That's what I was afraid of." Connie stroked Megan's hair and brushed it away from her face. Even Megan's face was different. It looked older, harder somehow. "You really have changed, haven't you?"

Megan nodded as she folded her hands in her lap. "I've learned so much about myself, about my lover, about what I want in life. I want a life with Delta Stevens; even if that means taking the back seat when she pursues some child molester or rapist, even if that means tending to her stitches and bullet wounds when she gets reckless. I want that life she was offering me but was too self-centered to see it for the gift it was. I want that life, and if Zahn has taken that from me, then I will spend the rest of my life hunting him down like the animal he is."

Connie inhaled slowly, realizing there were no words that would change Megan's mind. A woman just doesn't suffer sexual abuse and then forgive and forget. Some stay damaged for life; others try to drown the memories with alcohol or pills.

But for Megan, her choice was clear: to get even. "If I have anything to say about it, honey, you'll get that life and then some."

Megan's voice softened. "You know, I never thanked you for taking care of her while I was down here 'finding myself.' God, Connie, that's such a fucking cliché. How can you find yourself apart from the one who makes your heart beat?"

Connie sighed. "You seem to have managed to do just that, as did Delta, while you were gone."

"I'm sure she was quite a handful."

Connie grinned. "Quite. But then, that's what makes her so darn adorable; the way she gets in trouble."

Megan smiled. "Is that what it is? I thought it was the way she gets out of trouble. Guess she fooled me, eh?"

The expression on Connie's face suddenly changed. "That's it."

"What?"

Connie's fingers rapidly flew over the computer keys. "You gave me a great idea." She typed madly, screens whizzed by, until she came to a screen Megan didn't understand.

"What's that?"

Connie studied the encryption on the laptop before rubbing her hands together. "I say we call Manny's bluff."

"Meaning what?"

"Meaning, we fool him and his government drones into believing we've chosen to leave the country instead of playing into their hands. We'll make him think we gave up."

"How?"

"Easy. I can get into United's reservation databank and tell it we did, indeed, board the flight to LAX. If they check the flight log, they'll think we really returned home. It will take a few minutes to get in the back door of their system, but that ought to do the trick. When Manny checks to see if we went home, it will show that we have."

Megan beamed. "Brilliant!"

"We're not taking the fall for anybody."

"But what about the goons at the door?"

Connie shrugged. "The more red herrings we toss out to Manny, the better. We'll drop them, sneak out of here, and meet in Rivas, just as planned. He'll be looking all over for us and will be surprised to see that we've left the country."

"And just for good measure, I'll make it look at though Josh and Sal flew to Panama instead. Manny won't be able to find his butt with both hands!"

"Don't you think they'll have someone at the airport waiting for us?"

Connie shook her head. "Nope. He's not expecting us to take that flight. He's expecting us to jam out of here. Take my word for it; those two goons in the hall aren't the only two guys waiting for us to make our move. The most important thing is that none of us allows a tail. If Manny gets a tail on any of us, we're screwed, and he'll know where we're headed and that we're going in."

Megan chuckled to herself. "So, you've got him chasing his own tail, is that it?"

Connie nodded, a spark of reserved energy shooting from her eyes. "Wake everybody up and tell them we finally have a plan we can sink our teeth into."

FOUR

Delta sunk her teeth into a piece of chicken Flora's grandmother insisted she eat. She hadn't been hungry all day. The anticipation of returning to the mainland was filling her stomach with bat-sized butterflies.

"I wish I go, too," Flora said, as they walked to the boat.

Delta smiled at her. Warriors, it appeared, came in all shapes and sizes. "It's too dangerous. Hell, even I shouldn't be going."

When they reached the boat, Flora's father, William, waved Delta on board.

"I'm sorry the Colombians make your father work for them," Delta said as she watched him throw a plank over the side for her to walk on.

"If he did not, they kill him for boat."

Delta nodded. "I'm sure they would."

When the boat was ready, William said a few words to Flora, who translated for Delta.

"Papa say you good person. God be good to you."

"Tell him thank you, and that I hope to repay him someday." Delta took Flora's hands and looked deeply into her eyes. "And thank you so much, my friend, for taking such great care of me. I will never, ever forget you."

Flora blushed. "No good bye. Come see me. Send me picture cards. Flora Monge Murillo." Flora handed Delta a bota sack filled with water. "Water importante." Then, Flora pulled a small pouch from her pocket and handed this to Delta as well. "Eat. These will make you strong. They are cashews."

Delta took the proffered gifts and nodded. "Thank you. I will send you much more than postcards, Flora Monge Murillo. Gracias, mi amiga. Mi buena amiga." Clutching her bow and arrows, Delta watched Flora disembark and then wave as William pushed the boat away from the dock.

It seemed that Delta met incredible women no matter where she went. She vowed that she would do whatever she could to help Flora realize her dreams of returning to the states for her education. It was the least she could do for the woman who had pulled her through the worst fever Delta had ever suffered. Flora had proved wise beyond her years, and Delta knew she would forever have a warm spot in her heart with Flora's name on it.

Turning, Delta was startled to find William standing very close to her with a very sharp Bowie knife.

"Por usted," he said, handing her the knife, hilt first. It was about ten inches in length with an abalone handle, and it was beautiful. Then, he wrapped a leather belt around her with a sheath attached.

"Mate los," he said, making a stabbing motion.

Delta understood exactly what he said. William, who was tired of being threatened and used, wanted her to kill them. He wanted the Bri warrior to protect him and his family.

"Gracias, William," Delta said, taking the knife and returning it to the sheath. "Well, it looks like I'm about as armed as a girl in the jungle can get, eh?"

William grinned and went back to steering the boat. Delta wondered how he managed the pitch-black sea surrounded by dark nothingness. He must be an exceptional sailor to be able to navigate in complete darkness.

Complete darkness. Delta had been there and back and apparently, was going there again. What a strange life she led. Staring down at the black water, Delta sighed.

First, Miles, her beat partner and best friend, was killed before her eyes, dying in her arms from a gunshot blast. That darkness had been the loneliest moment of her life. After hunting down his killers, she had been forced to blow one away in a dark warehouse. Then, a psycho from Connie's past had kidnapped Gina and terrorized River Valley until Delta and Connie had managed to end his little game. Elson Zuckerman had killed a child, and the darkness Delta had felt as she held the lifeless little body in her arms was second only to the intense grief she'd experienced when she cradled Miles' dead body. They had exposed a child pornography ring specializing in snuff films, and Delta had been forced to kill her second perpetrator.

That darkness did not last long, as she and Carducci had each killed, and this had somehow brought them together.

Carducci.

The thought of him made her smile. There was so much potential in that young man. He had come through for her when she most needed it, had done what few human beings are capable of doing. He had shot a man right between the eyes, managing to save both Delta and a little girl. He had grown a great deal since she'd first been paired with him, and Delta actually found herself missing him. In the darkness of her beat, she had counted on Carducci and he had not failed her.

Delta had seen her fair share of darkness, but General Zahn and the things he had done to Delta's lover were darker than evil, darker than the feelings Delta had experienced at the brink of death. No, his was a darkness that had to end. And, one way or the other, it would end at her hands, hands far different from the hands that had first arrived in Costa Rica.

Watching the water skim past the hull, Delta touched the jaguar tooth on her necklace. She was a Bri warrior now. If she believed the things that happened to her during that ceremony, she should be able to make her way back to them. She wasn't just going into the jungle. This time, she was a part of it. And only the Bri could tell her where Zahn was. Every hour that went by meant one less hour for his hostages. She would find them, find him, and then find a way to end his darkness. All she needed was that phone Megan had seen. Once she got her hands on that phone, this would be a whole new ballgame.

"So, it's a whole new ballgame," Carducci said as he packed up the rifles. "I like it. It's something Delta would do."

All agreed.

"Indeed. I'm afraid she's rubbed off on me," Connie said.

"You could do worse," Taylor said, grinning.

"So that's it, huh? Everyone packed and ready?"

The room was still as everyone nodded solemnly. They were like athletes before a big game. There were nerves, butterflies, tension, and even, a sense of relief as they put into action the first leg of their plan. It was game time.

"Great. We split up and head for Rivas from several different directions. Once there, we'll double-check our equipment and then get moving. Have I forgotten anything?"

Josh shook his head. "Got weapons, maps, compasses, night scopes, machetes, flare gun, first aid, and a whole lotta energy. I haven't been this stoked since Da Nang."

Gina stepped up to Connie and slid her hand inside Connie's. "You just be sure you get your ass to that beach, you hear me?"

Connie nodded. "Loud and clear."

As they approached the beach, Delta felt the boat's motor shut down, and she saw William extinguish the lantern. The bow of the boat was dark and creaking as the water slapped against the sides.

"Ahora, acqui," William said.

Delta grabbed her bow and put it over her shoulder. She checked the arrows and made sure the knife was securely tied.

"Gracias, William," she said, shaking his hand.

"Bueno suerte, amiga," William said quietly.

Lowering herself into the warm water, Delta pushed away and began a slow sidestroke to the shore on the east side of the boat. It was like being in a vacuum again. There were no lights other than those from the men on the north shore, and she had no intention of going near there. The good news was that as long as there was gold, she figured there must still be hostages. General Zahn obviously discounted her as a viable opponent and boy, was that a mistake. From this distance, she could barely make out four or five torches or lights. Perhaps she could use their nighttime drops to her advantage. But first, she needed to find the Bri and see if they could help.

Quietly treading water, Delta figured another hundred yards or so, and she'd be back in the rain forest. Alone again. In the dark, again. Swell. At least she would be able to put this behind her. One way or the other, she would finish what she had started.

Not yet at shore, Delta was surprised when her feet hit bottom and she could walk.

It amazed her how shallow the shelves were in the Caribbean, and she was grateful she hadn't fallen into a shallow one the day she had dropped from the helicopter.

Stepping out of the water, Delta closed her eyes and inhaled deeply. The air on the island had seemed so salty, and thick, but this was the air felt fresher. She had noticed how good the air smelled once she got away from San Jose. The jungle air smelled like nothing she could ever remember smelling.

"Now, what, Storm?" Delta said aloud. She knew it was safest to travel at night, so she would have to push it while the darkness gave cover. Taking one last look out at the Cimmerian sea behind her, Delta descended into the dark heart of the rain forest.

It didn't take long for her eyes to adjust and, soon, she was moving at a pretty rapid pace, even through the dense brush. It surprised her how much easier it was to move through the jungle since she'd become united with the Bri. No longer did the strange noises bother her, or the moving shadows scare her. She was no longer a visitor to this place; she was a part of it. She felt a part of the twisting, gnarled root system of the forest floor. She sensed the movement of creatures she could not see. Inhaling the soft scent of the jungle, Delta wondered if there was any air purer than this. And although she was no native, she still knew she belonged. Just knowing that filled her with a sense of peace and contentment, which helped her move rapidly through the underbrush with only a dim light from the moon reaching the forest floor. Where she was headed, she had no idea, but she was sure, one way or the other, that the Bri would sense her presence and come get her. It was only a matter of time.

Time.

Time had such a different meaning down here than at home. Time governed her life in the states. She had certain places to be at certain hours. The clock was everyone's worst enemy, as it dictated when life began and ended. Here, time was different. The more time one had, the richer everyone thought you were. Time here, meant doing something or nothing, as long as it was your choice. The Tacos weren't concerned about owning the latest VCR. Hell, few of them even owned television sets. They didn't drive fancy cars, and Delta remembered how she had laughed when she saw several motorcycle riders wearing football helmets in order to obey the helmet law.

These people understood what life was really about. It wasn't about ownership, or trying to fill voids with electronic gadgets. It was about the quality of the time you could spend with the people you loved.

Now, it was time to round up her family and head home. It was time to take a really hard look at her life to see where it was going and see what she could do to change the things that weren't working for her.

Stopping in a little clearing, Delta smelled the air. There was the distinctive scent of death lingering like a black cloud, and it was close to where she stood. She had smelled this odor too many times in her life not to have it permanently embedded in her olfactory system. Was the source of this rotting, fetid stench?

Carefully parting two palmetto branches, Delta saw a canvas bag lying open with various items strewn about the ground. Walking over to it, she grabbed it by the bottom and dumped everything on the ground. Squinting through the dark, she spotted a canteen, a first aid kit, and a flashlight. Plucking the flashlight up like she'd just discovered a fine jewel, Delta smiled before placing the head of the flashlight against her stomach and briefly turning it on. "Yes!" she hissed, lowering the beam so as to not give herself away. Sweeping the ground with the light, Delta saw two corpses lying face down on the ground. She looked up through the dark foliage and wondered how far light could travel in the jungle and whether or not turning the flashlight on was wise.

Still, curiosity got the best of her, and Delta shined the flashlight on one of the corpses.

"Aw, yuck," she muttered, bending over for a closer look. As soon as she saw their clothes, she knew who they were. Poachers, men who catch exotic and endangered species to sell on the black market. They were the reason she was in this mess.

Well...sort of.

When Megan took her internship with a law practice down here, she had become interested in the preservation of scarlet macaws. She and a friend named Augustine had entered the jungle in the hopes of finding these poachers. While in the jungle, Megan had been captured by Zahn, and Augustine was killed.

Coming after Megan brought Delta, Connie and Sal into direct contact with these poachers, whom the three women had left gagged and bound to a tree.

Apparently, these two had escaped, but by the look of the bullet holes in their shirts, the Colombians, or someone else, had gotten to them anyway.

What was left of them now was barely enough to fertilize a kitchen sill herb garden.

Delta quickly checked for weapons, but these two had been cleaned out. They'd been shot and robbed, an ending, Delta surmised, fitting for men who stole animals from the forest. Grabbing their canteen and knapsack, Delta remembered Flora's words about the importance of water, and sipped some from her bota.

Looking around, Delta wondered what had happened to the other guy they had left taped up. Had he escaped and gone home to tell the tale? Had he been caught or killed by the Colombians? Perhaps a jaguar carried him off. In the rain forest, just about anything was possible.

Glancing up through the trees, Delta remembered letting the scarlet macaws free after taking duct tape off their beaks and feet. One of the birds had only one eye and Delta had guessed that it lost the other fighting these two maggot-condos now lying on the floor of the jungle.

"Karma," Delta whispered, straightening up. "You boys got exactly what you deserved." Turning the flashlight off, Delta continued through the rain forest, knowing she was ready for anything.

FIVE

"Ready?" Connie asked Megan for the twelfth time, as they prepared to execute their plan. Josh had taken care of the two government officials with a chokehold that had rendered them unconscious long enough to put into a cab and have them sent to the other side of the city. Now, it was time for action.

"I've been ready for nearly a week," Megan said slowly. "I can't wait to see that bastard again."

Connie held Megan's hand, looking uneasy. "Meg, this isn't about Zahn. It's about Delta and those women, and I need you to remember that."

"Don't worry about me, Connie. I won't blow it."

Connie cast a questioning glance at Gina, who said, "Megan, we all agreed, we'd get these women out and then beat it out of there. Don't let your vengeance put us in danger. It won't be worth it."

Megan shrugged. She couldn't expect any of them to get it. As much as she loved them, Megan knew no one could understand having been a prostitute didn't mean she could handle being raped and sodomized. "Until you've been fucked up the ass by a man who thinks you enjoy it, Gene, don't tell me what's worth it, and what isn't." Megan's voice was harsh and biting.

Gina glanced down at her belly and placed Megan's hand on it. Pressing firmly on Megan's hand, Gina didn't let up. "You tell me, Megan. Is she worth it? Would you honestly put her or us in danger just to kill him?"

Megan stared at the clouds, remembering his filthy hands groping her breasts, the way he rammed his dick into her so he could feel her breasts move. She remembered his foul odor and having to bathe him before giving head. And she remembered him on top of her, and pulling out as he came all over her stomach.

Megan remembered, all right. Her memories, like a glowing brand, were seared into her soul. "I won't put anyone at risk, Gina, but I am going to kill him."

Connie shook her head and looked down at her lap.

"What?" Megan asked. "You expect me to roll over and pretend it didn't happen? Well, it did! And we either get him now or I get him later. The choice is simple."

Looking up, Connie shook her head sadly. "You do so remind me of Delta right now, Megan, and I know there is no way in hell we can talk you out of this."

Megan stared down hard into Connie's eyes. "Absolutely no way."

Connie looked into a pair of eyes she did not know. Whatever force of rage had changed Megan's spirit, it had overwhelmed the soft, sweet woman she knew and loved, and turned it into something unfamiliar and harsh.

"Don't be blinded by your anger and hatred, Megan, okay? Think clearly."

"Clearly?" Taylor muttered, walking away from the intensity of the moment. Sal was on her heels in an instant.

"They're all loco," Sal explained to Taylor as she, too, sought respite from the tension.

Taylor stopped and stared at Sal. "From what I gather, dear heart, you could afford a couple hundred trips to a psychiatrist yourself."

"Being part of Delta's life really is to embrace a little lunacy," Sal agreed. "There's not a sane one of us in the bunch."

"Sane?" Carducci queried, joining Sal and Taylor. "Try flat-out nuts. Did you know," he said, turning to Josh, who had just finished loading his rented Subaru, "that Delta gave her gun up when not one, but two men had weapons? Now, that's insane. All the shit they teach us in the academy about never giving our weapon up, and she does. Delta doesn't follow rules. She breaks them. Megan's right, Con. Delta would sure enough go back in there. She'd be going the first chance she got." Carducci, Josh, Sal, and Taylor returned to Megan, Connie and Gina, forming a small circle.

Megan nodded. "And she would kill Zahn, wouldn't she?"

Everyone looked around at each other, until all eyes settled on Connie, the only one who knew, for sure, if Delta would find a way to kill Zahn. One silent minute turned into two as Connie studied each waiting face.

"Well?" Carducci asked, jamming his hands into his pockets.

Connie nodded slowly. "Yes, Megan, Delta would go back and kill Zahn."

Megan folded her arms. "And you're all okay with that, but you have a hard time with the fact that soft, sweet, sodomized Megan wants to? Delta's not the only one among us capable of killing." Megan looked into the eyes of every one of them. "With the exception of Gina and Taylor, every one of us has killed a man."

Taylor shook her head. "You don't know I haven't killed anyone," she said softly. Everyone stared at her, but no one said a word.

Megan nodded. "Then stop giving me shit for wanting that fucker's head removed from his body."

"Meg..."

Megan held her hand up to stop the protest. "No. If I have the opening to take him out, I will. End of story. Do not try to stop me."

There was nothing else to be said.

Connie stepped up to the group and inhaled deeply. "I guess this is it. We'll all meet in Rivas tonight, with the exception of Gina, who is flying to the coast, where Logan will be picking her up. You got everything you need, baby?"

Gina looked in her duffel and nodded. "I'm all set."

"Okay then. Time for a few quick good byes, and then you guys gotta shove off." Connie slid her arm around Gina's thick waist and pulled her closer. Walking away from the group, Connie leaned in and kissed Gina's neck. "I promise that when we get out of this, and we bring that beautiful little girl into the world, Delta and I both will start living for our families, okay?"

Gina reached out and stroked Connie's face. "I love both of you for the excitement you bring into life. Just think of all the wonderful stories we have to share with our child. None of it would be possible if you and Delta didn't insist on living on the edge."

"Me?" Connie was genuinely aghast.

Gina laughed. "Oh, my sweetest love, you forget how well I know you. You'd like the world to believe that you just spend your life getting Delta out of jams, but the truth is you need her even more than you need me. You need her fire, her spirit and her energy. She is what makes you, you. Good, bad, or indifferent, I love you both for the way you live life. Don't ever apologize for the gusto with which you live, my love. Just keep on living it."

Connie wrapped her arms around Gina and hugged her tightly. "I love you so much."

"I love you. And no matter what happens in that jungle, you remember that when this is through, we're going to have a boy or girl to tell the story to."

The boys and girls saw Delta before she saw them. After pushing her way through the jungle most of the night, Delta had stopped just to rest, but apparently, by the looks of the dawn peeking through the trees, it had turned into more than a short nap. Delta cursed herself under her breath for not being at full strength.

The little Bribri boy stopped still when he saw Delta rise. The look of fear on his face immediately turned to one of recognition, as he stared into Delta's eyes. It wasn't every day that an indigenous tribe had the opportunity to see a 5'9" white woman inducted as a warrior. It had been a time of celebration, a time when a tribe could be strengthened by a warrior's spirit.

Delta grinned at the children. "Hi there," she said, knowing they would not understand her. The Bri still had their own tongue, at least, they would until the damned missionaries infested their lives and changed their culture forever.

As if understanding her plight, the little boy took her hand and, a half hour later, Delta found herself on the fringes of the Bri village.

This was not the tranquil scene she'd been brought to before. This time, there was a heaviness, a pall hovering ominously in the air. Something had happened that affected everyone in the village. She could hear chanting in the corner where Shaman kept his home. There was definitely something amiss. She could feel it in her heart.

Taking Delta's hand again and pulling her to the other side of the valley, the boy brought her to the bonfire area outside Shaman's hut. Standing all around the hut were the warriors, wearing spears, war paint, and unreadable expressions.

Last time, Tamar was here to interpret. Unfortunately, Tamar fell victim a Colombian bullet, ending his young life far too soon. If Delta were going to communicate with her new people, she would have to do so on her own.

Pulling her hand from the boy's, Delta waited. Something was obviously going on inside Shaman's hut, and she didn't wish to disturb. Whatever it was included a deep sorrow because the warriors' expressions were like death masks.

Death masks.

Death.

Suddenly, Delta remembered thinking she had seen Shaman in the trees, alone, when they were forced to leave Tamar's lifeless body behind. Was that her imagination, or had Shaman followed them that day that felt like years ago? Delta could no longer contain herself. Something terrible had happened, and she needed to know what it was.

"Itka!" Her voice cracked as she called the chieftain's name. She had no idea what she would say beyond that, since verbal communication was virtually impossible.

Just then, Itka slowly exited Shaman's hut, his face rigid in a frown. When he saw Delta, he gave her a slight smile and nod, as if he'd been expecting her.

When the short, wizened old man stood before her, Delta bowed her head. He was, after all, her chieftain, and submission was required. Delta did not need a rulebook to know this, but it was odd how familiar, how normal being here was to her. In River Valley, Delta would have bowed to no man. It was what had gotten her into some of her troubles. But here, with this little old man standing before her, she knew her place and could acknowledge his.

"Del-ta," he said, taking her hands in his thick, callused ones.

"Itka," she replied, squeezing his hands. "What's going on?"

Itka looked over at the warriors, who were swaying and chanting, and beckoned Delta to follow him.

She was not prepared for what she was about to see. She was not prepared for the reaction her heart and soul would have when Itka motioned for her to step through the door. As soon as she did, Delta's heart sank.

"Oh no."

"Oh no," the little girl said, plopping down on a wooden stool. A black and white-faced Capuchin monkey hopped around in the trees behind her.

Connie nodded. "I'm sorry you had to find out from me, Bianca, but as you might have guessed, I'm desperate."

Bianca, a sixteen-year-old Costa Rican girl, shook her head sadly. "I wondered why Manny always came and left. Mama wondered, too. I couldn't figure out how he kept his tour guide job when he was gone so much." Bianca stared out the window, deep in thought. "And then there was his English. Manny had never spoken English as well as I, and suddenly, he could. I guess I was too preoccupied at the time to give it much thought."

Connie patted Bianca's shoulder. "Don't be too hard on yourself. Manny made a decision about his life. He didn't need to discuss it with his little sister."

Bianca sighed and turned back to Connie. "I wouldn't be surprised if papa knew. My father's a diplomat, you know. He probably helped Manny get the job."

"I'm sorry." Connie didn't really know what else to say.

Bianca turned back to the window. "We all change, I guess. I'm not one of those stupid little kids who don't know that." Bianca stared at a distant point before slowly turning around and locking eyes with Connie. "So, you're going back after her?"

Connie nodded, amazed at how bright this young woman was. Delta had told Connie how much Bianca had reminded her of how Con might have been at that age, and Delta was right. Bianca's eyes held maturity and wisdom beyond her sixteen years.

"I have to. She's my best friend."

Bianca nodded. Sixteen year olds understand the power and importance of friendship, and Bianca was no exception. She had taken a liking to Delta right off.

"When was the last time you saw any Colombians?" Connie asked.

"They were here for three nights a couple of days ago. I knew something had happened because they never spend one night, let alone three. They were obviously looking for someone. Two of the kids came to get me and told me they were asking about a tall American woman. They asked some of the adults if a helicopter had landed nearby."

Connie felt her throat tighten. "What did they say?"

It was Bianca's turn to offer solace to Connie, and she patted Connie's shoulder. "The people of Rivas are good, kind people, Connie. We take care of each other and the people we love. No one said a word."

Connie released a sigh. "So, the Colombians left?"

"Yes, and haven't been back."

"Good. I need a place with a phone."

"No problem. My uncle is away and has a nice house with a phone. Hot water, even."

"Excellent. I'll need another pair of eyes to make sure my friends get here okay and to show them the way here."

Bianca pointed to her own eyes. "Check. I'll put some of the kids on the main road, just in case."

Connie cocked her head at this amazing young woman. "How old are you?"

"Age is irrelevant. Next?"

Chuckling, Connie handed Bianca a list. "Those are the only supplies I didn't pick up. Would you mind getting them for me?"

Bianca scanned the list briefly before sticking it in her pocket. "Needle and thread? In case you have to sew anybody up, eh?"

Connie nodded. "Let's hope Delta's already been repaired."

Bianca rose and clicked her tongue. The monkey in the tree stopped eating the leaves and jumped through the window of the bar where Connie had found Bianca drinking a coke and talking to the bartender. "I'll put one of the Vargas kids at the entrance to La Amistad. They'll tell us if the Colombians come out. Those Vargas kids can really scoot."

"Excellent."

Bianca grunted, shaking her head. "Obviously, espionage activities run in the family. And here I thought Manny was just helping out a stranger when he offered to go into the jungle with Delta. I wondered why he went back after Delta. I thought maybe it was puppy love or something, but I never thought my brother was a special agent for the DEA."

"I'm really sorry you had to find out this way. Family issues should remain in the family." Connie understood the special nature of Latino families, and how important the privacy of family business was. In her family, airing family laundry was a good way to get a whipping.

Bianca shrugged, and the monkey on her shoulder appeared to do the same. "My family is this country, Connie. I may be going to school in Canada, but my heart is here. This forest, the animals in it, the Bribri, all of it make me who I am. I only wish Manny had felt the same way. The important thing is to get those poor people out."

Connie heaved a loud sigh. She was pushing the envelope of exhaustion and needed some rest. "Thank you so much for your help, Bianca. Seems we're going to need it."

"Not a problem. Someone needs to stop them. There's been too much loss and pain already."

Connie reached out and touched Bianca's shoulder. Kiki eyed Connie's hand with interest. "I wish there was something I could say to ease your pain, Bianca. I know how disappointed you must feel."

Bianca looked away and nodded. "If we can help get those people out, I'll feel a whole lot better about the pain in my heart where Manny once was."

Connie thought about the pain in her heart as a result of Delta's absence. If this was a permanent condition, she was afraid she didn't know what true pain was yet. She hoped she wouldn't ever have to find out, because if Delta was dead...

"Is he dead?" Delta couldn't believe it. Lying on a hammock in the middle of the tiny room, Shaman was dotted with red bullet holes. Miraculously, the bleeding had subsided, but Delta knew he didn't have much longer on the secular plane.

His wounds had taken their toll on him and even the Bri's great knowledge of medicines could not bring him back.

Dropping to her knees, she took his frail hand in hers and brought it to her cheek. This man had singularly affected her life. He had taught her so much in such a short amount of time. He had taught her just how precious life really was, and now he was, dying. This loss shook her every nerve, as she leaned over him and studied his pale features.

"No," she said softly, looking at his riddled body. "Not you. Please, not you."

Shaman's eyelids fluttered open briefly, and he turned his head toward Delta. She so wished she had the words, any words, to convey how sorry she was to have involved these people in this mess.

"I am so, so sorry," she said, pressing her cheek to his palm. "Not you."

Shaman whispered several sentences to Itka before looking back at Delta. He stared at her for a long time before smiling at her. Then, he motioned for Itka, the chief of the tribe.

Rising, Delta turned to Itka, who led her outside.

"Oh, Itka, you don't know how sorry I am." Delta did not care that they could not comprehend her words; sorrow had a universal tone she was sure Itka understood as well as felt.

Itka turned to Delta and gazed into her eyes for several moments before squatting on the ground. Delta followed suit, trying desperately not to cry. How could this have happened? These were gentle people; they meant no one harm. Shaman was their wise man, their spiritual hub, their center. Why had this happened?

Then, she knew. It was Zahn's way of keeping the Bri in line and out of the way. He took out the one person the tribe relied on. No wonder everyone was so quiet, so sad. Their rock had been shattered, leaving them to find another who was worthy enough to take his place. Zahn knew the Bri would try to heal their tribe first, expending energy on a burial, on choosing a new leader, on repairing their wounds. By the time they had finished, Zahn would be gone, leaving the rain forest and its people raped and bloody.

Itka grunted at Delta, causing her to rise from her pain and focus on him. He had drawn some figures in the dirt. He pointed to the figure lying down and said, "Tamar."

Then, he pointed to a group of three men with guns and made bullet marks going toward the figure that was obviously Shaman. He stopped to look at Delta to see if she followed him. She nodded, and he continued. Pointing to the lone figure to the left of Tamar, Itka said, "Delta." Then, he made a circle around Delta and the group on the left and drew an arrow pointing to the group on the right. With a swipe of his hand, he erased the three men with guns on the right. When he looked up at Delta, she shook her head. There was no way she was going to lead these people with spears, bows and arrows, and blow guns against fully-armed Colombians. Hadn't they suffered enough already? In the dust, Delta drew her response.

She pointed to the person in the middle and said, "Delta." Then, she wiped away each man, one by one, until there was none left. Itka looked at her and nodded solemnly. Perhaps his thirst for revenge was not so deep as his desire to see that Shaman received a proper burial, which would be very hard to do if all the warriors were gone with Delta. She had gotten them into this; she would get them out of it. Period.

Rising, she pointed to the hut and followed Itka back to the center of the room. If it were possible, Shaman looked worse. It was clear he would not last much longer.

Opening one eye, he coughed, rolled his head, and spat blood into a gourd on the floor. Then, with all the effort of his dying body could exert, he pointed to his open eye before succumbing to unconsciousness again.

"I am so very sorry," Delta whispered, reaching out to touch his cheek. By tonight, he would be dead, and for what? For what?

Backing respectfully out of the hut, Delta was surprised by two warriors who motioned for her to follow. On the other side of the bonfire, sat a prune-faced little man mixing something in a bowl. As much as she wanted to, she did not have time for another ceremony. She wanted revenge against the bastards who could do that to an old, harmless man. She wanted to fertilize the jungle floor with their body parts, water the plants with their blood. She wanted death.

Delta knew she had it in her. It was that dark side of her character she questioned most.

Delta had killed men before and had struggled in the aftermath with the notion that that made her a killer--which was no different from the scumbags she arrested. Delta knew the taste of death; she knew what it took to snuff the life from a man. More importantly, Delta knew she had it in her to bring down Zahn and his men. She had what it would take to shed their blood, to extinguish their lives.

At this moment, Delta knew it was time to come to terms with the truth about her soul, the truth that Delta Stevens was capable and willing to kill again. Perhaps that was what being a warrior really meant.

Standing in front of the prune-faced man, Delta realized this was no ritual. The little man had prepared for her curare tips, poison arrows. He handed her a bag of arrows and a blowgun, before dipping his fingers into some bluish muck. Stepping up to her, he opened her shirt and smeared the paint over the top of her chest. She still carried a light blue line from the last body paint job she'd received from the Bri. It must have worked, because two bullets and a 300-foot drop later, she was still here to talk about it.

When the man finished painting her chest, he chanted a few words, sprinkled something that smelled suspiciously like marijuana over her shoulders, and tapped her with a stick. When he was finished, he turned her toward the other two warriors, who inspected her arrows and nodded. Flora's arrows passed inspection, and they added the curare tips to her quiver, and handed her the blowgun. She was their warrior now, outfitted with their weapons, protected by their gods. Delta was the only one who could bring them the justice they deserved, and she relished the thought of administering that justice.

Armed with a knife, a bow, a blowgun, and poison tips, Delta was, at last, ready to take on General Zahn. The only problem was that, she didn't know where he was.

"Where are they?" Connie asked, as she paced back and forth in the little house Bianca's uncle owned. It was a nice place, actually, with a screened-in porch, a beautiful pocket garden, and an airy, open kitchen, like most Costa Rican homes.

It was too hot to cook indoors, so most kitchens were set up on the porch, where people from all over would gather to share stories, drink cervezas and enjoy each other's company.

"It's only been three hours since you arrived, and you've been here before. Rivas is not so easy for others to find."

Connie stopped pacing and stared at Bianca.

"Sixteen," Bianca answered before Connie could ask. "And age doesn't matter. " Bianca turned from the window and grabbed some nuts for Kiki. "They'll get here. If they're anything at all like Delta."

Connie sat in front of Eddie and dialed up the Internet while Bianca looked at the screen over her shoulder. Though Costa Rican by birth, Bianca's father was a Canadian diplomat, and she attended one of the finest boarding schools in Canada. She was fluent in Spanish, French, and English and was taking Japanese and Russian.

"The net, eh? Cool. What are you looking for?"

Connie quickly jumped out of the Internet and accessed some other on-line screen. "Not looking. Manipulating."

"My computer teacher at school says that data stored is data changed."

Grinning, Connie nodded. "Something like that."

Bianca glanced out the window and announced the arrival of a jeep. "Someone's here!"

Connie leaped from the chair and ran to the door.

"It's some cute guy."

Opening the screen door, which was the only door, Connie held it ajar for the bag carrying Carducci. "I was getting worried," she said, peeking in the bag.

"I suspected a tail, so I drove around for a while."

"A tail? You sure?"

Carducci nodded. "Yeah, but these guys suck. They may as well be wearing signs."

"So you lost them?"

Carducci nodded. "Absolutely." Carducci suddenly saw Bianca, and his whole demeanor changed. "Well, hello there."

Connie shook her head, remembering what a boy he often was. "Tony, this is Bianca. Manny's little sister."

Tony, surprisingly, caught Connie's inflection. "How little?"

Bianca took Tony's hand and shook it. "Never mind."

Connie shook her head. "Sixteen, Tony."

Carducci released Bianca's hand as if he'd been burned.

"I'm sixteen, cowboy. It doesn't mean I bite."

Connie chuckled as she moved the bag's contents around so she could see everything in it. More ammo, more supplies. He and Josh had done an excellent job of seeing to it they were well armed.

"I'm surprised the others aren't here," Carducci said, looking out the window. "Man, is this place bee-u-tee-ful or what? Wish this were a vacation." Carducci looked out the window at the variety of tree and plant life, and shook his head. "This sure isn't like San Jose. But then, I guess a capital is a capital no matter what country you're in." Watching children playing by a rushing creek, he sighed. "As weird as this is gonna sound, it sure is peaceful here."

Bianca walked up to him and looked out the window. "Here, in Rivas, or here in Costa Rica?"

"Both," Carducci answered without looking at her. He couldn't stop staring at this orange flower nestled in the crook of a tree branch next to an enormous pink flower.

"Rest up, Tony, because the jungle you're about to enter is just as dangerous as it is beautiful."

Bianca nodded. "Just remember that the brightest colored creatures are the most poisonous. Don't be afraid of the green or brown animals or insects but stay away from anything blue, yellow, or red."

Carducci sat on the worn couch and wiped the sweat from his forehead. "Well, that's easy to remember. In my life, it seems everything that's good looking is dangerous."

Connie thwacked him on the back of the head. "You're impossible. You know that, don't you?"

Carducci nodded. "So I've been told."

It would have been nearly impossible for Delta to decide which way the Colombian camp was. The two warriors who had escorted her out of the village had managed to find the old camp, but it had already been abandoned.

Wherever Zahn and his men were, Delta didn't have a clue as to
which direction they might have gone.

After rifling through the old camp, Delta turned to the
two warriors and signaled for them to return to the village.
Shaman's burial ceremony could not begin without them, and
Delta knew in her heart that the old man was dead. He needed his
warriors more than she did. With a slight reluctance, the two men
shook her hand before disappearing quietly into the jungle.

Sitting on a log about one hundred yards from the old
camp, Delta could hear the loud cawing from the scarlet macaws as
they flew overhead. She didn't blame Megan for her involvement in
protecting such a grand species from extinction; especially after
Delta had seen the way the birds were treated after being caught by
greed-driven poachers.

Delta had been pleased that Megan had found a cause she
could get involved in even to the point of risking her life to stop
them. It had helped Megan understand why Delta loved her job so
much and why she was willing to take the risks she took.

Fanning herself with a palm leaf, Delta rose and decided
she would travel to her left; a decision she always made whenever
there was doubt and boy, was she suffering from a huge case of the
doubts now.

Before she could take five more steps, she heard the sound
of one single, measured macaw screech.

Turning completely around, Delta was surprised to see a
scarlet macaw perched on a palm branch about twenty feet off the
ground. Not only was it an odd sight because it was so low, it was
strange to see just one macaw. Delta knew they mated for life, and
if they aren't mated, they hang out with other single macaws. Rarely
do they travel alone, unless...No, it couldn't be.

Walking closer, Delta squinted to get a better view of the
bird, which stood proudly in the sunlight, its yellow and blue wings
spread wide as if to get her attention. It was unusual to see one
down so low, since they favored the warmth and safety of the top
branches. It wasn't until the bird turned its head that Delta jumped
back. "You!" she said, seeing the one eye. Could this possibly be
the same bird she had saved from the poachers? No, it couldn't be.
That would just be too much of a coincidence.

Then she remembered.

Shaman had pointed to his one good eye shortly before she left. He was trying to tell her something. He had called this bird. He and this bird knew each other, and it had come to help her. Delta did not question how she knew this, any more than she would have questioned her instinct on her beat. It was an inexplicable knowing, like a mother's sense when her child is injured or ill. There were some things that science just couldn't explain. This was one of them.

Coincidence, Delta thought, was something that people who believe in nothing believe in. Well, Delta had been a non-believer and a disbeliever of a thousand things in her life, until she became a Bri. In that single, mind-jarring, life-changing ceremony, Delta learned there were things to believe in, and she believed them. All of them.

Stepping as close to the bird as she dare, Delta smiled up as it blinked its one good eye at her.

"Hello, again," Delta said quietly. "You have no idea how good it is to see you."

The bird made little grinding noises with his beak before ruffling its feathers. It looked much healthier than it did the day Delta and Connie had cut duct tape off its beak and feet when they had saved it from the poachers who capture them to sell on the black market for pets. Megan had explained that domestically bred Scarlets might cost anywhere from one to three thousand dollars in the states, but an illegally imported one sold for only hundreds. It was illegal as hell, but poaching was still alive and well in the jungle.

"So." Delta said. "What now?"

On cue, the bird flew to a tree fifty yards away, perched, cawed, and waited. As soon as Delta caught up, it took flight to the next tree. They did this dance for nearly three hours until the macaw landed on a branch with its head turned in one direction. It appeared that this was the end of the line, and Delta looked up at the macaw and smiled.

"Thank you," she whispered, and then, as if it had accomplished its task, it ruffled its feathers once more, shook out its long, scarlet tail, and took flight.

"Thank you all," Delta whispered, to the macaw, to Shaman, to Miles. When she looked up, she saw the entrance heavily guarded to Zahn's camp. All she had to do now was get to that phone and let someone, anyone, know she was alive.

⊕

"You still alive?" Connie asked Tony as she shook him awake.

"Huh? What?"

"Josh and Sal just arrived, and Josh wants to see you outside."

Rubbing sleep from his eyes, Carducci padded barefoot through the front door.

"You look worried," Bianca said, watching Connie stare out the window.

"I'll be better once Megan and Taylor get here."

Bianca set a glass of lemonade by the computer as Connie returned to the table to put Eddie through his paces. "You know, I hesitated coming back here. I honestly didn't want to put you in the middle of anything."

Bianca poured herself a glass of lemonade and stood next to Connie. "If innocent people are being killed and my brother chooses not to help them, then he's made the wrong choice. Maybe I'm the balance of the universe. You know, offsetting the things he does."

Connie grinned as her fingers flew across the keyboard. "How'd you get so smart?"

Bianca shrugged. "Old soul."

Carducci re-entered and pulled up a chair next to Connie. "Weapons are ready. Josh and Sal are going to fill the canteens."

Bianca quickly chugged her lemonade and wiped her mouth with the back of her hand. "We're on our way. It will only take about thirty minutes to get everything ready."

As Bianca headed for the door, Connie called to her. "Bianca?"

"Yes?"

"You're right, you know."

Bianca grinned. "I know."

"Bright kid," Carducci said, drinking from Connie's glass. "Hard to believe she's just sixteen."

Connie nodded. "There's a lot that's hard to believe down here."

"I'll say. Are you all set?"

Connie cocked her head to one side and studied him for a moment. She was liking him more and more. "Yeah, so far. I think that should do it. All we need is the rest of our little party, and we're set."

"Great. I'm itching to get going. You think Gina and Logan have hooked up yet?"

Connie shrugged. She hated the thought of sending Gina to the Caribbean side of the country all alone, but they had little choice. They couldn't afford to cut any of the others loose if the plan was to work.

Connie's plan was simple. Gina and Logan would wait off the coast on a fishing boat until they saw the flare. Then, they would send multiple faxes to every national and international police agency in Latin America, telling them of a paramilitary group in the jungle that was using Costa Rica as the staging area for drug sales. That way, if this whole thing turned sour on them, there would be some serious help; somebody out there would do something or, at the very least, investigate the claim. The faxes would be untraceable, and the little rescue troop would be able to slip into the Caribbean virtually unnoticed.

It was a good plan, but Connie knew no plan was foolproof, and this one, especially. There were simply too many variables to be able to make a plan that was truly sound.

Carducci looked at the screen. "So, is that what you've been doing, pounding on the keyboard, finding numbers for government agencies?"

Connie grinned and nodded. "May the wonders of the information super highway never cease to exist".

"Con, it's a good plan. I sure hope it works."

Connie turned and stared at him. "Are you having doubts?"

Carducci leaned forward. "Frankly, yes. I don't like the idea of women going into this kind of no-holds-barred combat, if you know what I mean."

Connie rolled her eyes. "Tony, your macho slip is showing."

"My...oh, I get it." Carducci blushed. "Sorry. Bad habit. Delta hasn't managed to break them all, you know."

"You know, Tony," Connie said. "It's quite possible we could get in there and out without killing anyone."

Carducci shook his head. "When pigs fly. There's no way those guys are going to let us waltz in there and take their laborers. No, I'll be surprised if all of us make it out alive."

As much as she didn't want to hear the truth, Connie couldn't disagree with him. Unless there was a more peaceful, quiet way to go about this, guns were going to be blasting, bullets were going to be fired, and people were going to die. She just hoped it wouldn't be any of them.

Carducci studied Connie for a moment before sighing.

"What's on your mind, Tony?"

Carducci looked down at his bare feet as a pink tint rose on his cheeks.

Connie nodded to him. "What's going on?"

Carducci very quietly said, "I was just wondering, you know, about the baby."

Connie turned to fully face him. "What about her?"

The pink tint suddenly darkened. "Aren't you worried? I mean, you know how kids are. They can be so mean."

Connie smiled warmly at Carducci. "You think the kids will be mean because she's going to be raised by two moms?"

Carducci nodded.

"Tony, kids are being raised by all kinds of configurations now. Blended families, single parents and their children living together, even communes haven't died out completely. This child won't suffer any more than a kid being raised by just a dad or a grandparent."

Carducci sighed. "I just hate the thought of kids coming down on her, that's all."

Connie smiled at him. Delta may not have broken him of all his bad habits, but she had certainly opened up his little mind. "People, in general, are cruel, Tony. It takes a village to raise a child. Our baby will be surrounded by people who love us and who will adore her. By the time she is old enough to go to school, she'll know the good people from the jerks."

Carducci nodded as he listened. "What if it's a boy?"

"Are you speaking in terms of a role model?"

He nodded.

"There will be plenty of those, regardless of the baby's gender.

What makes a role model a good role model has nothing to do with gender. It has to do with ethics, morals, and principles. Our child will have many good, loving role models, like yourself."

Carducci's face lit up. "Really?"

"Hell, yes. Tony, you didn't have to come down here and risk your life, but you did because you're a good person and you care. You're just the kind of person I want around my child."

The kindness of Connie's words turned the pink to a dark red, as an ear-to-ear smile spread across his face." Wow. You mean, you'd let me take him to a ballgame or out to shag flies or fishing?"

Connie laughed. "Well, I don't quite know what shagging flies is, but as long as it isn't pulling their little wings off, sure, why not?"

Carducci's smile widened even further. "Man, that'd be great."

Connie reached for his hand and held it between hers. "Tony, we've been so hard on you at RVPD because somewhere, deep down, Delta saw the potential of you to be a great cop. Delta doesn't let potential go to waste."

Carducci nodded, looking down at his big hand sandwiched between Connie's. "That why she rides me so hard".

Connie chuckled. "Trust me, Tony, you haven't experienced just how hard Delta can really be."

"That's a scary thought."

"Indeed. You know how she works. She has one speed. Fast. You either keep up, follow, or get the hell out of the way."

"Yeah. I've seen that. It's what makes her so good."

"It's one of the things that makes her so good."

"You don't think she'd mind if I took Junior to be with the guys, do you?"

Connie's eyebrows rose. "The guys?"

"Yeah, you know. The other little boys in the park."

Connie grinned as she shook her head. "What if it's a girl?"

Carducci appeared momentarily stumped before another smile spread across his face. "Then, I'll teach her how to kick ass!"

The front screen slammed open, and Megan pushed her way through it, hot, sweaty, and swearing.

"It's about time. Where've you two been?" Connie asked, taking one of Megan's bags from her.

"Someone," she shot a look at Taylor, who fell in beside her, "doesn't know how to read a map."

"Hey, I can't help it if the damn thing is in Spanish!" Taylor tossed her bag on the floor. "This place is out in the boondocks."

Connie put her hands on the smaller woman's shoulders. "I'm afraid, where the 'boondocks' are concerned, you ain't seen nothing yet."

SIX

Delta hadn't seen the interior of the camp yet, but it wasn't long before she came across her first sentry. Ducking down, she watched his legs as he strolled by. She was close, and adrenaline surged through her. Now, all she needed to do was find Zahn's trailer, get in, make a call, and get out so she could frame a strategy. One had already been brewing in the back of her mind. With the silence of the bow and arrow and blowgun, she could take out the sentries first. But she had to make sure that none of their weapons went off to alarm the others. She would have to bring them down quietly, one by one, just as she had told Itka.

But first, the trailer.

She'd considered waiting until night, but she couldn't risk either fumbling in the dark for the phone or shining a light for all to see. The odds were that Zahn would be there and confronting him right now was not part of the plan. Delta had to get help first. She might be able to weaken Zahn's numbers, but in the big picture, he had the hostages, and she couldn't afford to put them at risk. So, she would wait. Wait for back up to find her out here in the middle of nowhere. Wait for Connie to come running, as she had so often in the past. Wait. For how long, she did not know.

Delta silently made her way closer to the camp, which was set up much like the other camp, with one huge exception. There were no tents erected. What did this mean? Where was he keeping the prisoners? Delta squatted on her haunches and watched the minimal activity of the camp.

Days ago, when Delta and company had come down to find Megan, they'd arrived at the camp only to discover that Megan had cut her way out of her tent.

More than likely Zahn had fixed this "problem" by keeping the prisoners some place safer, someplace like the caverns themselves.

"Damn," Delta whispered, splitting a leaf with her thumb. It would be much harder to get the prisoners out of a cave than out of tents. She couldn't do that on her own, that was certain. She had to get to that phone and let someone know she was alive, know where she was. To the rest of the world, Delta was a needle in a haystack. But to Connie Rivera, she was the golden egg, and if Connie knew Delta was somewhere in the jungle, Connie would find her. Delta was counting on that.

For the next hour, she watched the comings and goings, until she saw Zahn exit the trailer, say something to one of his men, and walk toward the caverns. This might be the only chance she would get.

Carefully pulling out two of the small, feathered Bri darts, Delta loaded one into the blowgun and with a quick inhale and a push of air, sent a dart into the leg of one of the guards. Swatting at the protruding dart as if it were an insect, he collapsed in a heap.

Removing her bow, arrows and remaining curare tips from her quiver, Delta sent her second dart toward another sentry. He toppled over two seconds after the dart was embedded in his arm. Delta wished they could use these darts on the streets back home instead of a chokehold or baton. How easy it would be to subdue a perpetrator.

Covering up her weapons, her knapsack, bota, and canteen, for later, Delta plucked both darts from the men before quickly scooting around to the back side of the trailer. There, she found one window slightly open, and with a sharp tug, opened it completely and slithered through. When she landed, she was surprised her leg and shoulder had held up so well, and wished she would have had more time with Flora's grandmother to talk about the healing agents she'd used on the bullet wounds.

What she found inside surprised her even though Megan had described it. In the middle of the jungle, General Zahn was somehow managing to enjoy all the creature comforts of home. There was a loveseat, a desk with a computer, and a silver tea service on the coffee table with linen napkins arranged nicely around it. This crazy son of a bitch was living luxuriously, while both his men and his prisoners suffered through days of torment and hard work.

It was time, Delta decided, that General Zahn got what he deserved. He had hurt so many people, both directly and indirectly.

He was a Colombian in Costa Rica stealing gold that belonged to the Costa Ricans. He had murdered countless innocent people and taken Shaman from the Bri. She wondered what other atrocities he'd committed in his degenerate life. It was time to end his reign of terror here in the jungle, and Delta felt up to the task.

"Crazy bastard," Delta said, quickly moving to the desk. The computer was not on, but the phone, which looked like something out of Star Trek, lay next to it. The thrill of seeing a phone sent chills up Delta's spine. Finally, she could contact civilization.

Snatching the phone, Delta studied it for several seconds before pulling the antenna up and dialing the only thirteen numbers where she was absolutely certain someone would be.

The connection seemed to take forever, as sweat dripped down her back and between her breasts. Tick, tick, tick. Delta kept away from the window and waited for an eternity. Finally, the phone on the other end rang.

"River Valley Police Department. Sergeant McNeill speaking. How can I help you?" came the forced cheery voice. Sergeant McNeill was anything but pleasant.

Delta wanted to laugh. Well, for one, you could send in the US Army to get me out of this mess, she thought.

"Kim, it's Delta Stevens."

"Delta? Where the hell are you? Everyone here has been sick with worry."

"Well, I'm alive. Listen, Kim, I don't have time. Have you heard from Connie?"

"She called the other day to tell us that you'd gotten lost in the jungle and you'd be needing more comp time. And then..."

"Where is she?"

"Where else? Still in Central America somewhere, looking for you. Where are you?"

Before Delta could answer, the trailer door opened, and a very surprised General Zahn looked at her as if she were an apparition. He looked at Delta; she looked at him, neither quite knowing what to do. Time stood still as they sized each other up like two territorial cougars. It was Zahn, however, who made the first move.

Removing his gun from its holster, he pointed it at Delta and said something in Spanish. When she did not respond, he tried English. "I see I have an intruder."

Delta looked at the gun and smiled before saying into the phone, "Tell Connie I believe the story about her uncle-"

Zahn pulled the hammer back. "Another word, and you're a dead woman."

With regret so deep, she could feel it in her muscles; Delta pressed the zero and then hung the phone up.

Zahn motioned for Delta to move out from behind the desk. "Good. Before I kill you, you will tell me how you escaped."

Delta did not move. Her eyes swept from the gun to Zahn's deeply tanned face. He wore a thick, dark mustache, which matched his equally abundant eyebrows. Dressed impeccably in a khaki uniform, he reminded Delta of a modern-day Pancho Villa.

"Well?" Zahn raised the gun and pointed it at Delta's face.

Delta shrugged. "Escaped? I don't know what you're talking about."

"Come away from the desk." Zahn wagged the gun at her as he indicated that she should stand in front of the loveseat.

Delta did as she was told, never taking her eyes off his face. Should she jump him and take her chances, or play this charade out?

"Who are you?" Zahn asked, sitting on the desk and motioning Delta to sit on the couch. It was a wise move on his part, because it put him in a physically superior position. He'd made her decision for her. She would have to play this out. "I'm Dr. Rivera from Stanford University, and you are?"

"General Zahn, and I will ask the questions. What were you doing on my phone?"

"Isn't it obvious? I was calling for help. I am here with a biological team studying scarlet macaws, and I got separated from my group. I saw this trailer and was so glad to find a phone. I'm sorry if I upset you."

Zahn's eyes narrowed as he glared at Delta, and she knew he must have been weighing her words against his judgment.

"How many others are out there?" he asked, lowering the gun. After all, he had nothing to fear from a female biologist.

"There are only six of us, two biologists, one avian, one..."

"How did you get past my guards?"

"What guards?" Delta asked, all innocence.

Zahn jumped up from the desk and opened the front door, shouting a litany of orders to a man who saluted before running off in the direction of the sentries.

"They shall pay for their inattention," Zahn said, more to himself than to her. Back at the desk, he laid the gun in his lap and continued his interrogation.

"Who did you call?"

"The University of Costa Rica's Department of Biology."

Zahn picked up the phone and pressed redial. The only sound he heard was a single click.

"I had to dial the extension number," Delta explained, wiping the sweat from her lip.

"What did you say to them?"

"That I was lost and to radio the team that I was somewhere due north of our last research locale."

Zahn thought about the implications of this. "Your team has a radio?"

Delta nodded. "Oh yes. All of the major researchers..."

"Any weapons?"

Delta cocked her head. This just might work. "Weapons? No, of course not. We're biologists, General."

Suddenly, there came a loud, continuous pounding at the door. When the general answered it, the soldier he had dispatched was spewing Spanish like a punctured tire releases air. Zahn listened for a moment and then barked orders to the man who, in turn, sent half a dozen men scattering.

"What is it?" Delta asked innocently.

Zahn studied her for a second, and Delta knew he was trying to decide whether or not she, a woman, was capable of taking out two of his men. Her only hope, at this point, hinged on the predictability of the macho Latin American male. He would see her as a helpless woman lost in the jungle, not a veteran cop who, given equal circumstances, could kick his ass into tomorrow.

"Where is your equipment, Doctor?"

Delta sighed. "With the others. I got in a fight with another professor and went for a walk to cool off. That's when I got lost."

"Two of my men are dead, and I find you on my phone. I find that coincidence a little too hard to believe."

"Surely, General, you do not think one woman, a professor no less, capable of killing two trained soldiers? I abhor violence in any form."

"Right now, I am not sure what I believe. Until I know for sure, you will remain in that room."

Delta tried to look astonished. "What? You're not going to help me?"

"Doctor, you have stumbled on a top secret military excursion. Highly classified. You understand, I'm sure. It is for your own safety as well."

Delta shrugged. The perspiration on her back had spread to her waist and down the back of her legs. "I suppose. How long before you can let me go? I mean, my colleagues will be worried."

"Until I see what happened to my men. Then, I will have you escorted out of here."

Delta wanted to laugh. She imagined her escort meant a bullet to the back of the head and a shallow grave. The only reason she wasn't dead now was because the soldiers were scurrying around like army ants trying to find what killed those two men. Once the hubbub was over, she'd be tasting lead.

Zahn opened a small second room, filled with boxes, canvas bags, and assorted scales. "You'll be safe in here."

"You can't be serious!"

"Do not try my patience, doctor. If all is as you say, then you will be free to go shortly."

"I don't want to go shortly, I want to go now!"

Slam. The door was closed, and Delta quickly took survey of her prison. No windows, but there was a small closet. She opened up each box and found nothing but paper work. Checking the door to make sure it was locked, Delta was surprised when it flew open to reveal another soldier.

"Yes?" Delta smiled at the guard and retreated.

"Uh, nada. Gracias."

Slam. The door closed for a second time. Okay, she was in a windowless room with an armed guard at the door and probably more surrounding the trailer. That was the bad news. The good news was she was still alive. Now, if only her message was delivered to Connie, wherever she was.

Sitting on a large cardboard box, Delta looked down at her sweat-drenched clothes and covered her face with her hands.

This was not how she had anticipated her plan unfolding. Suddenly, Delta had the horrible feeling she'd just played her last card.

⊕

Carducci threw a trump card on the table and took the trick. "Come to papa," he said, grinning over at Taylor and Sal, who then threw their cards at him.

"Told you I was good," he said, picking the cards up. "Connie, are you sure we should wait until morning?"

Josh strode over from the window, where he'd been standing for more than an hour staring out at the jungle. "Ever been in a jungle?" he asked Carducci.

"Nope."

"Ever been someplace unfamiliar and the lights went out?"

"Yeah. Delta and I were on this call once in this field. There wasn't a damn light anywhere. Even the moon was a no-show. She, of course, insisted that we not turn our flashlights on."

Connie chuckled. "She told me this story. You turned yours on, didn't you?"

Carducci nodded. "Yep, and damned if the perps didn't shoot right at me. If Delta hadn't taught me how to hold my flashlight away from my body, I'd have been history."

Connie looked over her cards. "That's not the end of the story, Tony."

Tony started dealing another hand. "Well, it answered Josh's question, didn't it?"

Taylor picked up the bait. "Oh, no, Tonikins. Do tell. What happened next?"

Carducci glared over at Connie, who chuckled again. "Yes, Tony, do tell."

Carducci set his cards down and sighed. "I drew down, and Delta knocked my gun from my hand. I wanted to shoot the bastard. I was scared to death, man. It was the first time I'd ever been shot at."

Josh joined the group at the table and waited for the rest of the story. "I nearly crapped my pants the first time I was shot at."

Carducci sighed. "I think I was more afraid of Delta's wrath than being shot." He continued dealing. "It was so dark, and they'd already taken a pot shot at us. I couldn't believe she still wanted to move ahead." Carducci shook his head at the memory. "But that's Delta in a nutshell, isn't it?"

"More like nut case," Taylor added, scooping up her cards.

"Well, it seems Delta knew the woman who was shooting at us. Some homeless lady named Patty Packer, because she packs heat."

Taylor laughed. "Patty Packer? You've got to be kidding."

Connie punched in more information and shook her head. "All of the homeless people on Del's beat have nom de plumes. Most of which were given by her and Miles."

Carducci nodded. "Apparently, Patty had been raped a few years back, and so Miles gave her a piece he'd snagged from some drug dealer."

"What did she say when she realized it was Delta?"

Carducci's face started turning pink. "She apologized and said something about not thinking it was Delta, because she knew better than to turn her flashlight on in the middle of a dark field."

"Even the homeless have lessons to teach, eh, Tones?" Sal chipped in.

"Was Delta mad?" Taylor asked.

Carducci shook his head. "Nope. She just told me that that kind of luck runs out. That cops who rely on luck become prematurely familiar with their mortician."

Connie laughed. The words, though wise, were not originally Delta's. Connie had said them to Delta one evening when Delta was a rookie, herself, and had stormed her way into a situation where luck was the only ingredient that had kept her body intact.

"Well, Tony," Josh said, clapping Carducci on the shoulder, "that darkness is what it's like in the jungle at night. We have a reasonably good chance of finding those assholes pretty quickly in the day, but at night, we run the risk of moving farther away than we are now."

"The waiting is killing me. I feel like we ought to be doing something."

Connie turned from the computer and smiled at Carducci. "We can't risk it, Tony. We have to be smart about this."

Connie pressed the dial button and waited for the Internet server to tell her if she had mail. She did.

Carducci studied his hand. "Well, waiting around sucks."

Josh sat across from Carducci. "Tony, what we're about to do, man, could cause an international problem greater than you can imagine. Think about it. A bunch of renegade Americans in Costa Rica gunning down a major member of a Colombian cartel. The repercussions are gonna be felt in our government as well as Costa Rica, Colombia, and any number of our allies."

"I just can't believe a little shit hole country like Colombia has so much power."

"Money is power, Tones," Sal said, "and with 80 percent of the coke market, they got plenty of it."

"Amen," Connie said. Clicking open her mailbox, her heart leaped into her throat. The email simply said, ET phone home, Delta's alive! RVPD. Jumping to her feet, Connie let out a yell that scared everyone in the room. Grabbing the phone, Connie could hear the modem fuzz in the earpiece until she clicked on her computer to disconnect. "Delta called the precinct! She's alive!"

"What?" Megan came to her feet and joined Connie, as did the others. Everyone gathered around the phone as Connie waited for the other end to ring.

"RVPD, how may I direct your call?"

"Frances, this is Connie Rivera, I..."

"Oh my god, hold on! Hold on!"

Connie looked at the group and shrugged. "They're all very excited. My god, she's alive! I knew it!"

"Con? This is Kim. Delta called!"

"I got your email. What happened? How do you know?"

Without warning, Connie's hands started shaking, and tears filled her eyes. She thought she might break down, but the anxious faces waiting for her deserved better. Moving the phone away from her mouth, Connie let two tears fall as she reached out for Megan's hand.

"She's alive, Megan."

Megan's pace went pale and she blinked rapidly, as if trying to understand what Connie had just said. "She's alive?" Megan finally said.

"I knew it!" Sal said, giving Josh a high five.

"Where is she?" Megan whispered.

Connie returned the phone to her mouth. "Where is she?"

"Well, that's the thing. We don't know."

"You don't know? What do you mean you don't know?" Connie shrugged at the others huddled around her.

"She said for me to tell you she was alive, and then she paused, she said the strangest thing. Let's see, I wrote it down because it was so weird."

There was a rustling of papers and then Kim was back on. "Here it is. She said that she believed your story about your uncle, and then she disconnected."

Connie frowned. "That's it?"

"I'm afraid so."

Connie looked at Megan, her face filled with hope. Connie didn't know if she had the heart to tell Megan that the worst of her fears could still come true. "And that was all she said?"

"That was it. I made sure to write it all down, and one of the guys suggested emailing you. We all know what a computer geek you are."

"Thanks."

"You don't sound as thrilled as I thought you would."

"Delta may be alive, but she's far from being out of danger. Thanks a lot, Kim. If you hear anything else, I'm at 002-555-428-8082."

"Sure thing. Oh, and Connie."

"Yeah?"

"You both are sorely missed around here."

"Thanks." Hanging the phone up, Connie inhaled deeply and addressed the group longing for an explanation. "The good news is that Delta is alive. The bad news is I don't know for how much longer."

Megan swallowed so hard, everyone heard her. "Where is she, Con?"

Connie took Megan's hands in hers. "If my guess is right, Delta's been captured by General Zahn."

⊕

General Zahn was gone about an hour before the door to Delta's makeshift jail cell swung open and his large frame filled the doorway. He was a particularly scary-looking man, with the eyes of a hunter and a cruel mouth. He was fit and trim for a man who wore a general's uniform, and Delta wondered if he were truly a military general.

"While you were out doing your survey, did you see any natives?"

Delta's heart seized as she thought about her necklace. Looking down, she saw it had fallen inside her shirt. "Natives?"

"Yes, you know, Indians."

Delta shook her head. "We came upon no one until I stumbled in here. Thank god I found help. I don't think I wo..."

"It appears my men were killed by a poison of some sort. It would not be wise for me to allow you to go out into the jungle while those natives are on the warpath. It would not be safe for you."

"I have to stay here?"

Zahn nodded. "A few days, maybe less."

"In this room?"

"Si."

"That's ridiculous! Now, if you'll just let me go back to..."

Zahn blocked the door. "I am afraid you do not understand. I am in command here, and it is my responsibility to ensure the safety of everyone. That includes you, doctor."

"But I am no threat to anyone."

"My men and I are testing military equipment of a highly sensitive nature. No one else is allowed to see it."

"I won't look, then. Can't I just go back to my camp? You can have one of your men escort me."

Zahn shook his head. "I cannot spare any of my men at this moment. For the time being, you are safest here."

Delta nodded, not wishing to push him too far. How odd that they were both lying to each other. At least she knew she had a few more days. Maybe her message had reached Connie and help were on their way. Maybe...god, her life seemed made up of a patchwork of maybes.

"I understand. But, could I please have some water? It's very hot in here."

Zahn ordered his man to fetch a glass of water, which he did. In a plastic cup. "Now, I have work to do." With that, the door closed again.

Pacing the two steps it took to cross the room, Delta considered her limited options. She could try to take the first guard out, get his weapon and...and then what? Shoot her way out of a camp full of soldiers? Nope. She would have to give Connie and Megan a chance to get here. This time, Delta would have to wait for someone else to jump in feet first. This time, Delta's life was in someone else's hands. Looking down at the plain silver band she wore on her left hand, Delta sighed.

"Come on, baby. Come through for me. Please come through for me."

⊕

"We'll come through for her," Carducci said as they finished packing their provisions. "She's expecting that, and she deserves it. I don't give a shit how dark it is."

Sal nodded. "What's Con been working on? She hasn't left that computer since she got off the phone."

Carducci shrugged. "Beats me. I've found out that when Connie is glued to that screen, it's best to leave her alone."

Taylor watched Megan lay a semi-automatic gun on the top of her backpack. "You guys are really lucky."

Sal walked over and followed Taylor's line of vision. "Lucky?"

Nodding, Taylor sighed. "You have such a great support system. I mean, you guys really are family."

Sal nodded. "They're really good people. It's easy to be drawn to the four of them."

Taylor smiled warmly at Megan, a woman Taylor hadn't expected to like but did nonetheless. "She's alive, Meg. You need to focus on that."

When she looked up at them, her face was hard and dark. "I've always known she was alive. I just can't handle the thought of that bastard getting his hands on my Delta."

"She's a fighter," Sal said.

"That's exactly what worries me. Megan's words were measured and cold. "If he tries to do to her what he did to me, he'll have to kill her first."

Sal walked over and took her hand. "Delta always comes out on top. You have to keep believing in her the way she kept believing in you."

Megan nodded. "I'm trying. All I can feel right now is bloodlust. If he does anything to her, anything at all, his will not be a quick death."

The front door squealed open and Connie strutted out, beaming with confidence. "Damn, I'm even better than I thought." She held up the topographical map.

"What's that?" Carducci asked.

Connie crowed. "I know exactly where the Colombians are."

Everyone stared and waited. "How?"

"Eddie is a remarkable tool. He and I were able to hop on the Internet and with a great deal of fancy footwork and computer know-how, we were able to locate Zahn's modem."

"What?" Taylor said, shaking her head. "Locate his mother?"

Connie laughed. "Modem. Mo-dem. Megan said he had a computer. The only reason he'd have a computer in the jungle would be if he were using it to transmit data to the cartel. You know, updates, measurements, etc."

"Amazing," Carducci said.

"Not really," Connie shrugged. "The greatest weakness of the Internet is that once your modem is on-line, your privacy is nil. Just about everything within your computer is up for grabs."

"But aren't there security systems in place? Surely the cartel wouldn't allow access to their files."

Connie grinned. "No one allows me and Eddie to go anywhere. We go and do as we please, because we know what we're doing. Hacking is an art. Hell, if I were crooked, I'd be as rich as Taylor."

Gina nodded. "Connie's even managed to get into NASA. She's pretty remarkable."

Megan threw her arms around Connie's neck. "Yes, you are! God, I don't know what we'd do without you."

Josh strode over and offered a big paw to Connie. "Is that what you've been doing with that computer?"

Connie nodded. "It was difficult because I had to be on-line at the same time he was. I programmed Eddie to wave a flag, so to speak, every time a modem was used in the vicinity. Once Zahn logged on, we siphoned his information and came up with his coordinates."

"That's incredible," Taylor said. "I'm impressed."

"You should be. The surveillance software I have for this sort of thing was developed jointly by the CIA and Japan's secret service. It kicks ass over the old stuff. In today's technological society, knowledge and information mean power. We now have, my friends, the power to move forward. The night, the darkness be damned. We have the coordinates."

Megan threaded her arms around Connie's waist and hugged her tightly. "You are a remarkable woman, Connie Rivera."

"Yeah, well, this remarkable woman is ready to go. Everybody game?"

⊕

The game was winding down, and Delta was beginning to feel the pressure of the wait. More than anything, she hated doing nothing. Because of the intense heat in the small, confined space, she was losing body fluids by the quart. Though it was now night, the trailer had cooled off only slightly.

Pushing the boxes out of the way, Delta pulled the carpet up on one corner to see if there was any way she could slip out through the floor. The trailer perched on two cut trees, the way most motor homes sit on blocks. Maybe she could drop below the floor and shimmy out that way.

Feeling along the floor, Delta found a small piece of metal and tucked it in her sock. As she started further exploration, Delta saw a light flash under the door and the distinct sound of low voices right outside. Then, the door flew open, and there stood General Zahn, his two fiery eyes glaring at her.

"I contacted Stanford University doctor and it appears no one has heard of you, of this project, of nada."

"Well, I'm now..."

Slap! A lightning-quick backhand smacked into her cheek, sending her reeling against the wall. "Enough lies! Who are you, and what are you doing here?"

Wiping the blood from her lip, Delta stood erect and locked eyes with him. If it was possible, she hated him more than she had hated anyone in her life. "All right," she said through gritted teeth. "You caught me."

"I should kill you right now."

"And miss out on millions of dollars?"

Slap! This time was harder than the first. Delta tripped over one of the boxes and hit her head on the wall as she fell.

"Do not fuck with me, girl."

Raising back up, feeling her eye begin to swell, Delta pulled out the last bluff she had. "Look, I lied because uniforms make me nervous. I am an international jewel thief hiding out down here."

Zahn raised his hand, but Delta did not move. Their eyes locked together. Delta had already determined she would go down glaring at him in anger, and not like some sniveling, whining coward. "I've stolen over 30 million worth of jewels, which can be yours if you let me live."

Zahn slowly lowered his hand. He squinted as if doing so would enable him to find the truth. "Can you prove this, or is this another pathetic attempt to save your life?"

"I can prove it. If you call 011-555-827-1092, you'll reach the district attorney's office. The DA who handled my case is Alexandria Pendleton. My name is Taylor. Taylor Storm Stevens. Look, I am wanted by the FBI, Interpol, and some podunk city pd. I recently made some big scores there, but they couldn't catch me. Call that DA. She'll confirm it all. Go ahead, call. It could be the most lucrative call of your life."

Zahn stepped deeper into the room and glowered at her. "If this is another lie, you will die a most unpleasant death." With that, he turned on his heel and whisked past the guard, leaving Delta to ponder the minutes she might have left.

If Alexandria took the clues and confirmed her story, Delta had bought herself more time. Not much more, but enough. If Alex wouldn't confirm it, Delta had to decide just how she would try to take Zahn out. If he was going to kill her, he was going with her.

Five minutes later, he returned, and knew by the look on his face that he had been pleasantly surprised. "It seems as though your words were true."

"Who did you talk to?"

"Alexandria Pendleton, just as you said. She said your estimated worth could be one hundred million. You said thirty."

Delta shrugged. "I lost count."

For a moment, Zahn considered the information. "Fine, then. It will cost you one hundred million to save your life and not a penny less. When we are through here, you will hand over your jewels, and I will let you go."

"How do I know you won't kill me?"

The general grinned. "You don't."

"So that's it, then? I just have to wait here while you do whatever the hell it is you're doing? Can't you put me to work, or something?"

Zahn leaned closer to her and inhaled deeply. "The only work I would feel comfortable giving to you, my dear, would be lying on your back." Zahn laughed as he turned for the door. The room reeked of his body odor and aftershave.

"No thanks, General, I think I'd rather just stay here."

Zahn paused at the door, as if considering her fate. "Just be sure you remain quiet."

Nodding, Delta wiped more blood from her lip. "Oh, and General?"

"Yes?"

"If you ever hit me again, I'll kill you."

Zahn frowned, looked hard at Delta and laughed. "What is it with you American women?"

"We don't like bullies, General."

The general stopped in the doorway and turned to her. "And the next time, my dear, you talk to me like that, I will kill you.."

Delta nodded. "Then, I think we understand each other, don't we?"

"It would appear."

SEVEN

"It would appear we're ready," Connie said. The sun had already set, and the group was more than anxious to get going. Megan noted Connie's stiff demeanor and sidled up next to her.

"What's eating you?" Megan asked. "Scared?"

Connie's eyes slowly filled with tears. "Yes," she answered quietly. "I'm afraid we won't get to her in time. I'm afraid we won't all come out of this alive. I'm afraid. Afraid of what my life might be like after this is over."

Megan put her arm around Connie and pulled her closer. "It will be filled with joy and the memories of the crazy period in our lives when we followed Delta down a rabbit hole."

This brought a smile to Connie's sun-darkened face. "I hope so, Meg. Ever since she's been gone, there's been this gaping hole in my spirit where she used to be. Life would never be right for me without Storm causing chaos."

"Then you just make damn sure the two of you come home. No heroics, no grand gestures. Let's do what we came here to do and get the hell out."

"Right."

"I think we're all set," Megan said softly.

"Troops ready?" Connie asked, looking over at her friends who had guns and knives hanging from their belts. They were as prepared as they could hope to be under the circumstances, and Connie knew in her heart that these individuals were willing to die in order to save Delta Stevens. It was all she could do to keep from crying again.

"Ready and raring, Chief."

The nickname Delta often used for Connie came from Carducci's mouth before he could stop it, and Megan and Connie just stared at him.

"Um...sorry," he said, bowing his head.

Connie grinned at him. "Don't be. The Chief, I am, and
the Chief I will always be." Walking over to Bianca, Connie saluted
her. "I don't know how to thank you, Bianca, for the kindness you
have shown me and my friends."

Bianca smiled softly. "This rain forest is my home, Connie.
You and your friends have come to help it in one way or another.
First, Megan tried to save our beautiful macaws. Now, there are
lives at stake, and who knows, maybe even the country's life.
This is the least I can do for people who care as much as you do. I
only wish I could go, but I think it best if I stay home and deal
with Manny when he shows up."

"You think he will?" Carducci asked.

Bianca nodded. "Count on it. Don't underestimate my
brother. If he figures out you have not left the country, he will
return to Rivas. When he does, I have a few things to say to him."

"Well, you be careful, Bianca."

"You, too. And when you find Delta, please give her a
hug from me."

Connie nodded and she turned to go. It did not surprise
her that Delta Stevens had fans all over the world.

As the group began their descent into the darkness of the
jungle, Bianca patted Kiki's head. "Come on, Kiki," Bianca
whispered as headed back toward her house. "I think they're going
to need some help."

⊕

Delta knew she was going to need some help if she was
going to get out alive. She chipped away at the floor with a metal
stick, but nothing would give. The guard at the door hadn't
responded to her request for more water, and the air in the room
was stifling and stale. Slumping down against the wall, Delta
sighed, "Come on, Con, I can't do this by myself."

It had been hours since the general had left; yet Delta
could hear nothing outside. He must, she reasoned, be keeping the
hostages in the caverns. But why couldn't she hear anything else?
Surely, she should have heard soldiers laughing and talking;
something that indicated there were people outside. Only the
familiar night sounds of the jungle seeped in, barely audible
through the trailer walls.

Closing her eyes and leaning her head against the wall, Delta's mind bounced from subject to subject like a pinball in a 100,000-point arcade game. She thought about Flora and how eager the poor girl was to have a life, an adventure of her own. Adventures in Delta's life were a dime a dozen, some welcome, some not. She thought about Alexandria Pendleton's offer to come work for her as a special investigator to the DA. Now that could be an adventure. She and Connie could be partners. The thought was both exhilarating and intimidating. She thought about Connie and Gina raising a baby in an ever-frightening homophobic society. She thought about Carducci moving on to SWAT and finally fulfilling his John Wayne dream.

And she thought about Megan and the fear and anxiety she must be feeling at the prospect of living a life without Delta. Delta had been there, and she knew that it was one of the loneliest, scariest places in the world. She only hoped that Megan was too busy getting to her to think about the fear. The fear, like raging cancer cells, could eat you alive. She hoped Megan was stronger than that. Delta hoped they were all stronger than that.

When Delta's eyes opened, she realized she'd been asleep. For just how long, she didn't know. What she did know was that there was absolutely no sound. If the soldiers were drinking and partying like they used, they were doing it someplace else.

Placing her ear to the door, Delta held her breath as she listened. The murmur of low voices was all she could hear.

Exhaling softly, Delta was surprised when the door opened, the light temporarily blinding her. For a moment, the guard said nothing. Then, without warning, he cried, "Usted!"

Crouched low beneath some short palms, the small cadre looked down at the flickering torches surrounding the encampment. It was nearly 2 a.m. when they had come upon the camp, which looked much different than the last one they'd been to. Instead of tents ringing the camp, there were half a dozen torches, each manned by an armed guard. The trailer Megan had visited more times than she cared to remember had managed to find its way to this camp, though it sat awkwardly to one side, as if set down on a slope. Apparently, no one had bothered to right it.

There was a torch and a guard in front of the trailer as well, but there were no hostages to be seen.

"Where are the tents?" Megan whispered to the group.

Connie and Sal looked to each other for an answer. It was Connie who spoke first. "My guess," Connie said, "is that after you escaped, they made some changes."

"I'll say. You don't think..." Megan said, covering her mouth with her hand.

Connie shook her head. "No, I don't think they're all dead. If they were, he'd be long gone. He still needs them to pan and transport the gold. Zahn's not about to kill his pack mules until he's gotten all that gold to safety."

Sal took her cap off and shook her head. "Greedy son of a bitch. He could have been long gone already."

Connie nodded. "His greed will be his downfall."

Taylor, who had said little the entire trip, eased over to Connie. "Is that the place?"

Connie nodded. She hadn't realized how tight the security would be around the camp. There was no revelry, no partying, and no easy way in and out. The trailer may as well have been Fort Knox. "That's the one," Connie replied, pointing to the trailer and handing the night goggles to Taylor, who peered through them once before handing them back. They would have to kill many more men than Connie had originally thought. Either Zahn had reinforcements or she had severely underestimated the number of his men the first time around.

"Cake," Taylor said, a little too loudly.

"Shh. You can't be serious," Sal said, staring through the second pair of night goggles. "They've got the place covered."

Taylor grinned. "Au contraire, mon amie. In and out like that." Taylor snapped her fingers. "These bozos don't have the first clue about security. I can tell you right now, I've seen better security forces from the rent-a-cops in some podunky museums."

Josh scooted over to them and peered through his night goggles. "She's right. These guys aren't soldiers. They may look and act the part, but they're civvies, no doubt about it."

Megan rose. "That's good enough for me. Come on. Let's go find Del."

Everyone reached to stop her.

"No way, Meg," Josh whispered. "Get down."

"But she could…"

"We're didn't come all this way only to get careless now," Josh explained. "Connie and me will recon the area. When we get back, we'll figure out the best route for getting Taylor in and out. Like that." Josh snapped his fingers and winked over at Taylor.

"I agree with Josh," Connie added. "We'll do her no good dead. You guys stay here, check our weapons, and hang tight. We'll be back as soon as we can." Connie took Megan's hand and gave it a quick squeeze. "Hey, we made it this far, didn't we?"

Megan sighed. The thought of her Delta being treated the way she'd been tore at her heart. "Con?"

Connie pulled Megan into a hug. "I know. We'll be back as fast as we can."

Megan shook her head. "I was going to say, leave him for me. You get what you need, you get Taylor to Delta, and we get the hostages, but you leave Zahn to me."

Connie studied Megan for a fraction of a second before nodding. "Sure thing."

When Connie and Josh slithered into the darkness, Taylor slid over to Megan and whispered, "Let it go, Megan. Whatever he did, you have to let it go. That kind of anger is a dangerous place to work from."

Megan inhaled a jerky breath, forcing the memories of Zahn's abuse from her mind. "If he tries to rape Delta, she'd rather go down fighting. He'll kill her."

"Or she'll kill him," Carducci said, snapping together one of the rifles. "My partner doesn't go down easily. Soldiers or no, Delta won't go to the bone yard alone."

Megan closed the circle so they all sat elbow to elbow. "That's true, Tony, but this time, Delta may think she's alone. Who knows how she will react if Zahn puts his hands on her? I may have been able to force myself to do those things, but Delta? She'd rather be dead."

Taylor sighed loudly. "Sounds to me like you need to have more faith. She was able to contact Connie, right? That doesn't sound to me like a woman getting ready to throw in the towel. You guys need an attitude adjustment if we're going to pull this off. Delta is alive, she's unharmed, and all we have to do is get in there and whisk her away from them."

"Shh," Sal said. No one moved. Then, out of nowhere, Connie and Josh returned, silent, as if walking upon a carpet of grass and not piles of leaves.

"Any sign of her?" Megan asked anxiously.

Connie shook her head. "No. We didn't see anyone but the guards. There are two posted at the mouth of the cavern. We suspect Zahn may have the prisoners there, but we can't know for sure until we get in there."

Josh nodded and squatted next to the group. "It's much harder to escape from a cave. Zahn's no dummy."

Megan looked back down at the camp and the flickering torchlights. Yes, she had escaped into the protective darkness of the jungle, knowing full well the risk to the others. She had stolen a knife from Zahn's trailer and waited until nightfall before she cut her way out of the back of the tent and rushed into the wilderness, leaving Siobhan, who was too frightened to come with her, whimpering inside the tent. Megan had promised Siobhan she would come back for them if she reached safety. It was a promise she intended to keep. Megan could only hope Zahn needed the labor more than he needed a scapegoat or an example. Otherwise, her tent mate, Siobhan, was already dead, promise or no promise.

"And you didn't see anyone besides soldiers?"

Josh and Connie shook their heads. "He's sealed that place pretty tight."

"Any rovers?" Carducci asked.

"Not that I could tell," Josh said, lowering his voice. "But that doesn't mean there aren't any."

Megan took one of the night goggles and studied the camp. "Well, after seeing it up close, do you guys have a plan?"

Josh ran his hands over his face. "The way Con and I see it, Delta got cut off when she was on the phone in the trailer. Someone caught her, and she signed off. Since the general is a macho sort of guy, he wouldn't have the trailer guarded in order to keep anyone out. We think he's posted a guard there in order to keep someone in.."

Carducci nodded slowly. "Sounds reasonable."

Josh continued. "It's possible he's keeping her there so she's away from the others. No doubt, there's something precious in that trailer, or why the guards?"

Connie looked over at Taylor, suddenly aware of just how much they needed her. "Taylor, can you get in that trailer undetected?"

Taylor grinned. "I told you. It's cake."

Josh looked over the camp and shook his head. "Girl, you gotta be crazy. There's nothing easy about going through a bunch of would-be soldiers with their fingers on the trigger."

Taylor reached for her bag and then tousled Josh's hair. "Who said anything about going through them?"

For a split second, Delta thought her best chance was going through him; just ram him into the wall and take her best shot at getting out the trailer door.

"Puta!" The soldier spat as he stood in the tiny doorway.

When Delta's eyes adjusted to the light, she was staring into the face of one of the general's men who had chased her through the jungle. His face had the same branch marks across it as she wore on hers, and there was a butterfly bandage across one eyebrow. For a long moment, he stared at her, and Delta knew the ruse was up. Unless she could think of something in the next ten seconds, her life was going to come to that very unpleasant end the general had warned her about.

"You!?!" the soldier growled again, through clenched teeth. He snapped some quick Spanish over his shoulder to the general, who shoved him out of the way and backhanded Delta across the face.

"Fucking bitch! Where is Megan?" His voice was harsh and menacing, nearly cracking in its anger.

Licking her bleeding lip, Delta sneered, "Safe and sound and away from your sorry ass."

Slap! A second backhand rocked Delta's head again, and she struggled to maintain her balance.

"You lie." Zahn clenched his fists and stood ominously, breathing heavily into her face.

Delta wiped her chin with the back of her hand. She had about five minutes left to live if she couldn't come up with something to appease his anger.

"Okay, she's dead. They're all dead. Crashed into the cliffs. Gone in a puff of smoke. Is that what you want to hear?"

General Zahn grabbed Delta's arm and pulled her from the room. Pushing her forward, he shoved her roughly into another room. This one had a bare, stained mattress on the floor, a small light, and one window.

A mattress.

Shit.

Spinning her around, the general slapped her again. "I told you what would happen if you lied to me!"

"Lied? I didn't..."

Whack! Another blow to the side of Delta's face. If she took too many more of these, she wouldn't be in the game much longer. As it was, it didn't appear she had much choice but to take them.

"Where are the others?"

"I told you. Dead."

The general raised his hand again, and Delta held his angry gaze. "Do you honestly think I'd have come back here unless I had to?"

Hand poised to strike, the general slowly lowered it, his eyebrows lifted in question.

"Think about it, General. I came back here because I didn't make it to the helicopter and was left alone. Otherwise, I'd be dead with the rest of them."

"You're a dead woman anyway..." Zahn was at a loss for what to call her.

"Delta," she answered, for no other reason than she wanted him to know who it was that was going to kill him.

"Well, Delta, when my men get through with you, you will wish you had died with your friends. Although it is a shame that Megan had to die. She gave such good head. Perhaps you do as well."

Delta felt her insides begin to crumble. Her worst nightmare was coming to pass, and this time, it didn't appear as if the cavalry was anywhere in sight. Delta Stevens, officer of law, saver of lives, giver of gifts, was facing the kind of death she had always dreaded. In a heart-stopping panic, Delta knew one clear truth: she did not know how to survive this. She did not know if she wanted to.

Sensing her fear and apprehension, General Zahn smiled maliciously. "Yes, you're going to die tonight, Delta, but not before some of my more deviant men take their brand of pleasure from you. After all, they have earned it for killing your friends."

Eyes searching desperately for an exit, Delta felt the bile rise to her throat. Should she go for his gun and try to end it here, or should she allow her body to be abused in an effort to prolong what short time she had left? Suddenly, Megan's choice was profoundly understandable.

"Your men, like you, are pigs, General."

The general turned to Delta and flicked a smile at her. "Perhaps, but your friend, Megan enjoyed every moment of my piggish behavior."

Delta could stand it no longer. If she was going out, she was going out with her virtue intact. She lunged. "You son of a..."

But before she could get near him, the other soldier rammed his fist into her stomach and then slammed her head back with his other fist sending her to the floor.

Zahn turned and rattled off some orders to a second soldier who grinned widely and nodded before running from the trailer. To the soldier who had hit Delta, Zahn whispered something that made the man smile from ear to ear.

Slowly rising, Delta held her stomach and tried to stay conscious. If she went down now and stayed down, the things these fuckers could do to her body were too awful to contemplate. She had to stay to her feet, even as unsteady as they were.

Returning his gaze to Delta, Zahn sneered at her. "Hector, here, would like to be the first, my dear. But do be careful. He likes to bite. Hard. Hector has been known to bite the nipples off of women who fight him for his pleasure. So take your pick, Delta. That is about the only option open to you now."

Firing off a round of Spanish to Hector, General Zahn laughed at his own joke as he turned to leave.

"General?" Delta said, swallowing the lump rising in her throat.

Slowly turning, the general raised his eyebrows. "Yes?"

"You better kill me now, because if I live through this, you're a dead man."

Tossing his head back and laughing, the general walked out, locking the door with an ominous click.

Delta was alone in the filthy room with Hector, who gave her a depraved smile, revealing tobacco-stained teeth. "I get you first, puta."

Delta inhaled slowly and forced the bile back down her throat. This was it. She must decide here and now if she was willing to extend her life for a few more pain-filled hours.

"Take off your clothes," he ordered.

Delta breathed in again, as time slowed down.

"Don't make me mad, bitch." Hector grinned as he grabbed his crotch. "Muy largo," he said, laughing. "And you're gonna feel it up to your neck."

Gulping, Delta froze. God, this couldn't be happening. Not to her. The last time she had been in a situation similar to this, Sal and Josh had bailed her out by killing both men who were going to rape her and leave her dead body in the desert. Where were Sal and Josh now? And Megan? Where in the hell was Connie? Connie, who had never let her down, not even once? Where in the hell was everybody?

When she finally found her voice, it sounded detached, like it wasn't hers. "I thought all you macho types fantasized about being sucked off." Maybe she could do that. Maybe, if she visualized something else, she could bite the fucking thing right off.

Hector's facial expression didn't change. "Si. Especially by smart-assed American bitches."

Delta looked at his crotch. God, she had no clue. She had tried to give head once to a guy in high school, and put the damn thing in her mouth like a piece of corn on the cob. She was so bad, the poor guy had to jerk himself off. Searching the corners of her mind, she found some lines from movies she'd watched. "Are you hard?" It was the only thing she could think of.

Delta was surprised to see a red blush creep across his face. She realized he'd been drinking. Score one for her side. Maybe, just maybe, there was a slim bit of hope.

Before Hector could answer, the door flew open and banged against Hector's back, as a second uniformed guard came in. He muttered something to Hector before closing the door behind him. Now, there were two in the room, and Hector did not appear pleased.

He spat something at the soldier, who snarled right back and pointed to Delta. The alcohol fumes from their breath filled the room, mingling with the odors of fear and perspiration.

It took everything Delta had in her to stay standing. The room seemed to spin around her, and she grabbed the wall to keep from falling. If she attacked them, they'd probably enjoy the fight. If she let them do what they wanted, she would only prolong her agony before they killed her.

It looked, for once, as if there was no way out.

Bowing her head, tears welled up in Delta's eyes. Not for herself, not for the fate awaiting her, but for two women she knew would never find her remains. She knew Connie and Megan would spend their time, their energy, and every dime they had trying to find a body that would probably end up shark food. The thought of them never knowing what had become of Delta ripped at her spirit. As a tear slid off her nose, Delta closed her eyes and thought of Megan, her love, and Connie, her soul mate, and was glad they would never know what was going to happen in this tiny, dirty room in the middle of a jungle. Megan would get over it, eventually. She would move on, telling stories about her life with the irrepressible Delta Stevens. Megan would laugh that little laugh whenever she spoke of Delta's idiosyncrasies and exploits. She would see things and hear things that would remind her of their time together but eventually, Megan would recover.

Connie was another story.

It had taken thousands of dollars, plus three thousand miles for Delta to understand who she couldn't live without. It had taken a Shaman, a vision, a moment of peace, a minute of pain for Delta to finally realize that she was only half a person without Connie Rivera. They were like a lock and key, a bullet and a gun, the moon and the sun. It was Connie who would never fully recover from Delta's death. Connie would carry her grief like a ball and chain until it drove her around the bend. Delta acknowledged this now because, if the roles were reversed, she'd be lost without Connie Rivera. Without Connie, Delta was a body without a spirit.

It was fitting that Delta's final coherent thoughts were of Megan and Connie. After all, she knew what was coming. She'd interviewed half a dozen gang-rape victims during her tenure on the force. She knew what was in store: the pain, the drifting in and out of reality, and the loss of consciousness.

They would strip her clothes and try to strip her dignity from her, but Delta would not let them have the latter. They could hurt her physically, crush, bruise, penetrate, and cut her body, but they would never reach her spirit. Of that she was certain.

Delta looked up at the two men, unsure about how many seconds or minutes had elapsed.

"If you won't take them off, we'll be happy to cut them off." Hector grinned at his cohort as he pulled a ten-inch bowie knife from a sheath strapped to his thigh.

Looking at the knife, Delta made her choice. She could not do what Megan had done. It wasn't in her character; it was not an act her body would allow. If Delta Stevens was going down, she would do so under her own terms, and like the woman she was. As a fighter. As a warrior.

When Hector stepped toward her, she lunged at the knife at the same time her left fist shot out like lightning toward his Adam's apple. Feeling it crunch beneath her fist, Delta tried to grab the knife's handle, but felt a huge fist smash against her wrist. As Hector bent down, choking, his amigo rammed Delta, face first, to the floor, pinning her arms beneath her. All his weight crushed down on her, forcing the breath from her.

"I like it rough, puta."

Squeezing her eyes shut, Delta struggled, but his full weight was too heavy, and she couldn't move.

"God...damn...it," she gasped, feeling his thick fingers tear at her shirt. The buttons pulled hard before popping off.

"I'm gonna hurt you," he growled, ripping her shirt. "You're gonna bleed."

Unable to breathe, Delta willed herself to pass out. She did not want to feel what was happening to her. She could no bear the experience. Inhaling the dust from the filthy tile floor, Delta wondered if she could bang her head hard enough against it to knock herself out. The floor, while grimy and gross, was better than the stained mattress on the floor.

Closing her eyes and focusing on not breathing, Delta felt the soldier's weight as he rubbed his crotch on her backside. It was beginning, and she couldn't stop it or save herself.

Suddenly, there was a loud thump right next to her face.

Opening her eyes, Delta was shocked to see Hector lying next to her, eyes closed, unconscious, blood gushing out of the side of his exposed head. Something had happened to Hector, and as she squirmed to get out from under the other soldier, she realized that he, too, had stopped his bumping and grinding and was merely dead weight.

"Lying down on the job, gorgeous? Looks like I got here in the proverbial nick of time. Mama always said I had great timing."

Struggling out from under the soldier's weight, Delta looked up at the open closet door and went slack-jawed when she saw Taylor crouched in the top of the closet below the small crawl space.

"You?" Delta shook her head, as if to clear her vision. Had they knocked her out and she was dreaming this? "How..."

"Explanations will have to wait, love. We're sorta on a deadline. Pardon the pun." Taylor reached a hand down from the top of the closet, where she was perched. One hand extended toward Delta, the other held a gun with a silencer.

Delta glanced down at the two men, each bleeding from a bullet hole through the head. "But..."

Taylor shook her head. "Later, sweets, climb up."

Needing no further prompting, Delta took Taylor's hand and climbed into the top of the small closet. Taylor closed the closet door behind them before they moved along the tight passageway. Delta could hear talking or music or something farther down, but Taylor stopped and pointed to an opening in the ceiling. Looking up, Delta grinned. It was the opening for a swamp cooler that was not there. Swamp coolers were the main form of cooling in many mobile homes and trailers, but this unit had had its cooler removed. Taylor had somehow managed to get to the top of the trailer, and slipped into the cooling unit.

Pushing herself through the opening, Delta turned and easily jerked the lighter woman up on the roof with her. Lying on their stomachs, Delta and Taylor could see the surrounding camp. From this position, Delta could see where all the guards were, the size of the camp, and the opening of the caverns. What she didn't see was how Taylor had managed to get to the trailer unnoticed.

Taylor? Delta blinked. If Taylor was here, that meant Connie and Megan weren't far behind.

"Up," Taylor whispered, reaching above her in the
darkness and grabbing a rope. In the darkness of the jungle, one
would have to be standing next to the rope to know it was there.
Taking the rope, Delta realized it was knotted every two feet or so,
and all she needed to do was pull her weary body dozens of feet in
the air to the branch it was hanging from, and she'd be free.

Delta climbed, pulling herself up, hand over hand, feeling
the burn in her arms, thankful the burn was in her arms and
nowhere else. Her shoulder ached a bit as she struggled up the
rope, but the adrenaline surge made up for the slight pain. She
climbed forever until she came to a large branch. Her entire body
was sweat-drenched, and her arms and legs were rubbery, but she
was alive! As she straddled the branch, she peered through the
dark, wondering what was keeping Taylor.

Taylor.

The international jewel thief who had plagued Delta's beat.
Was it only a few weeks ago? Taylor, the irresistibly charming
criminal who had left Delta's house after delivering both a present
and a kiss. Taylor, the woman who had gotten in and out of several
well-guarded national museums, archives, and residences as easily
as walking in her own front door? Delta grinned. This had to be
Connie's doing. Connie was brilliant. Somehow, some way, Connie
had tracked Taylor down and convinced her to help get Delta out.

But how?

Feeling the rope move, Delta squinted through the
darkness and saw Taylor barreling up the rope after her. When she
hoisted herself over the branch, Taylor leaned into Delta and
whispered, "Follow me, love."

Delta did, although keeping up with Taylor in the trees
was much like trying to keep up with an Indy 500 pace car on a
ten-speed bicycle. It was no wonder Taylor had been able to leap
from one rooftop to the next when Delta was chasing her. She was
either insane or fearless. Delta bet on the latter.

After spending some time navigating through the trees,
Taylor began her descent, for which Delta was grateful. She had
never imagined a human could move through trees like a monkey,
but Taylor appeared to be as comfortable off the ground as Delta
was on it. More than once, Delta almost lost her footing, barely
managing to hang on, until Taylor could help her get back on track.

When it appeared Taylor was working her way down, Delta let out a sigh of relief. She doubted she would have been able to climb with as much ease if it had been daytime, since she could have seen just how far up they were.

Once on the ground, Delta turned to Taylor, who smiled brightly. Standing in a rare patch of moonlight, she looked beautiful. "Miss me, gorgeous?" Taking Delta's face in her hands and wrapping her arms tightly around Delta's neck, Taylor kissed her passionately. It was a kiss Delta returned with gusto. Whether it was because of the near-death experience, or simply because she had always found Taylor attractive, Delta did not know, nor did she care. She had been saved from a fate worse than torture, and she was grateful.

When Taylor finally pulled away, she breathed warmly into Delta's mouth. "Well, that was a close one, wasn't it?" Taylor said, her hands lingering on Delta's face.

Delta wasn't sure if she was talking about the incident in the trailer, her near-falls from the tree, or the kiss. "How in the hell did-"

"Shh." Taylor put her fingertips to Delta's mouth. "Very shortly, General Zahn is going to know that you escaped and that you had help doing so. We gotta dash. Connie's orders."

Delta nodded and waited for Taylor to move. When she didn't, Delta asked quietly, "What's the matter?"

Taylor pulled Delta to her one more time and kissed her hard. "I sure missed you. For a minute there, I thought I'd lost you for good."

Delta gently pushed Taylor away from the kiss and grinned. "You and me both, Taylor." Looking down into Taylor's face, Delta grinned. "I just can't believe it's you."

Taylor kissed the back of Delta's hand and urged her to follow. "Believe it."

Carducci adjusted the sight and returned his eye to the scope. "I can't fucking believe it."

"What? What's happening?" Megan took the night goggles and peered through them. She couldn't see anything except the top of the trailer. "What? I don't see them."

A big grin spread over Connie's face as she looked through the second pair of goggles. "Damn if Taylor didn't get her."

Megan couldn't see Delta or Taylor or anything. "I don't see them."

"That's because they shimmied up that rope faster than lickety split," Carducci replied, training his eye back on the night scope attached to his rifle.

Sighing loudly, Connie struggled to maintain her calm. Delta was alive. Alive and free, and it was now up to this little group to keep it that way.

It was odd. Connie had never, ever doubted that Delta was alive. As deeply as Connie loved and adored Gina, there was never a doubt who Connie was most connected to. That connection, that sixth or seventh sense of knowing another being so well, was like knowing yourself.

"They're in the trees," Connie whispered to Megan, who appeared like a granite statue staring into the night. "Goddamn, but that woman is good."

"Delta?" Megan asked.

Connie shook her head. "Taylor. No wonder she's never been caught."

Megan continued to peer through the goggles, but she had no idea what direction they had headed. "And you're sure you saw both of them come out of there?"

Carducci and Connie both nodded.

The revelation seemed to enter Megan's awareness in slow motion. "Then she's really alive?"

Connie grinned. "Alive enough to climb up a rope three stories high. Did you ever doubt it?"

Megan shook her head. "We're not out of here yet. Tony, can you see Josh and Sal?"

Carducci swung his goggles over to the other side of the camp and nodded. "Yep. They're getting into position as we speak."

As Josh and Sal maneuvered into position, Josh held up his hand, and they both froze.

They had been chosen to get as close as they could to the caverns, since Josh's Viet Nam experience and Sal's size made them the most obvious candidates. Josh had served hard time in Viet Nam, and killed his share, and Sal had slit a man's throat once, keeping Delta alive. They could do what the job required.

Josh lowered his hand as the pair stalked closer to the camp. So far, no warning signals had gone off, so the guard or guards inside the trailer were either dead or oblivious to the fact that Delta had escaped. Either way, there would be some serious commotion once Delta was discovered missing, and this place would explode.

Creeping as close to the camp as they could get, Josh stopped and knelt on the ground.

"What?" Sal whispered, staring at the camp.

"Here. I can see most of the camp from here."

Sal looked back at Josh, his face painted with the camouflage paint he always carried with him. Always. He was the consummate soldier, and Sal had seen him come to life ever since they'd arrived in Costa Rica. She had often wondered if he missed war, or missed being with his buddies, most of whom had left body parts in Viet Nam. Seeing him so alive, so full of energy made her wonder if Josh shouldn't still be in the military. After all, they had volunteered not only to come down and help Delta, but tonight, they were the ones who would do most of the killing.

Their job was to pick off as many men as they could once the alarm sounded. Confusion, Connie had explained, and the element of surprise, were on their side. At night, from out of nowhere, the soldiers would become human targets, not knowing who was shooting at them, how many were shooting at them, or where the shooters were. In the excitement, Delta, Taylor and Megan were going to slip into the caverns and rescue Megan's friends.

At least, that was the theory.

The practice was another story. Josh and Sal didn't know how many men there were. No one had any idea if there really were any people alive in the caverns, nor did they know what shape they were in. If Taylor did her job well, the general would have no reinforcements and would have to fight the small attacking army in the dark, not knowing how many there were or even where they were. It was a great plan.

In theory.

Casting her eyes over the camp, Sal sighed. She wondered if her dad would be proud of her humping through the jungle to rescue good friends, as he once had. Was he smiling now? She had dreamed of him during surgery to remove the bullet one of the Colombians had planted in her upper leg, dreamed that he smiled at her before fading like a fog passing through. It had been so long since she'd seen him, he seemed to be fading from her memory, and he only came to her now in her dreams.

But here, here in the jungle, her memory of him was alive and well. She could see the strength of his strong jaw, the fierceness of his eyes, the tautness of his body. She could understand now why he went back after his friends in Nam. Because how good would the quality of your life be if you left your friends to die? What kind of person could turn their back on a friend in need? Her father hadn't, and neither would she. When his body was shipped back to the States for the funeral, Josh had taken care of all the arrangements, including a headstone that read, "An honorable death is far greater than a dishonorable life."

Looking over at Josh, Sal grinned. She understood the demons he was exorcising from his past. Josh had failed to bring her dad home alive. It was a failure that haunted him nightly. Cold chills, hot sweats, thrashing about, and crying were all part of his nightly ritual from which, it seemed, he would never wake up. Maybe bringing Delta and Megan home would alleviate some of the guilt looming over him. Maybe, just maybe, Josh could even the universal score.

As Sal pulled out one of the HKs, she leaned over and whispered, "How ya doin'?" In the light of the moon, she could see his teeth as he smiled at her and whispered, "Kick ass and take no prisoners."

Sal nodded. Megan had asked her some time ago why Josh chose to hang out with a bunch of women, most of whom were lesbians. Sal had told her that war had taught Josh that quality people come in every shape, color, gender, and size. These crazy women were his family now. He'd already killed once to save Delta from death, and for a soldier, that act bonded you for life. But it was more than just the killing, it was the camaraderie, the loyalty, the love and devotion that drew him to them.

Since Viet Nam, Josh had longed for his buddies, his unit, his family, but they were all gone, killed either by the Cong or by a society that never accepted them when they returned from doing a job nobody wanted to do in the first place. And when he'd found a genius, a prostitute, a shrink, and a rebel cop, he'd found the family he was looking for.

And Josh wasn't about to let any of them go.

"Ready, Salamander?" Josh whispered, raising the cannon he called a rifle.

Smiling with admiration, Sal nodded. "And take no prisoners."

No longer a prisoner of Zahn's, no longer facing an ordeal that would surely have been the worst experience of her life, Delta felt her strength returning. She was grateful to Taylor, who had somehow managed to join Connie and Megan in the jungle. She could hardly wait to hear that story. She could hardly wait to see Connie and Megan.

Delta could have sworn Taylor was leading her in circles. It felt as if they had initially traveled away from the camp but were now heading back.

"This is the wrong way," Delta whispered, pulling Taylor to a halt.

Taylor stood close to Delta. "Connie's plan, sweets. Pretty soon, old General Zahn will know you're gone. When he does, all hell will break loose."

"My point exactly. Shouldn't we be getting out of here?"

Taylor lightly ran her finger across Delta's jaw line before gently caressing Delta's puffy cheek. "Lover, we're going back and getting the people you came for."

"Tonight? Now?"

Taylor nodded. "Shh. Look. If we give them a chance to regroup, they'll kill everyone first before coming after us. We can't afford to fight them in the daylight. At least, that's what that big hulking Josh-guy says. This way, they'll never know what hit them. We're ready, don't worry."

Delta shook her head. It was one thing to look up from a near rape to find Taylor grinning down at her, but it was quite another to hear her sound like Connie.

"Who's we? Taylor, please slow down a minute and tell me what's going on. I need the whole picture."

Taylor took Delta's face in her hands and started to kiss her, but Delta held her at bay. "Not now," Delta said, stepping back from Taylor's embrace. "Will you please tell me what is going on here?"

Slowly pulling away, Taylor held Delta's hand. "There's not much time..."

"Taylor, goddamn it, where's Connie? What are you doing here?"

Taylor flicked her hand in the general direction of the group. "Connie and Megan knew you were still alive, so they rounded up everyone they could to come get you out of here."

Delta nodded and waited for the rest. "She received my message then."

Taylor nodded. "Loud and clear. But by then, she had already dropped a quarter to call yours truly. They knew you'd either go to the Bri or come back here. Frankly, I bet you'd return to the Bri first."

Delta nodded. "I did."

Taylor smiled. "Well, your resourceful buddy found me. How, I haven't a clue. But she did, and I guess she figured there was only one person who can get in and out of just about anywhere undetected. So, here I am."

Delta couldn't help but grin. "You're incredible. Thank you. How's Megan?"

Taylor grinned. "A pretty gutsy woman, that one. As much as I'd like to say I hate her, I must admit, she's a good one."

Delta sighed. "Yes, she is. But then, so are you."

"I think she's hanging in there, Delta. She will be awfully glad to have you back." Taylor took Delta's hand and started moving east. "The rest will have to wait. We gotta move fast. Any second, those men are going to find two dead soldiers and no prisoner. Connie thinks that's the perfect time to strike."

"Strike? Don't tell me..."

Taylor chuckled, almost too loudly. "We're attacking. Damn right. Gonna shove that gold right up the general's wazoo."

"Taylor, this is the jungle, for Christ's sake. You'd need someone who..."

"Got one. Josh, who, strangely enough, seems to really be enjoying himself. The guy knows his shit."

Delta nodded. "But he'll need good cover. He'll need someone who can pick these guys off from..."

"Got him, too. Tony."

Delta's jaw dropped open and she stopped moving. "What?"

"Yep. Your cute boy partner packed up his toys, took a leave, and right about now is getting ready to put a bullet between some unsuspecting slob's eyeballs."

Delta was speechless. Carducci, here, in Costa Rica? "But how..."

"People care about you, Delta Stevens, enough to risk their lives for you. Don't worry your pretty little head. We've taken care of everything."

"Including attacking a small army?"

Taylor nodded. "Yup, and saving the village. Right now, Megan's making her way to the mouth of the caverns."

"Alone?"

"Yup. She figured she was the only one who could convince the hostages to leave with us."

"You guys let her go alone?"

"Give her more credit than that, Delta. Megan's one tough lady. This place doesn't scare her anymore. She can handle herself." Taylor quietly unzipped her bag and pulled out two broken down automatic rifles. "Here. You'll need this." Handing a stock and barrel to Delta, Taylor slammed hers together with a loud click, as if she had been doing it all her life. Delta stared at her, amazed at how quickly she had her weapon ready.

Taking the rifle pieces from Taylor, Delta looked at them in the moonlight. " Josh?"

Taylor nodded. "That man has some golden connections." Slinging the rifle over her shoulder, Taylor motioned for Delta to follow. "Come on. We're Megan's ground cover."

As Taylor turned to go, Delta touched her arm. "I don't know how to thank you, Taylor."

Taylor reached up and lightly touched Delta's swollen cheek. "I do."

Delta looked down into her partly shadowed face. "I'm serious. Do you realize you just killed two people back there?"

With her hand still on Delta's cheek, Taylor whispered, "Wasn't the first time, love, won't be the last. Besides, anything for you. Don't you get that yet?"

Delta realized that she hadn't gotten anything. She hadn't comprehended the depth of Carducci's loyalty to her or the strength of Taylor's passion. Delta had been so busy trying to right the world's injustices that she had missed many important opportunities to connect on a deeper level with the people she cared about.

When she got out of here, all of that was going to change.

Connie was sure the men would discover Delta missing at any moment. Megan had just made her way to the outskirts of the east side of the camp, where the mouth of the caverns was. Connie was amazed at the stealth with which Megan had moved in the darkness of the jungle. Perhaps they had been here too long, if they were becoming accustomed to moving about in the thick darkness as if they belonged. Connie hoped it was not an ill omen.

Suddenly, it started just the way Connie had predicted it would. Two men entered the trailer and immediately came flying out with their arms waving, yelling in Spanish, and trying to extinguish the torches. Connie waited for one torch to go out before quietly saying "Now," to Carducci.

Three cracks of his rifle later, and three soldiers were down before they could even reach their weapons.

Four cracks resounded in the distance, and two more men went down onto the jungle floor, dead before their faces hit the ground.

Carducci squeezed off more rounds, taking more lives with each pull of the trigger. Even Connie was amazed by his unerring aim. SWAT, she decided, was getting much more than its money's worth in this man.

The camp burst into chaos while men ran around looking for cover and firing wildly into the dark forest. Connie watched as the soldiers were killed or wounded by her team.

They had succeeded in catching the Colombians unaware, and the surprise attack was far more successful than Connie had dared to hope.

Through the night goggles, she saw Megan leap over the first casualty of Carducci's bullets and disappear into the caverns. This was where the plan got sticky. If Megan took too long, the General might attempt to enter the caverns for cover, possibly killing all those they had hoped to save. If the hostages became too frightened to leave, or were somehow incapacitated, they would have to move to Plan B, a plan not nearly as well devised.

Suddenly, the camp went totally dark and, to everyone's surprise, no one was firing back..

"What the fuck?" Carducci exclaimed, not moving his eye from the scope. "They've disappeared."

Connie watched through the goggles as the soldiers uncovered foxholes and disappeared down inside.

"That son of a bitch was expecting trouble," Connie said, as the last soldier vanished into his foxhole.

"We got nothin' now," Carducci said, relaxing his finger on the trigger. "Not unless we move closer."

"Where is Megan?" Connie growled, looking at the entrance to the caverns.

"She comes out in the next thirty seconds, or we're in deep shit." Carducci checked his ammunition and waited for Connie's orders.

Connie lowered the night goggles and looked at Carducci. "You got to keep them down in those holes."

Carducci nodded. "Will do. There's only one problem."

Connie waited.

"I don't think these are foxholes."

Connie looked back at the top of the pits. "What do you mean?"

"Not one guy's looked up since they dropped in. That's not normal."

Connie could only stare as the realization of her miscalculation hit her. "Oh my god, Tony..."

Carducci nodded. "Shit! They've gone underground."

Connie stared hard at the foxholes, willing herself to see that which she could not. Had they managed to dig foxholes that led to underground caverns and had evaded them?

She couldn't even bring herself to think about what that meant to their rescue efforts.

"If they've escaped to underground tunnels, we're fucked!"

Everyone stared at the jungle floor, afraid that they may have fallen into a trap; a trap they might never escape from.

EIGHT

At first, Siobhan didn't recognize her, since the light from the torches was dim and the shadows were deep. It wasn't until Megan stood next to a lit torch that Siobhan recognized her old tent mate, and saw that she was alone.

"Megan?" Siobhan blinked hard and squinted.

"I promised you I'd be back, and here I am."

Siobhan's eyes grew wide. "But how..."

"Long story. Right now, we have to get out of here."

Nodding slowly, Siobhan looked around. "We?"

"Remember those two friends I was telling you about?"

Her face registered surprise, and Siobhan took Megan's hand. "They're here? Now?"

Megan nodded.

"Is that why all the gunfire?"

"Yes. Listen, Siobhan, we have to move quickly. I need you to gather everyone up and move to the mouth of the cavern."

"But...we were told..."

"I don't care what you were told, Siobhan. You have to trust me! If you want to live, you're going to have to get moving!" Turning to a small group huddled in the corner, Megan realized these people did not trust her.

And why should they?

Megan had received preferential treatment at the hands of their captor. She had been given better food, days off, even a bath. They had every right to be suspicious of her.

Every right.

Only now was not the time to exercise that right.

Turning to the group, she held her hands out in supplication. "Listen to me, all of you. My friends and I returned to rescue you. If you want to get out of here alive, to go home and see your loved ones, then you must follow me outside."

"There are soldiers..." one voice called out.

"Who told us they would shoot on sight."

Megan held her hands up. "Listen to me! Those gunshots you hear are my friends. We..."

"How do we know who won outside?"

"How do we know you're not part of his plan?"

"Whore!"

Megan shook her head. Maybe she deserved that, maybe she didn't. It didn't really matter. What mattered was getting these people to safety. "Don't you understand? You'll die tonight if..."

"Why should we believe a whore?"

"Yeah!"

"Yeah! You and Zahn could be in this together!"

"Please," Megan's voice was pleading.

But the voices rose louder, and Megan cast a hopeless look toward Siobhan. "My friends are risking their lives for you, goddamn it!"

Siobhan looked from Megan to the others and back to Megan, the fear firmly embedded in her eyes.

"Siobhan, you saw me escape. Why would I have come back, if not to save you? I promised, don't you remember?"

Slowly, Siobhan nodded. "Yes."

"Here I am, then, just as I promised. And I brought help with me."

As Siobhan nodded, the fear seemed to dissipate, replaced by a look of understanding and acceptance. "Then, it's true?"

"Yes! And there isn't much time. We must get out of here quickly!" To the others, Megan cried, "If you want to live, follow me. If not, look around you, for the cavern will be your grave." Taking Siobhan's hand, Megan started for the mouth of the cavern. Only two other women were behind them as they turned and started toward the entrance to the cave.

"Are we really going to be free, Megan?" Siobhan asked, casting a doubtful eye toward the dark forest.

Megan did not look back at Siobhan. "I sure as hell hope so."

⊕

Delta watched the mouth of the cave in desperation. "Where the hell are they?"

"Keep your shorts on, sweetie. That cave could go on for hundreds of yards, and she doesn't even know where they are. Give her time."

Hefting the HK against her shoulder, Delta felt an all-too-familiar pang in her gut. Something was wrong. She knew it as plainly as she knew her name.

"We don't have time. We have to get down there."

Taylor shook her head. "No way. Connie made it clear..."

"That we what? Wait forever? Come on, Taylor, something's not right."

Suddenly, a single shot reverberated through the air.

"What in the hell?" Delta squinted through the dark.

"Someone made a run at the cavern," Taylor said, also squinting in the dark. After years of looking for valuables in the darkness of people's homes, Taylor had the best night vision of anyone she knew. "And your wonder boy dropped him in his tracks. Damn, he's good."

Delta felt too cut off, too isolated from the others. She was blinded by the near darkness, frustrated by the waiting, and too conscious of the warning flares bursting in her stomach. If someone had made a break for the cavern, they were after something.

"Why would one of them try to get to the cavern?"

Taylor did not answer. Instead, she squinted more until she could make out the action happening at the mouth of the cavern.

"Oh no," Taylor said, dropping her rifle. "Come on!" As fast as their legs could propel them through the dense underbrush, they ran toward the cavern, Delta plowing quickly past Taylor when she saw what it was the soldier was going for.

"Come on, Taylor, we have to get to it before they do!" Delta pumped her arms faster and harder as she scrambled down the hill and into the camp just as one of her guys took out one of theirs trying to make it to the mouth of the cavern.

"There goes another," Connie cried, seeing a soldier jump from his foxhole and run toward the cavern.

This time, the other men in the hole shot into the jungle darkness in order to cover him.

Carducci inhaled before slowly letting his breath out and squeezing the hair trigger of his rifle. Five steps from the foxhole, the soldier's chest blew out, and he collapsed.

"What the fuck are they doing?" Carducci asked, not taking his eye from the scope.   Connie whipped the goggles to her right and saw Delta and Taylor rushing closer to the camp. Then, she swung the goggles back to the mouth of the cavern, searching for some reason why the soldiers had left the safety of their foxholes.

"I don't know, but Delta does. She's making a break for the cavern."

"Shit! She knows something we don't."

"Oh my god," Connie muttered when her eyes fell on a small box nearly invisible at the mouth of the cave.

"What?"

Connie peered hard into the goggles. "Those men are trying to get to a detonation device sitting in the front of the cave."

"Damn it! You don't think Delta will..."

"If she does, Tony, she'll set off the blast. Delta doesn't know squat about explosives."

"Then, what is she thinking? What's she going to try to do?"

"I have no idea. But if she messes with that detonator, they're all as good as dead."

With thirty yards to go, a crash of gunfire exploded around the camp, and all Delta could do was hope Carducci was laying ground cover for them. If it wasn't Carducci and Josh firing, there was no way in hell she and Taylor would make it to the cave alive.

Turning on the final burst of speed she had left, Delta sprinted into the open and leaped over the dead soldiers who had failed to reach the cave. Quite suddenly, she found herself inside the cave, her lungs heaving in and out, working for much-needed oxygen.

"Well?" came Taylor's voice behind her, startling her. "You gonna unplug that thing? We don't have all day."

Delta shook her head. "Can't. I don't know diddly about explosives. If I did something wrong, I could blow us all up."

"Great. Now what?" Taylor asked, pulling out a standard River Valley Police Department six cell flashlight from her bag and flicking it on, illuminating the cavern room where they stood.

"We grab Megan and get out of here before someone reaches that thing." Delta hefted the HK to her shoulder and threaded her finger through the trigger guard. She was not about to be ambushed inside the cave.

"Can I ask if you're sure you know what you're doing, love?" Taylor stuck the flashlight under one arm before also readying her rifle.

Delta shook her head. "You can ask, but the only answer is I'm improvising. Want to bail?"

"And leave the love of my life to uncertainty? I think not. Come on, babe, I've come this far, don't doubt me now."

Wiping the sweat from her forehead, Delta grinned at Taylor. "Sorry."

"Don't be. Let's get Megan and get the hell out of here. I'm ready for a shower. This place really stinks."

Delta nodded, carefully picking her way about fifty yards into the cave. When intensive gunfire rang out from the mouth of it. Delta's gut told her everything she didn't want to know. Grabbing Taylor's hand, Delta started running deeper into the cave.

"Don't let go!" Delta yelled above the distinct pinging sound of bullets ricocheting against the rocks of the cave walls.

A few more shots rang out, and Delta pushed harder, trying to get as far away as possible from imminent danger. As she pushed her legs and lungs to their limits, Delta felt the explosion before she heard it.

The first explosion brought rocks tumbling down in front of the opening. Huge, two-ton, three-ton boulders fell heavily from above as the sides of the cavern collapsed in on itself. Dust, debris, and rocks fell, instantly blocking the cavern's opening. With Taylor's hand in hers, Delta ran through the tunnel in a panicked attempt to escape the succeeding blasts she was sure would come.

It was as if the boulders falling behind them were nipping at their heels, chasing them deeper into the dark catacombs. Blast after blast rang in Delta's ears, each one coming closer until a final blast sounded directly above them. The deafening roar sounded like thunder crashing inside the cave. Air choked with dust became unbreathable, and Delta pulled her shirt up around her nose to filter the dust particles.

"Hang on!" Delta yelled, as the stone walls gave way after an eternity of sleep. The sound of crumbling stone filled her eardrums like the power of a nuclear explosion.

As an oven-sized boulder nicked past her shoulder, Delta felt Taylor's hand slip from her own. Knocked off her feet by the tumbling rocks, Delta covered her head and lay in a fetal position while dust, boulders, and sediment pounded. Struggling to stay conscious, the last thing she heard before blacking out was Megan screaming, "Delta!"

"Delta!" Connie cried, seeing the cavern collapse in on itself. "Oh my god! No! Delta!" Before Connie could take off, Carducci grabbed her by one arm, mindful of her martial arts skills, but determined to stop her from running down to the cave.

"You'll be killed, Connie!"

Connie struggled to free her arm, but Carducci held on with all his might. "I don't care! Let me go, god damn it! Delta!"

Carducci wrapped his meaty arms more tightly around Connie and pulled her closer to him. "You may not care, but there's a baby who does!"

Connie kicked out at him, striking a blow that would have felled a lesser man than Tony Carducci. "She's in there!" Connie's body shook violently, but Carducci didn't let go.

"And we're out here! We're alive; Connie, and we need to stay that way. Delta needs us to stay that way. Listen to me!" Carducci squeezed Connie even harder, waiting for her to pull one of her patented maneuvers few ever walk away from.

Before Connie could respond, a loud crashing noise startled them, and as Carducci reached for his rifle, Connie shook off his grasp and ran right into Josh and Sal.

"Whoa, Connie, where the hell you going?" Josh asked, holding her biceps in his large hands. Josh knew Connie's famed ability to take down men his size, but that was the least of his worries now. He needed to keep her panic from spreading.

"It's Delta! She's in there!"

Josh studied the camp for a split second before nodding slowly. "What're we waiting for? Let's go get her." As Josh turned, Sal grabbed his arm. "Josh, if she was in there when those rocks gave way, she's not alive. Not this time. Not even Delta Stevens could have survived that."

"No!" Connie's screamed, pulling away from Josh. "I will never believe it. Not until I see her bloody corpse will I ever believe she's dead. I'm going after her!"

"Whoa," Sal cried, grabbing Connie's arm with her free hand. "Reaction, my friend, is not your bag. You're the thinker. The planner. Right now, we need to think and plan. Connie, right now, we need to keep our heads together. Capische?"

Connie's jaw ground back and forth, and she swallowed hard before nodding slowly. Breathing in slow, measured breaths, Connie tried to get control. "Okay, then. You want me to plan, to think? I say we kill all those fuckers once and for all and get Delta the hell out of there!"

Josh stepped out of the shadows and into the moonlight, his face sullen. He'd left Sal's father behind, at the cost of his inner peace. He would not do the same with Delta. Perhaps this was his chance to balance those scales after all. "If she's alive in there Sal, she ain't got much time. She could be outta air in an hour or a week."

Carducci nodded and said softly, "If she's alive."

For a silent moment, no one spoke. No one spoke or moved as the soldiers began making their way out of the foxholes.

The first one to speak was Sal. "Con, this is going to sound bizarre, especially coming from me, but, with all that mumbo jumbo about warrior spirits and soul mates and shit, can't you somehow tell if Delta is still alive?"

Slowly turning from Carducci, Connie looked hard at Sal. For a long minute, she just stared at her, as if she hadn't heard a word Sal had said but was still trying to puzzle it out.

"What?"

"I mean, you either buy into this spirit thing or you don't, right?"

When Connie finally spoke, her voice was barely audible. "You're right, Sal, that's bizarre even for you."

Sal bowed her head. "I know. But we're on the edge of desperation here."

Connie nodded. "You're right, though. You either buy into it or you don't, and I do. My heart tells me she is alive. My head tells me there are thousands of tons of rocks blocking that entrance. There's no way we're going to be able to dig her out of there. Even if we had a backhoe, there's too much that would have to be moved. It would take days, weeks, even."

"Which means what?" Josh growled.

"It means it's time for us to double-time it to the boat and get help."

"Help? But you just said..."

"I said a backhoe might not help. Dynamite is one solution. A better topo map of this particular region is another."

"A topo map? How the fuck is a topo map going to help Delta and Taylor and Megan?" Josh asked, keeping an eye on the soldiers as they peered cautiously around the camp.

Connie hoisted her rifle to her shoulder and shot two men who had slipped out of their foxholes. "I learned a thing or two from our little jewel thief when she was playing around on Delta's beat. There's always more than one way in or out of anywhere. Always. And I don't give a damn how many governments we piss off. Megan, Taylor, and Delta are in there, and we're not leaving here without them..."

Megan silently wondered if she should have just left without them. If she had, Delta wouldn't be covered under a small mountain of rocks and boulders. If only she hadn't made that promise to Siobhan.

As Megan and the hostages furiously clawed at the fallen debris atop Delta, she realized that Delta had just missed being crushed by a boulder the size of a small car.

"Be careful!" Megan ordered, as the women began digging Delta out. Megan estimated three; maybe four feet of rocks covered Delta, who had run just far enough in to escape the larger, more powerful explosions that had dislodged the supporting walls. Still, it took them twenty minutes beneath the flickering flame of their lone torch to uncover Delta.

When Delta was finally uncovered, Megan knelt down and cradled her head gently in her arms. Delta's body was limp and lifeless, and Megan pressed her face closer to see if Delta was breathing. When she felt Delta's breath against her face, Megan closed her eyes and sent a small prayer to the heavens. Not even hundreds of pounds of rocks could stop her Delta Stevens.

"Delta, wake up," Megan urged, surveying Delta's body for signs of broken bones. She did not see everyone frantically pulling and pushing boulders off of Taylor.

"Delta, you've got to wake up," Megan commanded, slapping Delta's face. Oh, how she wanted to gaze once more into those emerald green eyes that could say so much with a single glance.

After several long moments, Delta's eyelids began to flutter, and she slowly opened them. Wiping dust from Delta's face, Megan peered closely into Delta's eyes. With the single torch now barely burning, Megan could just make out Delta's features. "Honey, it's Megan. Are you okay?"

Delta blinked twice before slowly nodding her head, which felt as if hundreds of tiny jackhammers were beating different tunes. "I think so." Looking at her arms and then at her hands, scraped and torn from acting as a shield for her head, Delta turned her hand over and stared at her open palm. Something was missing. What was it?

"I thought I'd lost you," Megan cried, wrapping her arms around Delta and pulling her closer. "Thank God you're okay."

Delta buried her face in Megan's chest and breathed in Megan's familiar scent. She could not believe how good a hug could feel. "Miss me, did you?"

Megan pulled back and smiled into Delta's face. Tears rolling down her dusty cheeks made muddy track marks. "You have no idea."

Pressing her lips to Delta's, Megan kissed her hard and deep, a kiss Delta eagerly returned. Megan's scent may have been familiar, but Delta would have known those lips if she'd kissed a thousand other women in a contest.

The idea of kissing another woman jarred Delta's memory. "Taylor!" She cried into Megan's face as she withdrew prematurely from the embrace.

"Easy, hon," Megan said, putting her arms around Delta. "The others are digging for her now. Have a seat for a min..."

Shaking Megan off, Delta stepped toward the massive pile of rocks the other hostages were busy clearing, ignoring the throbbing of her body and head. She felt like she'd been steamrolled. "I have to get her out." When Delta bent over to help, her world swam before her, and she fell face first into the rocks.

"Baby, let the others do it. You just sit still for a minute." Megan slipped her hand into Delta's and gently pulled her from the group furiously pawing at the rocks covering Taylor.

"We don't have a minute," came Delta's answer. "This whole fucking cave is going to go." Delta pointed to the roof of the cave, where huge crevasses poured dust like a waterfall.

Megan looked up at the enormous cracks in the ceiling above them. "Will you just rest for a second then?"

Delta nodded. Her head felt like one of the boulders lying at her feet. Turning to Megan, Delta reached out and lightly touched her cheek. "When did you get so bossy?"

Megan grinned and stepped into Delta's arms. "When have you let me be?"

Delta kissed Megan softly at first, paying no heed to the stares of the hostages. As she crushed Megan to her, Delta's kiss became penetrating, consuming, as if it might be the last kiss they ever shared. "I'll let you now. How's that for starters?"

Taking Delta's hand in hers, Megan kissed the back of it. "I suppose it will have to do. You scared the shit out of me, you know. Plunging into the water like that."

Delta nodded, casting an anxious glance to where Taylor was. "You knew I was alive, didn't you?"

Megan nodded. "Not as much as Connie did. She's a wreck."

"Well, she's not gonna be the only wreck if we don't find a way out of here before this whole thing falls on our heads."

Delta used Megan's arm to steady herself as she returned to Taylor. "We have to get Taylor out."

As everyone continued digging, a section of the cavern ceiling fell into the underground river where the prisoners had panned for gold. Picking Taylor's flashlight off the ground, Delta made a mental note to tell the department just how well their mag lights held up under pressure. Shining the light up at the ceiling of the cavern, Delta saw the streams of dirt and sand running the length of it from foot-long cracks.

"Damn," she muttered, shaking her head.

"What?"

"See those cracks? See the dust falling in one steady stream?"

Megan looked up and nodded.

"There isn't much time. That ceiling is going to come tumbling down any moment now."

Megan turned to Delta with a puzzled look. "And you know that because...?"

Delta grinned. "Because..." Delta considered her answer. "Because me and the land are one. It is what the Bri believe, and I am one of them."

In the light from the flashlight, Megan reached up and wiped a stream of blood from Delta's forehead. She had waited so long to have Delta back, and there was so much she wanted to say, but nothing could come out of her mouth except the fear that was building inside her. "Indeed, my love, you are. You're not going to let us die in here, are you?"

Taking Megan's hand and kissing it, Delta shook her head. "Not if I can help it."

Megan watched a drop of blood fall off Delta's chin. "You know, women all over the world dream of having a super hero like you for a partner. Will you stay mine always?"

Delta kissed Megan's mouth tenderly. "Eternitas." Delta pulled slowly away and surveyed the situation. "But there's not much time."

"At least we're together," Megan whispered.

Delta turned and kissed Megan's cheek. "We will always be together. Don't you lose faith in me now, kiddo."

"Here's her hand!" one of the diggers cried.

Delta and Megan climbed over the rubble to help clear the rest of the rocks off Taylor.

"Get a pulse," Delta ordered, praying to the gods who had saved her countless times to save Taylor now. She was not ready to let Taylor slip away into nothingness.

"Got vun!" came a voice with a distinctive German accent. "Faint, though, but then, I'm no doctor."

Delta knelt by Taylor's side and checked her vitals. "Taylor, can you hear me?"

Before Taylor could respond, another section of the ceiling plummeted into the water, splashing all of them. The cracks in the ceiling were growing wider. It was only a matter of time now.

"Del?" Megan quietly reached for Delta's hand, but Delta wasn't listening. Instead, she watched a piece of straw bob with the current. As the straw floated toward the wall of the cavern, it spun around three times before disappearing beneath the surface.

"That's it," Delta cried, clapping her hands together.

"What?"

"There may be a way out."

"No, honey, there isn't. Not unless we can dig."

Delta shook her head. "Not that way. This is an underground water source. It goes somewhere."

As the third section of the ceiling fell dangerously close to them, Megan looked up at the cave roof, then back at the water before turning to Delta once more. "You have got to be kidding."

"It's our only hope, Meg. This whole cave is going to collapse. We stay here much longer, we'll all be crushed."

"We don't know that it goes anywhere."

"And we don't have time to find out." Turning to the diggers, Delta asked, "Are any of you above-average swimmers?"

Dropping a football-sized rock, Siobhan raised her hand. "I used to swim in college."

"Would you be willing to swim under that water and lead these women out of here?"

"Delta," Megan said softly. "You have no idea what you're asking."

Delta squeezed Megan's hand. "Megan, that water is our only way out. It goes somewhere. Anywhere is better than here."

"But the next air pocket could be hundreds of yards away. We could drown before we reach the other end."

"Drown, suffocate, or be crushed, honey. Those are our options. But if we stay here, we are all surely dead."

"Hey! We got most of her free!"

Delta went back and shone the light on the tiny, frail body of Taylor. She was completely uncovered from debris except her left leg, which was pinned by a boulder the size of a refrigerator.

Suddenly, the cavern rocked, and more debris fell.

To Megan, Delta said, "There's no time. You all must follow Siobhan into the water. If you stay here, you'll die. The choice is yours."

Megan's voice was cold and flat as she swung Delta around to face her. "You all?"

Nodding, Delta released herself from Megan's grasp and took Siobhan by the shoulders. "Listen, you lead them out of here. You swim close to the surface looking for places where you can come up for air. I'm not saying those will even be there, but the possibility is far better than the chances of living through a cave-in."

Siobhan nodded. "I understand."

"As soon as you can, surface and help the others." Taking her belt off, Delta hooked it around Siobhan's waist and handed it to the next woman. "All of you do the same! You must stay together."

As more rocks crashed into the water, the hostages finally realized the hopelessness of staying in the cave.

"The rest of you, follow her!"

"You're crazy," one of them said. "I am not going under water not knowing if I'm ever coming out."

Delta knelt down and checked Taylor's pulse. She was breathing, but her leg was pinned beneath a boulder too big for them to move even if they had the time to move it.

"I'm not going to argue with you," Delta said over her shoulder. "Stay here and die. That's your prerogative." Feeling Taylor's breath on her hand, Delta rose, just as a huge boulder crashed in front of Siobhan. "Get going!"

Siobhan stepped into the water and motioned to the others to gather around. "Megan told me about these two women who save people's lives.

Megan, herself, kept her promise to me and returned. Well, I for one am willing to put my life in their hands. It is better than dying here. Anyone who wishes to save their own life comes with me." Siobhan turned to Megan and hugged her. "Thank you, my friend." With that, Siobhan disappeared into the same pool the straw had vanished into.

One by one, the others followed suit, stopping to inhale deeply, before going under. When the last person was submerged, Megan turned to Delta, just as the entire left side of the cavern gave way, splashing a wall of water across them.

"You're not coming, are you?" It was a flat statement, devoid of emotion. Megan knew Delta. She knew what Delta would and wouldn't do under most circumstances. And what Delta would never do was leave a friend to die alone, especially one who had risked her life to save her. Anyone knowing Delta Stevens would expect no less of her.

Delta looked away from Megan and shook her head as more rocks began falling. "No, baby, I'm not."

"Then, neither am I."

Rising, Delta brushed Megan's hair from her face. "You have to. Someone has to get those people to safety. You're the only one who can. Without you, they'll all wind up shot in the back, or worse. They need you."

"And you?"

Delta looked hard into Megan's eyes. There was so much to say; so much she wanted Megan to know. The Delta standing before her was not the same woman Megan had fallen in love with a lifetime ago, yet here they were, again, in the familiar and painful place of doing what was right over doing what was best. And again, Delta's life, her woman, her love of Megan took a back seat. But she was Delta Stevens, after all, and anyone who understood her knew she wasn't about to leave Taylor to die alone. Doing so would be to consign the rest of Delta's life to a huge black hole; a void only death could sew back up.

"She saved my life, Megan. I can't aban..."

Putting her fingers over Delta's mouth, Megan smiled softly. She could only hope that, someday, Delta would have the chance to see just how much Megan had grown and changed, just how much Megan now understood why Delta did the things she did.

She could only pray that the lessons learned were not too late to be put into practice and that she and Delta would live to love another day. Megan Osbourne could only wonder if this would be the last time she would ever look into her brave lover's eyes.

"I wouldn't expect less of you. I love you, Delta Stevens."

There was so much more to say, so much more for them to share, but time was not their ally, and Delta could feel the rumbling of the cave in the souls of her feet. It was time to let go. "I love you, Megan. I will love you always." Delta pulled Megan to her and kissed her with a passion borne out of intense love, fear, and desire. She wanted to die in that kiss. If their time together was to be extinguished, let it be snuffed out in an embrace even the Gods of Olympus would have envied. Delta didn't want to let Megan go, but she didn't want her to stay, either.

Pulling away, Delta lightly brushed her fingers across Megan's lips one more time. "Go, before it's too late."

Megan kissed Delta softly on the lips before stepping into the water. "Del?"

"Yes, love?"

"Know one thing for me."

"What's that?"

"You are now, and shall always be, the one true love of my life."

The ceiling was really falling now.

"I know, sweetheart. I have always known."

Nodding, Megan inhaled deeply and dropped beneath the surface, leaving Delta and a partially covered Taylor alone to face the burial the others may have just escaped.

Looking around, Delta realized the only thing she could use for leverage was the six-cell flashlight. Placing it in a crack in the boulder, Delta moved around to Taylor's other side. As she did, Taylor's eyes begin to flutter.

"Taylor?"

Taylor groaned and coughed. "Fuckin' A, it hurts."

Delta knelt beside her and grinned. "I know. There's a boulder on your left leg I'm gonna have to roll off you."

Taylor slowly, gingerly sat up and looked around her, and then at her pinned leg now drenched in her own blood. "I think my head is going to burst open."

Delta did not answer as she tried to move the rock. It would not budge.

Taylor watched her for a moment before shaking her head. "You can't seriously think you're going to get that off me, do you?"

"I'm going to see if I can use the flashlight as a lever. When the boulder moves, slide your leg out. Can you do that?"

Taylor nodded. "I can try. There's a machete in my bag, if you think that might help."

Delta reached over to the bag and retrieved the machete. "Cutting your leg off isn't an option, but this might come in handy later."

Taylor laughed and then coughed. "Later?" Taylor covered her head as rocks started falling closer to her. Looking up from under her arms, Taylor frowned. "Where are the others?"

"They took the Mississippi express," Delta said, jerking her head toward the water.

Taylor looked at the water and then up at Delta. Reaching out, Taylor grabbed Delta's wrist. "Don't do this."

Delta pulled her wrist free and continued putting weight on the flashlight. "What?"

Taylor inhaled slowly and winced. Whatever slight pain she'd felt initially was gathering strength now, and her thigh began throbbing in time with her head. "Get yourself out of here, Delta. You and I know you can't get that boulder off by yourself."

Delta kept working at the boulder, which hadn't moved an inch. "Oh, ye of little faith."

"And even if you do, there's one more problem."

"Oh?"

"I can't swim."

Kneeling down, Delta cupped Taylor's chin in her hand. "I don't care if you can't fly, Taylor. We're either leaving here together, or we're dying here together. It's that simple."

Taylor studied Delta's face. A single tear made track marks as it slid down her dusty cheek. "I don't understand, Megan..."

"Knows who I am. She knows I'd never leave someone I care about. Never, Taylor."

Through the pain, the fear, the certainty of death, Taylor's eyes sparkled, covering the agony Delta knew she felt. "You care about me?"

Delta bent over and kissed Taylor's forehead. "Taylor, this world needs you. I need you. And in another life, in another time, I'd fall so hard in love with you, I would see anyone else. But either way, I'd make the exact same decision I'm making right now."

Taylor wiped the tear away. "Does that mean..."

"It means I'm not letting you die here alone. I'm not letting you die. Period."

Taylor nodded as she reached up and touched Delta's face. "In my dreams, you are always there, rescuing me or some other silly damsel in distress. Why is that?"

Delta sighed and held Taylor's hand in hers. "Because I love you, you silly, eccentric jewel thief, that's why. Now, can we talk about your dreams later?"

Taylor grinned and nodded, instantly regretting her quick movement. "Be my heroine, Delta Stevens. Get us out of here, and I'll love you from a distance for the rest of forever."

Delta kissed Taylor's forehead again. "Good. Now I'm going to put all my weight on the lever, and as the rock gives, slide out. Can you do that?"

"Yes."

Standing on the flashlight, Delta put her weight on it, but the rock wouldn't move. The rocks above them, however, had no such problem, as they littered more debris all around the two women.

"Delta?"

Delta tried jumping on it, as the rocks and debris became a steady stream.

"Delta?" Taylor's voice rose slightly in panic.

Nothing Delta tried could get that boulder to move.

Taylor reached for Delta's hands and brought them to her chest. "Save yourself, Delta. Come on. It's time to cash it in and call it a day. You've given it your best. Go, while there's still time."

"No." Delta pulled the flashlight out and beamed it around looking for something, anything. Even the machete was no good to her now.

"Goddamn it!" Delta cursed, ignoring the baseball-sized rocks bouncing off her head and shoulders. "There has to be a way."

"Delta..." Taylor's voice was weak and fading, and Delta knew it was from shock.

"No, Taylor, I will not give up!"

"Delta."

Pacing, Delta stopped for a moment to center herself. Becoming unbalanced would do them no good. Closing her eyes for a few seconds, Delta ignored the rocks and dust polluting their small domain. If she had learned one thing from this jungle, it was that nothing was as it seemed. She had thought to kill a crocodile that eventually ended up saving her life. Moths looked like leaves, bushes looked like trees, and innocent-looking frogs were poisonous creatures. If nothing was really as it seemed, then what she needed to do was go with her instincts and against her head.

Opening her eyes, she shone the flashlight on the boulder perched on Taylor's leg. Her head told her to try to push the boulder off of Taylor's leg. But Delta's instincts told her that was the exact wrong thing to do. So, if the opposite of up was down, then Delta needed to...

"That's it!" Getting on her hands and knees, Delta grabbed the machete and started burrowing underneath Taylor's leg.

"Delta, that won't work. There isn't time! Get yourself out!"

"I told you. Live together or die together, Taylor." Digging in the hard ground, Delta felt the dirt begin to give way. Taylor swept the debris away and tried to keep the falling rocks from Delta's head.

As Delta struggled to move as much dirt as she could before the rest of the cave collapsed on them, a thousand pictures flooded her mind: her mother, the baby of Gina's she was never going to see, the life with Megan she might never get to live. Using her hands to clear another patch, Delta looked up and knew she only had seconds.

"Hold this," Delta said, handing the machete to Taylor before digging faster and deeper, tearing the skin from her fingers. Delta knew the shallow hole she'd dug would have to do if they were to get out alive. They were out of time.

"That's as good as it gets, Taylor. I'm afraid there's little time left."

"What now?"

"I'm going to pull you out."

"And leave the rest of my leg there?"

"If I have to. Are you ready?"

Taylor inhaled a shaky, frightened breath and nodded. "Go for it, sweets."

Moving behind Taylor, Delta hefted her under her armpits and leaned back, pulling a screaming Taylor free from the boulder, and landing Delta flat on her back. With Taylor free, Delta scrambled around to the front of her and slapped Taylor's pale face. "Stay conscious, goddamn it!"

"Fucker." Taylor said through parched lips. "I bet you enjoyed that."

Delta shook her head. Taylor had more guts than anyone she'd ever met.

"Is my leg still under the fucking rock?" Taylor grumbled, looking down at her broken leg before glancing up at Delta. "Hey...did you just slap me?"

Delta nodded. Taking her shirt off and slipping out of her bra, she used it as a tourniquet below Taylor's knee. "I thought you'd fainted."

"Well, think again, gorgeous. In the future, try finding out first before you go smacking your number one fan around. It's bad for business."

Delta grinned. "I'll do that." Then, she stood Taylor up on one leg and grabbed her by the shoulders. Delta didn't know how much time she had before shock set in, rendering Taylor incapable of moving on her own.

"We have to get going, Taylor."

Taylor's face was sweating, and her eyes were glazing over. "Told you. Can't fucking swim."

"How in the hell can a woman born on an island not know how to swim?"

Taylor shrugged. "I took boats."

As the far wall cracked and crumbled onto the shore, Delta picked Taylor's bag up, took the machete from her, and jammed it back in the bag before handing it to Taylor. "Hop on."

Taylor grabbed the bag and hooked her free arm around Delta's neck. Delta helped Taylor wrap her good leg around her waist. "Hold on, Taylor."

"You're not..."

"No other choice. Take a big, deep breath and pray it's not your last."

Just as Delta got the two of them into the water, the ceiling opened up and dropped everything it had. In one dive, Delta found herself in the murky water with nothing but a flashlight, a canvas backpack, Taylor, and a lungful of air.

NINE

"They expected us to come after the hostages," Connie said, as the four of them hurried from the camp and back to their home base near a hollowed-out tree stump. "They weren't as unprepared as I imagined. I'm sorry."

Sal looked behind her as they moved through the bushes. "They'll be coming after us, won't they?"

Connie did not slow down. "Count on it."

Josh stopped, forcing the others behind him to stop as well. "Tony and I should stay and pick off as many following as we can. You guys get to the boat and see about getting us some help."

Connie started to reply, but Josh stopped her.

"This is a war they can't afford to lose, Connie. There's a lot at stake here for them. Failure here means death back home. They have to stop us. Go. Take Sal and don't stop. Tony and me'll keep them from following."

"But..."

Josh shook his head. "No buts, Connie. You know I'm right, and you're wasting time. The sooner you're outta here, the sooner you'll bring back help."

Nodding, Connie sighed loudly and hugged Josh. "I know you're right. I've just never left Delta when she needed me most."

"Take it from a soldier who's been there. If retreat can save lives, then there's no dishonor in it. Delta would do the same if it was you buried under tons of rock. You can't work on emotions now, Connie. You have to think."

Connie knew he was right, but that didn't make leaving any easier. "We'll be back for all of you," Connie said reluctantly.

Sal reached up and kissed Josh's cheek. "Don't do anything stupid, big guy. I need your ugly puss around, okay?"

Josh nodded once before he pushed Sal toward Connie. "Take care of her, Con."

"You betcha," Connie replied, as she and Sal picked up their rifles and started back through the forest, leaving Carducci and Josh to face the general's men.

Putting his eye to the scope, Carducci squeezed off a few rounds at two men coming from the back of the trailer. Both exploded in a fury of blood. "Think they're alive in there?"

Following suit, Josh picked off two more men who had carelessly crawled from their holes. "Nope."

Carducci sighed, "Me, either."

"But Delta don't die easy. I've seen that with my own two eyes."

Carducci chuckled as he scanned for more moving targets. "Ain't that the truth?"

"And anyone who doesn't die easily deserves the chance to try to get herself outta another mess like this one."

Carducci looked at Josh and nodded. "If anyone can, she can."

Josh nodded, without taking his eyes from the sight. "That's what I'm countin' on."

*   *   *   *   *   *

Delta was counting on there being at least a six-inch space between the water and the cavern's low ceiling. If there wasn't, she didn't know how much longer she'd be able to hold her breath.

Delta didn't know how to keep from panicking when she reached up and felt the low ceiling of the cavern as it touched the water. There wasn't three inches of space the first time, let alone six. The river cut a path through the rock, filling the entire space. There was no breathing room at all, and the claustrophobic sensation was almost over-powering. Feeling her way along, she wondered how far the current would take them before they ran out of air.

Ten seconds turned into twenty, and the pressure building up in her lungs began to burn. She had felt this burning sensation once before when she was trapped in a house on fire with no place to go. Then, she had nearly broken her neck jumping through a plate glass window. Now, she'd give anything for there to be any window. She figured she had forty seconds or less to find an air pocket before they drowned.

Thirty seconds, and still no space could be felt. Her only consolation was that she hadn't bumped into any floating bodies.

The others must have gone farther than this or, if the gods were willing, they'd made it all the way.

As she pushed harder, Taylor started gripping Delta tightly around the neck. If she didn't find an air pocket soon, she might have to carry a drowned Taylor through the caverns, and Delta didn't know if she had it in her to carry that off.

Forty seconds, and Delta's lungs felt ready to burst. Her chest burned as her lungs screamed at her, and her arms ached from reaching up to see if her hand would ever come out of the water. Her whole body yelled at her to give up, but she could not.

One whole minute went by, and Delta's lungs really hurt now. Her chest was on fire, and her head pounded. The edges of darkness threatened to collapse in on her, consigning her to oblivion. It took every bit of will power she had not to give in to the pain in her chest.

But no dead bodies in the water had to mean something. Somehow, they had made it this far, and farther. If only she could keep her wits about her. Panic was her constant companion now, and she fought to keep it from becoming her master.

Seventy seconds, and Delta's fingers reached up and felt...nothing. Air! There was a small space between the water and the ceiling. Quickly surfacing, Delta and Taylor hungrily gulped the stale air of the cavern, like a starving man would consume moldy bread.

"Jesus!" Taylor said as she exhaled the near poisonous air from her lungs. They had about a ten-inch space, so they were able to float with their heads above water without smacking into the ceiling.

As they bobbed up and down in the water, slowly moving with the current, Delta shone her flashlight around. They were in an air pocket about eight feet wide, where the water gathered to form a pool before running down one of two forks in the underground river. Without the flashlight, they would be in a Cimmerian blackness. The thought alone made Delta shiver.

"Damn, that hurt," Taylor said, touching her chest. "Felt like I was going to implode."

"You okay?" Delta asked.

Taylor nodded, loosening her hold a little. "Barely. For a second there, I thought I was gonna have to suck up river water."

"Me, too." Shining the light in the water, Delta breathed deeply. "The good news is there aren't any bodies floating around here."

"What now?"

"We'll keeping following the river."

Taylor looked over Delta's shoulder. "Ummm, which one are you taking?"

Delta shrugged. "As a lefty, I always go left."

"Then left it is." Taylor winced as pain shot through her leg. "Why do you suppose this area didn't collapse as well?"

"We're quite a ways down from the explosions. This current is swifter than I first thought, and this cavern may not even be connected to the caves that blew."

Taylor kissed Delta's neck. "That was close back there. Thank you."

"We're not out of danger yet. Who knows how far or deep this river goes?"

Taylor sighed, trying to ignore the throbbing of lower leg. "Gee, and I thought my life was exciting."

"How's your leg?"

"Honestly? Hurts like hell. I could use a stiff shot of bourbon. Or maybe a bullet to bite on."

Delta ran the back of her hand along Taylor's cheek. "Careful what you wish. You ready?"

Taylor winced as she readjusted her legs around Delta's middle. "Sure you can handle both of us?"

"No."

"Oh, good."

"Did you want me to lie?"

"Yes."

"Next time, then."

Taylor nodded. "Thanks."

"It doesn't look like there's any room for air pockets in either of those tunnels. More than likely, the water fills up the entire chasm. We'll have to hold our breaths until we can find another air pocket."

Taylor nodded. "We don't have much of a choice, do we? Let's get this over with, Storm."

Delta inhaled as deeply as she could and pushed them toward the left chamber.

In an instant, they were carried down the river by a current stronger than the last. The current was so swift; she could not slow down enough to check for air pockets and wondered if this would be the end of them.

Ten seconds, twenty, thirty, and still, they were propelled like two leaves carried by a strong wind. The flashlight did little to illuminate the darkness, and Delta had to squint to see anything in the murky water. The light was more of a comfort. It made her feel less vulnerable to the darkness around them.

Forty seconds, fifty, and then wham! Feet first into a wall.

A wall?

How could that be? Feeling upwards, Delta knew their time was about up. There was no air pocket here. But the water had to go somewhere. Feeling along the lower part of the wall, Delta discovered a hole where the water exited. Swimming lower and shining her flashlight on the small aperture, Delta pushed them through the hole and the next rush of the river quickly carried them away. Realizing, too late, that Taylor had been wrenched loose; Delta was carried alone down the current.

As her chest burned again, Delta knew she was finished. She would inhale buckets of water and drown. The current was moving too quickly for her to stop and check for air pockets. When this river emptied out, it would carry their lifeless bodies into the sea, or wherever this underwater river came to rest.

As the fog of unconsciousness crept into her, Delta suddenly found herself thrust into a large body of water, free of cavern rooftops and stale air. She'd made it out of the caverns alive.

"Aaargh!" Delta cried as she gulped down fresh air to cool and soothe her aching lungs. The underground chamber had erupted into a lake, and her lungs rejoiced at the fresh, rain forest air filling them.

Turning back to the water pushing against her, Delta made her way back to the edge of the lake where the river had spit her out. Reaching into the opening, she reached in and found Taylor's shirt and yanked her to the surface. Taylor popped free like a cork from a champagne bottle.

"Breathe, goddamn it!" Delta cursed, shaking Taylor hard.

Taylor gasped and spluttered as she inhaled both air and water. Delta held Taylor afloat with her right arm while she pounded on Taylor's back with her left.

"Slap me...again, love...and I'm going...to start...taking it personally." Taylor put her arms around Delta's neck and coughed once more before inhaling her first clear, waterless breath.

"You had me worried there for a minute."

Taylor nodded. "My leg started hurting, and when I reached down to loosen the tourniquet, I was ripped away from you. Sorry."

Looking around at the calm lake they now floated in, Delta studied Taylor for a moment. Her face was pale, but she appeared alert. "You gonna live?"

Taylor nodded. "I think so."

Still holding Taylor with one arm, Delta rested as she got her bearings. "Wonder where the right chamber led to."

"You think that's where the others went?"

Delta shrugged. "We're not that far behind them. They must've taken that one. Damn." Delta positioned herself in front of Taylor and threaded her arm under Taylor's armpit and across her chest. "Relax. Pretend you're dead and let me carry your weight."

"Pretend I'm dead? Could you at least choose a better phrase?"

Delta grinned. "Lay back."

Taylor smiled. "I thought you'd never ask."

Side stroking the floating Taylor to the nearest shore, Delta's feet soon hit muddy bottom. It was still too dark out to assess their whereabouts, but at least they had found land. "I don't think I'll ever swim again," she gasped as she dragged herself out of the water.

"Same here." Collapsing next to Delta, Taylor rolled on her back and looked at her leg. "Mind shining that light over here so I can assess the damages?" The moonlight trickling through the trees cast eerie shadows across Taylor's face, and Delta shuddered at the thought of how close they had come to not making it out of there alive.

Delta shone the six-cell on Taylor's leg.

Pulling the wet pant leg up, they could see the white bone of her lower leg, but it was hard to tell if it was broken or if the skin and muscle had been torn from the bone. "Does it hurt much?"

Taylor winced. "Sometimes. I can't feel it mostly."

"I think you've climbed your last building, Taylor."

Taylor sighed and lay back down. "I had retired anyway."

Putting a new tourniquet ripped from Taylor's pant leg, Delta leaned over Taylor and touched her face softly. Facing death always brought people closer together, but Delta knew that the feelings she had for Taylor were there long before Taylor arrived to save her from a brutal rape and death. Delta had meant it when she said she loved Taylor, and though there was no place to go with that love, Delta was glad, at least, for having the opportunity to tell her.

"Feel well enough to travel?"

Taylor nodded slowly. "The real question is do you feel strong enough to carry me?"

Nodding, Delta started to rise when Taylor stopped her. "I don't know what to say."

Delta smiled warmly into Taylor's moonlit face. "How about 'dinner's on me when we get out of here'?"

Taylor grinned weakly. "Dinner? Can I have you for dessert?"

Delta laughed. "You never give up, do you?"

Taylor shook her head. "I told you, love, we're cut from the same cloth. It's what sets us apart from the rest."

"Well, right now, we need to reach the rest."

Taylor took Delta's face in her hands and softly kissed her cheek. "Thank you."

Delta smiled. "No, Taylor, thank you." Rising, Delta gently lifted the lithe Taylor up and wrapped her over her shoulders. "Let's go home."

When Megan and her party of eight surviving hostages finally surfaced, she looked around and had no idea where they were. The only indication she had for navigation was the gunfire echoing through the forest.

As much as she hated to admit it, her only hope of meeting up with Connie and the others was to head back toward camp, toward the shooters. If the Colombians were chasing the others back toward the shore, then it made sense to be moving in that direction.

"Megan?" Siobhan's voice was soft.

Megan turned to her. "Yes?"

"Thank you for coming back, for saving us."

"We're far from safe, Siobhan. I'm afraid we're going to have to follow the shooting of my friends. It's our only hope."

A tall, blonde woman shook her head. "I am not going back there."

Tired, scared, and afraid to think of what had become of her lover, Megan snapped. She didn't know how Delta had managed to save people from themselves for all these years, but Megan didn't have what it took. She was tired of their suspicions, their opposition, and their lack of trust. If they didn't want to return to their families, then fuck them. Fuck them all. "You know what? I don't give a shit if any of you come with me. I left my lover back there! Stay or go, it really doesn't matter to me anymore."

"Megan..."

Megan turned on Siobhan, her rage erupting. "Don't 'Megan' me, Siobhan. Our only, and I'll emphasize that word; our only hope of getting out of here is to find my friends. I'm done playing heroine, Siobhan. I can't do it, so don't ask me to. Make your own choice, but I'm going to my friends."

As Megan turned, she felt Siobhan fall in behind her. "We need you, Megan."

"No," Megan said, whipping around. "You need guts! Because, goddamn it, that's what it's going to take to get out of here, and frankly, I only have enough for myself right now." As Megan turned to leave, Siobhan grabbed her, and Megan coldly peeled Siobhan's hand off. "Siobhan, I'll hurt anyone, including you, who tries to stop me again. We probably have two hours before dawn, and I want to be far away from here by then. So, if you stop me again, I'm going to hurt you."

Megan forged through the bushes; only dimly aware that Siobhan and five others had fallen in behind her. The rest, it appeared, had had enough of this crazed woman and had moved in the other direction.

"You sure you know what you're doing?" Siobhan whispered.

Megan nodded. "Someone out here is on our side and is shooting back at those bastards. Once we find them, we can get help and go home."

"In that order?"

"Yes, Siobhan. In that order."

TEN

It was dawn when Connie and Sal stumbled to the coast, the lavender light of the sky skipping across the water's surface. They had not stopped moving for many hours, and they were fatigued, dehydrated, and scared. When they finally reached the sand, which lapped right up to the forest, Sal collapsed on her back, exhausted.

"I sure hope Gina's out there," Sal said, looking up at the lightening sky. "Are we at the right beach?"

"Close enough, Sal. She's out there looking for us as we speak." Connie reached into her bag and pulled out the flare gun. "It's a risk to use this right now, with the others still so far behind, but I don't know what else to do. We need help."

Sal stopped Connie from firing and pointed to their six-cell. "You shoot that thing off prematurely, and our boys are screwed. Use the mirror from the flashlight."

"What if she doesn't get it?"

"She might not, but Logan will. He ought to be expecting it. Trust me, Con. You give away our position too early, and we're fucked."

Connie nodded and unscrewed the cap of the flashlight, carefully removing a round mirror. "God, I hope you're right."

"There's some things vets from a war like Viet Nam will always remember and hand-to-hand combat is one of them. Logan will be looking for it." Sal rolled over and glanced back at the jungle. "How far behind do you think the guys are?"

Connie shrugged as she maneuvered the mirror to catch the morning rays. "Hard to say. They should have laid enough cover and then gotten out before the general's men had a chance to surround them or figure out how few opponents they were facing."

Sal sat quietly while Connie continued catching the dawn's sun with the mirror.

She had wanted a radio for communication, but the chances of their mission being overheard by any number of armed bands of drug dealers, cartel members, or government agencies was too high to risk it.

"Con?" Sal asked, rolling on her side.

"Yeah?"

"What if they didn't make it?"

Connie did not turn from her task. "Who? Delta and Taylor?"

"Yeah. What if we risk going back there for nothing?"

Connie looked at Sal. It was time to tell the little soldier the truth. "We aren't going back. I am."

Sal sat up quickly. "No way!"

Connie nodded. "I'm afraid so. We've risked enough as it is. I want all of you on that boat safe and sound. I'll take whoever answers our SOS back to the caverns, but the rest of you are done with this disaster."

"But you have a baby on the way."

Connie looked over at Sal and grinned. Sal's face looked like someone had used it for a canvas, but instead of using a paintbrush, they'd used a razor. Branches had left their slash marks across her face as they plowed through the dark jungle. Even with blood on her face and fatigue in her eyes, Sal still looked like an army cherub.

"Delta is my first responsibility, Sal. I'm not leaving this jungle without her."

Wiping a drop of blood that was trickling down her temple, Sal nodded in understanding. "You really love her, don't you?"

Connie grinned. "More than life itself."

"What I don't get is if you two love each other so much, how come you're not together?"

This made Connie chuckle. "Oh, Sal, if I had a quarter for all the times people asked me that."

"Well?"

Connie brushed the wet hair off Sal's forehead. "If Delta was my lover and did the shit she does, I'd kill her."

Sal laughed. "No foolin'?"

"No foolin'. My bond with Delta runs deeper than the lover relationship. We're connected on a plane that transcends the physical realm."

"You love her more than Gina?"

Connie sighed. "It's a different kind of love. Delta makes me a complete person. I need her fire, her energy, and her strength. She needs my earth, my calm, and my rationality. We need each other."

"You've never wanted to go to bed with her?"

Connie laughed. "Hell, no."

"I would. She's something else."

Connie maneuvered the mirror once more and caught the sun just right. "Like I said, the physical aspect of relationships isn't what we're about. It's about our spirits."

"Gina and Megan sure are understanding about the crap you two go through in the name of friendship."

"Yes, they are. But then, they're both remarkable women in their own right. Gina is the most remarkable woman I have ever known, and although she isn't a warrior like Delta, she has the biggest, kindest heart I have ever known."

"I guess you four are pretty lucky to have found each other."

Nodding, Connie looked back at the forest. "Yes, we are. And that family has extended to include you and Josh, Carducci, and even Taylor. I won't risk losing any more of you by going back. I want you and Josh to see Gina home safely."

"But Zahn..."

"Zahn will be long gone by the time help arrives. He may feel confident to clash with a bunch of wayward Americans, but the cartel frowns upon any sort of international incident. I'll be fine."

"If it's so safe, why can't the rest of us go?"

Connie lowered the mirror and stared at the sea. There was no getting around Sal's probing questions, except to say the truth. "Whether she's dead or alive, I'm not leaving here without her. It could take weeks to dig them out of there. I want the rest of you to go home and live your lives. Take care of Megan and Gina. There's no need for all of us to wade through tons of boulders."

Sal's mouth dropped open. "Are you telling me you think she's dead?"

Connie sighed. A single tear dropped off her eyelash. "I don't know what to think anymore, Sal. My head tells me not even Delta Stevens could have survived a blast like that, but my gut tells me it isn't over until I see her corpse. And that's something I will have to do myself."

Sal took Connie's hand in hers. "Promise me you'll come back, that you won't do anything stupid."

Connie barely nodded. "My days of doing stupid things are over, Sal. After this, all I want is a quiet life with my lover and child and aunt Delta coming over to be a bad influence."

"Come on, Con, you're scaring me! What about that native spirit shit? How come you can't tell if she's still alive?"

Connie closed her eyes for a second and listened to the rhythm of the sea. She didn't want to tell Sal that she was afraid to listen; afraid to hear the sound of a spirit no longer connected to Delta's living being. Connie Rivera was too afraid this time to know the truth, so she had blocked out; completely blocked her spirits, like drawing a curtain against the glare of the sun. She knew the odds of Delta living through a cave in of that magnitude were remote at best, and Connie could not bear the thought of listening for Delta and hearing the empty, tortured sound of her own soul echoing back at her.

Turning to Sal, Connie opened her eyes. "I can't tell if she's alive, Sal, because I am too afraid of hearing the truth."

"And what truth is that, Connie?"

Connie looked at the beautiful dawn and shrugged. "The only truth in the universe that scares me more than death."

Sal scooted closer to Connie and hugged her. "Living without Delta?"

Connie shook her head. "No. Failing her."

"God, don't fail me now," Megan muttered as she ripped through the foliage toward the sounds of the gunfire. Pushing quickly through the forest, she followed the shots until she was right on top of them. She had managed to avoid two soldiers making their way through the jungle, but she knew there must be others searching for them as well.

She figured that as long as there was gunfire, there were two sides still fighting. All she had to do was reach her side.

When she did, Carducci whirled around at the sound of their approaching steps. He took one look at Megan, dropped his gun, and took her in his arms, holding on to her tightly.

"How the hell did you get out?" he asked, seeing the party of women standing sheepishly behind Megan.

"There was an underground river and..."

"Did Delta make it?" Josh asked, pausing for only a moment to ask the question before continuing to fire at the men coming from the camp.

Shaking her head slowly, Megan buried her face and tears in Carducci's chest. "I...I don't think so. She...stayed with Taylor."

Carducci squeezed his eyes closed. "You sure? Did you see her?"

Pulling away, Megan wiped her eyes and tried to compose herself. "We keep expecting her to perform one miracle after another, Tony. This time, I'm afraid, she couldn't pull it off. She and Taylor... There just wasn't enough time."

Nodding slowly, Tony released her and retrieved his weapon.

"Got no time for a memorial, either," Josh announced. "It'll be full daylight soon, and then they're all comin' after us. We gotta double time outta here."

Carducci nodded. "Can those others travel?" He jerked toward Siobhan's group with his head.

"They're going to have to."

Josh plucked several rounds of ammunition from the ground and tucked the night goggles back into his bag. "Wait a second," he said, as he rummaged through the assorted debris in his bag. "I told Logan to put a few goodies in here. Let's see if he ever figured out how to follow orders." Pulling out a hand grenade, Josh smiled. "Can't leave without sayin' goodbye. Tony, you, Megan, and the others go on. I'll catch up to you in a bit. Here're the compass coordinates. Just continue southwest at that coordinate. I'll meet up with you there."

Nodding, Carducci snagged the piece of paper from Josh and, with the other hand, reached out to shake his hand. "You're a hell of a soldier, man."

Grabbing Carducci's hand, Josh grinned. "Yeah, but you can shoot the tits off a gnat. Take care of the girls, Tony."

"Will do."

With that, Carducci, Megan, and a handful of exhausted women headed southwest, toward freedom.

"Megan?" Carducci asked as they shoved branches and bushes out of the way.

"Yes, Tony?"

"If you didn't see her die, maybe she's still alive."

Megan held back a large branch while the others followed Carducci.

"With my Delta Stevens, anything is possible."

Delta had no idea where they were, but it was possible they were headed toward the beach. Her instincts told her they were headed in the right direction, but she couldn't tell for sure. If she could stay alive until sunrise, she would know which was east and which was west, but until then, her gut was the only compass to rely on. Once or twice, she had heard the distant echo of gunshots, but she could not tell from which direction the sound came.

Taylor had given Delta a brief rundown of the plan, but it didn't help that neither of them could figure out the way to the water. What was worse, Taylor was beginning to fade in and out of consciousness, and as she made her way through the thick brush, Delta stopped every now and then to make sure Taylor was alive. The fear that Taylor would die from shock before they could reach help motivated Delta's exhausted, aching legs. She was operating on adrenaline alone and knew it was only a matter of time before fatigue became her worst enemy.

"Del?" Taylor's voice came weakly from behind.

Stopping, Delta gently lowered Taylor to the ground. It was hard to tell in the soft early morning light, but Taylor's face appeared pasty and lifeless. "You hurting?"

Taylor nodded. "Been thinking."

Delta looked around the forest floor for a moment, before finding the same type of bush Flora's grandmother had shown her.

The leaf, when chewed and mixed with saliva, had some sort of healing agents in it, and though Delta couldn't remember what those were, she would eat dirt if she thought it would ease Taylor's pain.

"Are you gonna listen or not?"

Delta jammed two of the bright green leaves in her mouth, chewed them to a paste, and then spit them out in her palm. "I need to put this on your leg."

Taylor looked into Delta's palm and winced. "Eww. Do you know what you're doing?"

Delta grinned. "Sort of."

"Um, Delta? What, exactly happened to you out here? I mean..." Taylor reached out and caressed the dark blue painted line running just beneath Delta's collarbone. "You're all tattooed, you're chewing leafs and shit, and you're...well...acting a lot like some kinda native."

Delta pressed the paste to Taylor's leg before retying the tourniquet. "It's along story. What was it your were thinking?" Sitting down next to Taylor, Delta wrapped her arms around her and held Taylor close. Two, maybe three hours had elapsed since they had emerged from the caverns, and Delta feared she wouldn't be able to get started again once they stopped.

"About what?" Cradling Taylor in her arms, Delta lightly stroked Taylor's hair. She was cold and sweaty at once; sure signs of shock.

"In case I don't make it..."

"Taylor..."

"No, let me finish."

Delta rocked Taylor gently as she waited. "Okay."

"In case I don't make it out of here, I want you to know why I came."

Delta kissed Taylor's temple and continued rocking her, trying to forget the time she had held another dear friend in her arms as his warm blood drained onto the cold pavement. "I know why."

Taylor coughed as she shook her head. "Are you gonna let me talk or not?"

"Sorry."

Shivering a little, Taylor put her arms around Delta's waist. "I fell in love with you long before I met you.

I romanticized who I thought Delta Stevens was in my head. There's quite a bit of press about you and your exploits, you know."

Delta nodded but said nothing.

"Then, when I finally met you, I was surprised to see that I hadn't romanticized at all. You were exactly the heroine I'd fantasized about."

Pulling Taylor closer to her, Delta continued to rock.

"But I was also surprised that my feelings for you were deeper than sexual or physical. You were a woman whose life I wanted to be a part of in whatever capacity you'd let me."

Taylor snuggled closer before continuing. "When Connie called, there wasn't a moment's hesitation in me. You needed my help, and I saw it as the perfect opportunity to become part of your world."

Delta nodded.

"I guess...I guess I just want you to know that I think you and your friends are tops in my book, and if I die, I'll go knowing that I was a part of that, a part of them."

Squeezing her eyes, Delta sighed. "Yes, Taylor, you are."

"I never had a family, you know."

Trying to contain her tears, Delta swallowed hard. "Well, you do now, sport."

Taylor winced from some pain and stiffened in Delta's embrace, her voice starting to take on a dreamy sound. "I think that's all anybody wants in this life; a place to belong, people who care whether or not they live or die. Don't you think?"

Feeling tears run down her cheeks, Delta nodded. "I care, Taylor. We all do."

"That's my point. If I die in here, you have to know it's a way better death than living without people who truly love you. If I had to do it all over again, a herd of Tasmanian devils couldn't keep me away."

Kissing Taylor's forehead once more, Delta held her tightly. "I know."

"Do you?"

Tilting Taylor's face up so she could see her eyes, Delta smiled warmly. "I'm so glad you came into my life."

Kissing Delta lightly on the cheek, Taylor returned her head to Delta's chest. "Me, too. Megan is a lucky woman, and so are you."

Closing her eyes and feeling Taylor's weight sag against her, Delta nodded. Right now, lucky was just about the last thing she felt.

⊕

"And if you're lucky, it will be right where it's supposed to be."

Sal looked at Connie, her right eyebrow arched in question. "Now we're relying on luck?"

Connie dug through her bag and opened a package of trail mix. Offering the bag to Sal, Connie waited for her to dig out a fistful before helping herself. "Luck helps. But, no, I am relying on a hell of a lot more than that."

"So what, exactly, is it you want me to do?"

Connie had received confirmation from the boat by way of a flashing light that someone had seen her signal.

"If my rusty Morse code is still any good, we're about a quarter of a mile off track. We don't have time to comb the shore looking for the raft Gina and Logan were supposed to leave. We need you to swim out to the boat and bring one back. Think you can do it?"

Sal looked out at the boat and estimated the swim to be a quarter of a mile, maybe more. "If that's what needs to be done, then I'll do it. Are there sharks out there?"

Connie grinned. Sal had some kind of phobia about being eaten alive. She had voiced these concerns even when they had first run into the Bri. "I don't think so."

Sal looked up at her. "You don't think so? Con, you're the smartest woman on the planet. Could you at least lie to me and say there's no way in hell sharks hang out here so that my little ticker doesn't get overly excited?"

Connie grinned. "How's your leg?"

Sal shrugged away the pain. "It works."

Connie looked hard at Sal. "It hurts, doesn't it?"

"Is it now time for me to lie?"

Connie grabbed another handful of trail mix. "No. I know the answer to that question."

Sal reached for the trail mix and poured more in her hand before opening her canteen and swallowing three huge gulps of water. "So, I'm supposed to just let you go back in there by yourself?"

Nodding, Connie removed a compass, a Bowie knife, and her canteen from her bag. "Have to."

"Gina'll kill me when I tell her."

"She'll understand. Just get me some help as soon as possible. Given the size of the explosions in the caves, the nationals might already be on their way."

Sal nodded as she removed her backpack and set it beside Connie's. "How much time should I give you?"

"Before calling it quits?"

Sal looked away. Neither wanted to admit the possibility that Connie or the boys might not make it back. "Yeah."

"Forty-eight hours. You take the boys and go back to the Gran Hotel in San Jose. Stay out of Panama. The Panamanians won't be very pleased to learn we're back in La Amistad. At least in Costa Rica, we have Bianca."

"The Gran Hotel. Got it."

Watching Sal take her shirt off, Connie grinned weakly. She had never been so tired in her life. "Sal?"

"Yeah?"

"Thanks. For everything."

Nodding, Sal took a few steps toward the water. "None needed. Just bring her back."

"Will do."

"What should I tell Gina?"

Connie had been thinking about that ever since they left the jungle. "The truth, Sal. Always the truth."

"She'll be okay, won't she? I mean, this won't take her into premature labor or anything, will it?"

Connie shook her head. "Nah. She's tougher than she looks. She'll be fine."

"I'll be back in a flash." With that, Sal waded into the clear blue Caribbean water, leaving Connie to wonder if she'd ever see her again.

Just when Binaca wondered if she'd ever see her brother again, the kids she'd put on watch detail ran excitedly through the open front door, telling her that Manny had just arrived in town.

Her new friends had already been gone several hours, and Manny had actually arrived sooner than Bianca anticipated. Still, he was too late, and for that, she was glad. She had been hoping for a chance to tell Manny what she thought of the way he had treated these people and the ones he had yet to save.

After sending the children back to the main road, Bianca poured herself a glass of lemonade and stood by the window overlooking the small town. Rivas was nothing like the city of Vancouver, British Colombia, where she attended school. It had one main street, several small bars, and a grocery store. Even the gas station was in the town ten miles south of Rivas. There was little for children to do here except play in the jungle, and swim in the river winding its way in and out of town. She had grown up here and loved every moment. Even with its small size with little for her to do, she often found herself longing for the peacefulness of Rivas when she was away at school, but that calm had been broken by Colombians, Americans, and even her brother.

Manny.

She felt so betrayed by him. And now, she was going to have the chance to tell him just what she thought of his clandestine activities. She could hardly wait. It wasn't easy to realize that her big brother had opted for money over morals. These days, poor people seemed to be doing that more and more. Farmers were selling their rain forest property to large American, Canadian, and German companies, who clear-cut it for grazing land in order to feed the Americans lust for beef. While the farmer became rich, the land, and the people on it, were forced to adapt or die, like any other creature in the jungle. She had thought Manny knew better than to turn on his country, but she had been wrong. Like the farmers, Manny's lifestyle was more important than the big picture of saving a country from the capitalist nations that threatened to destroy it. Perhaps the Americans' gluttonous way of life was poisoning everyone it touched.

Be that as it may, she was not about to let her brother pursue her friends into the jungle.

He may have chosen politics over pride of his heritage, but Bianca would not let him choose to harm her friends. There may have been little to do in Rivas while she was growing up, but that meant spending quality time with her friends, and Bianca had many friends. She had friends who wrote her weekly, friends who shared her love of adventure, and friends who were also disappointed that Manny had sold their country out. She had had enough of his lies and deception. Bianca had faith in the group of Americans who had befriended her, and she was going to give them every possible chance of success, because that's what friends do for each other.

Picking up the phone, she dialed and waited for someone to answer the call. When a deep, husky voice answered, she said, "Ahora, acqui," and then hung up the phone and continued staring out the window.

Ten minutes after her call, Manny came bursting through the door, his eyes red-rimmed, and his face haggard. "Binaca!" he shouted, before he saw her standing at the window.

"I am right here, Manuel." Binanca crossed her arms and leaned against the wall. Manny looked like he hadn't slept in days, and he sported a three or four day old beard. Deception seemed to have prematurely aged him.

"Where are they?" He said, looking frantically about.

"Whom are you speaking about?" Bianca slowly picked up her lemonade and took a sip. This was not the boy she had grown up with, and her heart sank at the prospect of having lost him already.

"Do not trifle with me, Bianca. I know they must have come here!" Manny's eyes swept the room looking for evidence. "There was no place else for them to go."

"Are you asking as my brother, who has turned his back on his friends, or as the agent working for the United States government, who has turned his back on his country? Tell me, Manuel, to whom am I speaking?"

Manny's head whipped around and he stared hard at his little sister. "Then they were here!"

Bianca shrugged. She was angrier with him than she realized. "They were not here, Manuel, Connie was. The rest of them went back to the States." If he could deceive to catch them, she could do the same to release them.

Manny plopped down in a chair, his eyes still working over the room. His eyes were bloodshot and there were horrendous bags beneath them. Bianca wondered what job was worth putting yourself through this. "Just Connie? And don't lie to me Bianca. I know when you're lying."

"It's a shame I can't say the same about you."

Manny released a bone weary sigh. "It is not a child's world I live in, Bee. There's much more to this than..."

"Than what? Than friendship? Than patriotism? You know what saddens me the most, Manuel, is that it was you who taught me about both."

Manny rubbed his stubble and looked away from her. "I don't have time for this."

"It was also you who told me that our people valued time together more than money or riches or possessions. Were you lying about that as well?"

Manny looked back at his little sister. She was not the little girl she was when last she'd come home. "When this is all over, I will explain global politics to you, Bee, but right now, I need to know if you're being honest. Did only Connie go in the jungle?"

Bianca nodded, feeling her heart slowly breaking. "She is the only one who thinks Delta is still alive."

Manny laid his face in his hands and sighed loudly. "Damn them."

Setting her drink down, Bianca shook her head sadly. She had never felt like any of her siblings were strangers to her until now. "Damn them for not acting the way you wanted them to?"

Manny waved her off without looking at her. "You don't have any idea what this..."

"I most certainly do. I know far more than you imagine. I know that you have turned your back on those people. How could you do that, Manuel? Is that how Papa raised you?"

"Bianca..."

"No, you are going to hear me out, big brother. Josh carried you out of the forest, took you to a hospital, saved your life, and this is how you repay him?"

Manny looked at her through his empty, bloodshot eyes. "It's not about me, Bianca."

"It is to me! You were my idol, Manny. I thought you were the picture of virtue and ethics. I was proud to call you my brother. But not today. Not any more."

"You don't know what the world is about, Bianca."

"I don't need to know what the world is about to know that you betrayed someone who saved your life. And if that isn't bad enough, you've betrayed our people, our country, even our family." Bianca shook her head sadly. "You've used people who only wanted to make the world you seem to think I know nothing about, a safer place for everyone. So don't try to rationalize your behavior, Manny, because you're wasting your time. I am not a little girl any longer."

Manny rose to leave, but suddenly found the door blocked by a very large younger man about Bianca's age. Behind him stood two more young men who could have passed for teenagers. All three men wore machetes around their waists. Manny turned to her, anger and frustration on his face. "Don't do this, Bianca. This does not concern you."

"That's where you're wrong, Manny. Saving people, saving the rain forest, saving my beautiful country does concern me." Bianca nodded to the man blocking the door. His name was Enrico, and he had grown up with Bianca. "Gracias, Rico."

Enrico nodded, glaring at Manny. "No problemo." Enrico motioned for Manny to sit down, which he did.

"You've lost your way, Manuel," Binaca said, folding her arms across her chest. "You've given up what's important for something that doesn't even matter. Well, those people and this country matter to me, and I'm not going to allow you to go after them or get in their way."

Manny's eyes grew larger. "You lied! They did go after Delta, didn't they?"

Bianca cursed herself beneath her breath. "It doesn't matter who went after her, Manny, because you're no longer in the game."

Manny studied Bianca a moment before turning to Enrico and reeling of a barrage of curses at him. Enrico only grinned and put his hand on his machete handle.

"Relax. Enrico, Saldovar, and Javier are here to make sure that you don't go anywhere." Bianca walked over to her brother and held her hand out. "Both your guns, please."

Manny stared, slack-jawed at her. "My..."

Bianca grinned. Connie and Delta would have been so proud. "Your guns, Manny. Give them to me."

"You think I would use weapons against Enrico?"

Bianca shrugged, sadness covering her face. "I don't trust you any more, Manny. I don't believe you know what's right and wrong any more. I can't take the chance that you might hurt one of us for your American paycheck." To her surprise, Manny's eyes filled with tears.

"I can't believe..."

"Neither can I. And I can only hope that you haven't set this whole thing up to explode in our faces."

Manny impatiently wiped his eyes. "What does that mean? What do you mean our faces?" Manny pulled out his two handguns and handed them to Bianca.

Taking the handguns, Bianca walked over to Enrico and handed them to him. "It means that those Americans need help, and I'm going to give it to them."

Bianca and Kiki had been in the jungle for nearly three hours when she sent Kiki scurrying up to the highest portion of the canopy. She knew Kiki understood what they were looking for, and who better to find the invisible beings in a rain forest than a Capuchin monkey? It wouldn't be long now before Kiki located their quarry. She always had.

Following the group's trail through the jungle had been child's play, and Bianca wondered if she might not come upon her new American friends' corpses. The Americans had created a wide swath that would have told even a novice tracker that they had come this way. Bianca could only hope that wasn't the case. She had grown fond of the Americans, who had shown her more courage than what she'd read about in school. It was odd to see Americans act the way these people had. Most Americans were so busy strutting about, acting like gluttons, consuming everything any country made, that they were unaware that they had become the laughing stock of so many other nations. Even her own beloved Costa Ricans thought the haughty nature of Americans was both sad and amusing.

But these Americans were different. They had come to her not once but twice, asking for help, and Bianca had delivered. Sure, she had delivered them to her secret agent-spy-undercover cop-operative-brother, but that didn't mean she couldn't make up for Manny's poor judgment and even poorer job choices. She loved her brother very much, and the Manny she'd grown up with would never have allowed innocent people to get hurt, even if it meant political hurricanes would sweep down. He had changed. Maybe it was just about growing up. Whatever it was, she was not about to let him sentence these courageous Americans to death in order to fulfill some kind or obligation he had to some other government.

No, Delta and her friends deserved a fighting chance. Manny surely must see that. He couldn't possibly send people to their deaths knowing that one of them had come down and immediately gotten involved in a rain forest preservation project. That had to matter to him. Watching Kiki scamper among the branches, Bianca listened carefully to the sounds of the jungle. It didn't matter how long she had been away, a kid who had grown up in the jungle knew it better than any place in the world. It was as familiar to her now as it had been when she was ten years old and had spent a month in the Bribri village with her father. The world around her may have changed, but the jungle was as beautiful and as dangerous as ever.

Suddenly, Kiki made clicking and popping noises that told her Kiki had seen what they were looking for. Kiki, too, had managed to stay relatively unchanged since Bianca was a child, and Bianca could recognize each of her many sounds like a mother knows what her baby is saying when it first learns to talk. Kiki had spotted them. There was a certain noise Kiki made with the tip of her tongue. Kiki had learned that sound during their month in the jungle six years ago.

As Bianca neared a huge mango tree, she clicked her tongue to call Kiki back. As the monkey descended from her perch high in the trees, Bianca heard the slightest cracking of the jungle floor. Turning around, she had found what she was looking for.

"Well, it's about time," she said, opening the top of her shirt to display a thin light blue line that resembled a tattoo. "I need your help."

It had taken them more time than they realized, but when the sun started peeking through the thin blue line of the horizon, it was a welcome sight. When you are running for your life, nighttime in the jungle feels like an eternity.

When Meg, Carducci, and Josh finally made it out of the jungle and onto shore, Sal was just returning to the beach in a rubber raft large enough to carry them all. Even the ex-hostages had managed to keep up with the three of them as they scurried through the jungle.

Sal was about one hundred yards from their exit point, and when she saw them flop on the sand. She paddled furiously before jumping into the water and swimming as fast as she could until she found herself being yanked out of the water by Josh's large hands.

"Salamander! You made it!" Josh crushed Sal to his huge chest and lifted her off the ground.

When Josh finally released her, Sal stared, slack-jawed, at Megan. "You got out? How?"

After a brief explanation of how they had all arrived, Megan examined the shore and posed her own question.   Sal knew by the tone in Megan's voice that she wasn't going to be pleased with the answer.

Megan frowned. She knew Connie well enough to hazard a good guess. "No, don't tell me..."

Nodding, Sal sighed. "There was no talking her out of it. You know how she gets. Sometimes, she's more pigheaded than Delta."

Megan looked over at Carducci, who shrugged. "Damn her. I should have expected as much. Those two would rather die here together than live without each other."

Josh cleared his throat. "Ladies, we don't have time to sit here and discuss the relationship of two crazy broads, we have to get these people some help and get the hell outta here."

"How long ago did she leave?" Megan asked Sal, who was rubbing the back of her leg.

"Not long, about thirty or forty minutes. She sent me back to the boat to get a second raft. We were off-course when we landed here."

Megan nodded as she turned to Josh. "How far behind do you think the General's men are?"

Josh shrugged. "Not far. You can just bet that asshole will send men after us."

"I'll go get the raft," Carducci offered, stripping down to the army fatigues Josh had loaned him.

Megan wiped some wet hair off Sal's forehead. She was still breathing hard from her swim. "Did Gina and Logan get help?"

Sal smiled. "She's a smart one, that woman. She told both the Panamanian police and the Costa Rican cops that there were Nicaraguan rebel forces here. Their responses were immediate anger and irritation. Nico rebels are a zit on the face of Central America, and apparently, that means the Panamanians and the Ticos are more than willing to jump in. We should be seeing choppers over the horizon any time now."

Josh rubbed his hands together. "Smart thinking. If they can get a bird in the air soon, the general's men will be forced to disperse. Once they scatter, we can get back to their camp and see about getting Delta and Taylor out of there."

Megan looked up at Josh's tired, sweaty face, "You think she could have survived those blasts, Josh?"

Josh looked away for a moment before returning his gaze to Megan. "Delta just doesn't go down easily, Meg."

"That's not what I asked."

Inhaling deeply, Josh rubbed his beard. "No, Meg, I don't. But in Nam, you never believed your buddy was dead until you carried his lifeless body off the field. Until I see her body, Delta is as alive as if she was standin' here with us."

Throwing her arms around Josh's neck, Megan stood on tiptoe to hug him. "Thank you, Josh. Thank you for believing in her."

"I've seen her pull outta too many scrapes not to, Meg."

Sal looked at the horizon at the small dot that was their boat. "Let's get these people to the boat and figure out how to get us all home safely."

Everyone turned and look at Sal, who seldom issued orders of any kind. When she realized everyone was staring at her, she grinned sheepishly and shrugged. "Connie told me to take care of everyone until she got back, and that's what I'm going to do. Now double-time your asses and get to that boat."

ELEVEN

Connie double-timed through the thick forest, fueled by an oddly familiar mixture of fear and anger. She pushed herself as if she'd been hiking through the rain forest all her life as if she had a fresh pair of legs and nothing to fear. She was not afraid to die.

Like so many others before her, Sal's questions about her relationship with Delta made Connie smile. Delta hadn't just blasted into Connie's life; she had filled a void that only one's true soul mate could fill. She had brought with her all the pieces Connie needed to feel whole. When Delta Stevens had landed in Connie's life, she had lit it up like a halogen headlight illuminates the dark. Oh sure, Delta was unpredictable, quick to react, and broke all the rules, but she was also the most loyal person Connie had ever met, and her level of integrity was second to none.

As Connie pushed her way deeper into the jungle, she didn't even stop to wipe the sweat off her forehead. The what if syndrome began playing in her head like a song she couldn't let go of. What if Delta hadn't made it out of the cavern? What if she were alive and suffering? Shaking her head, Connie knew one thing. She wasn't leaving without Delta.

Period.

After a period of time, Delta woke, her head pillowed on Taylor's soggy backpack. Delta was still holding Taylor, and had no way of knowing how long they'd been asleep. By the looks of sky, dawn had graced the world, shining small bursts of sun through the forest canopy.

"Damn it," Delta cursed under her breath. She knew it was more dangerous to travel in the daylight and wished she hadn't fallen asleep.

"Taylor?" she whispered, gently shaking her. When there was no response, Delta's heart leaped into her throat. "Taylor?" This time, Delta shook her roughly. "Wake up, Taylor."

"Is this how you treat all the women you sleep with?" Taylor's eyes slowly opened, and a slight smile played on her lips. Her face was paler and had an unhealthy grayness to it.

"Feeling better?" Delta knew the answer but hoped for a different response than the one Taylor's face reflected.

"No, but I was afraid you'd slap me again. I feel like shit."

Delta felt her forehead. She was clammy. "Yeah, well, if you have any thoughts about dying on me, forget it."

Taylor chuckled. "You gotta be kidding. After your super-human effort to get us out of that fucking cavern and then spitting some green shit in my wound? Not hardly. Even I have to stay alive to see how this adventure turns out."

"Good." Easing out of Taylor's embrace, Delta checked the tourniquet. "At least in the daylight I'll be able to get a good look at your leg."

"It's busted."

"Now you're a doctor?"

"I busted it once before. Took a bad fall from a four-story condo in Spain. Good air time, poor landing, lots of loot. Felt a lot like it does right now, only sans the loot."

Delta looked at her leg. It was swollen and had a purple tint to it. "You're going to need help soon, or you could lose it."

Taylor smiled in the pink and green morning and lightly touched Delta's cheek. "Lover, if we get out of this godforsaken jungle alive, a leg will be a small price to pay."

"You're not going to lose it, and we are getting out of here. One way or the other, Taylor, we're living through this."

"It'll read great in my memoirs."

Delta chuckled. "Now that's a book I'd pay hardcover price for."

As the morning light burst through the foliage, Delta knelt and studied Taylor's leg more closely. It did look broken, but the bleeding had stopped. Loosening the tourniquet, she looked at Taylor's pale face. "You don't look so hot."

"Told you I feel like shit. Are we leaving or are you going to play doctor all day?"

Delta grinned. "You wish."

Taylor smiled back. "Can we play doctor just once later, when I feel better?"

Delta shook her head and pulled Taylor's pant leg down. "You know that's not how I work."

"I wasn't talking about work. I was talking about playing. Come on, Delta, play with me."

Delta gazed down into Taylor's eyes and smiled warmly. "Don't you know that people in shock aren't supposed to be cantankerous?"

Taylor looked into Delta's green eyes and sighed, "Can't help it. You bring out the sexual beast in me."

Delta rummaged through Taylor's bag and pulled out a canteen. "Here, oh-saucy-one, have a drink."

Taylor took the canteen and sipped a little before handing it back to Delta. "You know, you keep saving my life, and I'm going to have to be indebted to you forever."

Delta recapped the canteen, and pulled a bag of trail mix from the backpack. "Nah. I told you. You're family now. My family. We don't run out on each other." Delta poured some trail mix in her mouth and started to hand the bag to Taylor, who shook her head.

"No, thanks. Family, eh?"

Delta ate another mouthful before putting the rest back in the bag. "Yep."

Taylor studied Delta through exhausted eyes. "Then how could Megan leave you?"

"Megan knew I'd never leave you. Hell, it's the first time I think she ever really understood me."

"She's not the one who truly gets you, is she?"

Delta shrugged. "Con doesn't believe I'm dead, if that's what you mean."

"How can she not? That blast was probably felt all the way to Brazil."

Retying the tourniquet, Delta helped Taylor up. "You gotta understand one thing about me and Connie. We're connected. Before all this shit came down, I took a spiritual journey."

Taylor held up her hand, signaling for Delta to stop. "Whoa right there. You took a what?"

"A spiritual journey. She and I discovered something I'd known all along, but I was hesitant to admit for fear of sounding like a lunatic. Connie and I are more than friends, much more than colleagues, and more important than lovers. We're creatures whose spirits coexist in the warrior realm together. We're connected...Delta's voice trailed off, her thoughts with Connie, who she knew was searching for her now.

"Uh, Del?"

"Oh, sorry. I was just thinking."

"For a minute there, I thought you were communicating with the spirits."

Delta grinned slightly, and then her face froze. "What did you just say?"

"I said, oh, never mind."

Delta stared hard at Taylor. "Wait here."

Taylor pointed to her leg and leaned against a tree. "Gee, okay. Where are you going?"

But Delta did not hear her. Moving to a slight clearing, Delta knelt down and closed her eyes. As she did, she dug the fingers of one hand into the soft dirt at the base of a plant, and placed her other palm against a tree. She had seen Connie do this once when they first met. It had appeared crazy at the time, but now, Delta realized how little she truly knew about her best friend. Too busy scoffing at the intangible, Delta had never fully understood or accepted the spiritual gifts Connie possessed, until now.

It wasn't until Taylor had joked about her communicating with the spirits that Delta realized the impact of her own journey. During her warrior's initiation, Connie's spirit had somehow managed to join Delta's on the spiritual plane. That meant Connie's spirit was so tied to Delta's that she could locate her even in another realm. If she could do that on an astral level, the chances were high that Connie could find her on the physical plane.

Opening her eyes, Delta took one quick look around before closing them again. She wasn't sure what to do beyond this except open her mind and let the images float freely. After several minutes, she opened her eyes and felt a peacefulness she hadn't felt since before Megan had left the States.

Yes, Connie was out here. Of that, Delta was sure. Now, if only they could find each other.

Rising, Delta walked back to find Taylor still leaning against a tree. "We'll move faster if you don't have to carry me."

Smiling, Delta threaded her arms around Taylor's tiny waist. "You sure you're up to it?"

"No, but we don't have much choice. If I don't take a bath soon, I may get suicidal."

This made Delta laugh. "Doesn't anything get you down?"

Taylor nodded. "A few things do."

"Like what?"

"Let's see. I hate it when I miss a sale at Nordstrom's. I get depressed when Susan Lucci doesn't win a much-deserved Emmy, and it really bums me out that you won't sleep with me."

"Taylor!"

"Hey, you asked."

Moving toward the southwest, Delta helped Taylor walk. "You're nuts."

Taylor stopped abruptly. "I'm nuts? I'm nuts? You go off to commune with the spirits, and you think I'm crazy? Look again, Sherlock. The clues about which of us is crazy are right in front of your eyes."

Pushing branches out of the way, Delta and Taylor forged silently ahead, trying to make it to the beach before the sun completely gave them away.

"Will you always be my hero, Delta Stevens?"

Delta chuckled. "You bet. As long as you'll always be my number one fan."

Taylor nodded. "Count on it."

Josh counted the remaining rounds of ammo left before looking over at Carducci's stack. "How much you got?"

"Not much. A hundred rounds, maybe. Give or take."

Josh nodded as he reloaded his rifle. Lowering his voice he said, "Gettin' all of us outta here alive ain't gonna happen."

Carducci sighed and nodded. "I know."

"We gotta make sure those in the boat get outta range first."

Carducci looked up from his rifle. "First?"

Josh nodded. "Never seen combat, eh?"

Carducci, a Gen Xer, barely knew what the Viet Nam War was about. "Nope."

"You're lucky. We have a chance to get some of us to safety. That's first. In Nam, if half your unit returned, you considered that a success."

"Pretty harsh."

"War's harsh, man, and that's what we're in."

"So, what's second?"

Josh studied the ever-lightening forest. "Second rule in Nam was you go back after those you left behind."

"With less than a hundred rounds? Is there a third rule? A Plan B?"

Josh shrugged. "Sure. We can cover the boat and then get the hell outta here ourselves."

Carducci reached out and touched Josh's rifle. "You're kidding right?"

Josh shook his head. "Saving your own ass is always an option."

"Not for me it isn't. Dead or alive, I'm bringing her back. I may not have seen war like you have, Josh, but that doesn't mean I'm a coward. I'd be nowhere if it weren't for Delta. Any dream I ever had about becoming part of SWAT will only come true because I was taught by the best. I won't leave her in this fucked-up wilderness."

"You sure about that? She could be under tons of rocks and shit."

"She'd do the same for me," Carducci said quietly. "For all of us."

"Yeah, she would. She's a helluva gal."

Checking his sights, Carducci nodded. "Hope she made it outta there."

Sal returned to the two men after seeing Megan and the others into the raft. "Sure you can't come with us?"

Josh looked over his shoulder at the forest before looking down at Sal. "They'll kill us all if they get to the beach before we can get safely out of range. Can't risk it."

Sal hugged Josh hard, lifting her feet off the ground as she wrapped her arms around his thick, sweaty neck. "Be safe," she whispered. "I need you."

Josh turned his head and listened intently. "They're coming. Get outta here, Salamander. And don't take any wooden nickels."

Sal wanted to respond to the stupid phrase, the same one her dad used to use before sending her to the store for those pink bubble gum cigars, but Josh's expression told her to get moving. Running to the raft, Sal hopped in with the others.

"You can see them?" Carducci looked through his scope, seeing nothing; he tensed his finger around the trigger

"Nah. Hear 'em. There's a sound the jungle makes when men are slithering through it. I heard it so much; I still hear it in my sleep. The Cong could do it better than anyone. They'd slither along, slit your throat, and slither out with barely a noise. You learned to listen for that sound. You also never forget it. "Josh glanced over his shoulder and watched as the raft's tiny engine sputtered to life, and zipped away. "But it'll be a cold day in hell before a bunch of bean-eaters hurt Sal. These boys are rookies, about to experience their first American Marine." Josh returned to his rifle, took a deep breath, and fired off a few rounds, instantly killing two men who hadn't even emerged from the jungle yet.

Carducci followed suit, carefully squeezing the trigger to take out one more.

"How many?" Carducci asked, a single bead of sweat running down the side of his face.

Josh fired again. "Too many."

"Meaning?"

"We're fucked."

When the first shots reverberated through the jungle, Delta stopped in her tracks. "Fuck!" she growled, regripping Taylor.

"What?" Drenched with sweat, Taylor hung like a rag doll from Delta's left arm.

"That's gunfire. The general's men must have caught up to the group. Damn it!" Delta's voice was low and gravelly.

"Our escape route is blocked, huh?"

Delta refastened her grip on Taylor's waist and continued pushing through the jungle.

"Not necessarily. It just means we'll have to work our way south and hope the general's men have stayed together."

"You think everyone got out?"

Delta shrugged, pausing to wipe sweat from her forehead. "Well, someone got to the beach or they wouldn't be firing. Unless..."

"What?"

"Unless they caught up to them before the beach. Hell, anything's possible out here." Delta listened carefully to the sounds in the far distance. There was much more shooting than had expected. It could be another group in the rain forest. Or maybe help had already arrived and was fighting off the renegade soldiers. Or maybe the Colombians were trying to take down her best friends in a standoff at the beach.

"You scared?" Taylor asked softly.

Delta shook her head. "I'm way past being scared."

"Are you too scared to stop and loosen the tourniquet? It's really hurting."

Delta stopped and leaned Taylor against a tree. As Delta retied the tourniquet, she felt Taylor's body stiffen. When she looked up at her, Taylor's face was pale and her eyes wide. "Taylor? Did I hurt you?"

Taylor's eyes were fixed on a point over Delta's shoulder, and as Delta turned to see what she was looking at, Taylor muttered, "I sure as hell hope help is somewhere nearby."

When Delta turned around, she was staring down the barrel of a rifle. "Oh, shit."

"Oh shit," Gina cursed when she and Logan helped everyone into the boat. "Where are they?" she demanded, grabbing Megan by the shoulders and staring into her eyes. "Be straight with me, Megan. All Sal would tell me is that we're in trouble. Are they dead?"

Without warning, Megan's eyes filled with tears, as she quickly updated Gina about the explosion and Connie's decision to go back after Delta and Taylor.

When Megan finished, Gina took both of Megan's hands in hers and inhaled slowly, attempting some semblance of composure for Megan, for herself, and for the baby within her. "So, Connie went back?"

Megan nodded. "I'm sorry, Gina, but no one could stop her."

"Nor should you have." Gina's eyes filled as she smiled warmly at her friend. "If Connie believes Delta is still alive, then we must believe also."

Megan sighed and slowly shook her head. "It's a very slim possibility, Gina. The cavern..."

Gina held her hand up for Megan to stop. "Connie would never have risked it if she didn't feel Delta was alive. You must believe also."

Megan looked down and shook her head. She was running out of faith and hope. "I believed when Delta fell into the water, but this..."

Gina shook her head. "You believed because of what you saw. You saw Delta plunge into the water, therefore, you believed she could be alive."

"But..."

Gina shook her head and held her hand up again, signaling for Megan to stop. "No, hear me out. You saw the cavern beginning to collapse, and you believe Delta and Taylor could never have survived it."

Megan nodded.

"For Connie, seeing isn't believing. It's always been about how she feels, and Connie's feelings have seldom been wrong. I can't tell you how many times I have counted on her feelings to do what was best for us. Her spirit guide is a very intelligent source of direction for her. She trusts it. So do I."

Megan looked down into Gina's brown eyes, wondering how this woman could stand here so poised when their lovers could be dead, lost forever to them. She'd always know of the deep bond between Delta and Connie but hadn't ever given much thought to how two women so different could be so connected. It wasn't until Megan met Tamar and spent time with the Bribri that she'd given any thought to the spiritual component of life. As a prostitute, only the physical was important.

The corporeal world had been her bread and butter, her flesh her greatest attribute. When she met Delta, Megan finally allowed herself the chance to know emotional fulfillment as well. She learned what love felt like, and how to give it as well as receive it. Even then, Megan held no spiritual beliefs at all. She didn't care if there was a higher power or Supreme Being. All that mattered was learning how to love, how to live a completely new life, and how to accept the many changes Delta Stevens had brought about in her life.

And now, another layer of life was unfolding for her, giving her a little more hope that maybe Delta was alive.

"As it stands, Meg, there are people who could use our help, and that's what we need to be doing now, not worrying about our partners."

"So, what now?" Megan asked, as Sal and Logan appeared from the cabin of the small fishing boat.

Gina turned and introduced Logan to Megan and the others. "This is the other man in Sal's life."

Logan, short and stocky with a thick head of black hair and a fu manchu mustache extended his hairy hand. "Heard a lot about you ladies. Josh promised this would add some adventure to my life. He wasn't kidding."

Megan took his hand and grinned. "Your boat?"

Logan nodded. "Sorta. And I'd like to keep it in one piece, so we better get moving."

Megan's heart raced. "Moving? We can't go anywhere yet. Not without the others."

Logan shook his head. "Darlin', if we stay here and catch a bullet in the engine, we're all going down. We have to get these people some help, and we gotta give ourselves some distance from them guns."

Megan turned to Sal, who nodded before handing Megan a pair of binoculars. When Megan looked through them, she saw Josh and Carducci pinned behind some rocks. Raising the binoculars slightly, she could see about a dozen muzzle flashes coming from the fringes of the forest, as the Colombians made their way closer to the two men on the beach.

"Oh my God," Megan muttered, lowering the binoculars. "They'll be killed."

"Isn't there anything we can do?" Gina asked Logan.

Logan shook his head. "Nope. Nothin' we can do from here. We've already radioed for help. There ought to be so many government agencies crashin' this party, we'll feel crowded in this damn sea."

Suddenly, a familiar beating sound could be heard in the distance.

"There's nothing more we can do, but plenty the Panamanians can do." Lowering the binoculars, Logan grinned. "When we called the Costa Rican cavalry, we told them Nicaraguan drug runners were attacking a group of American and German tourists. Both groups bring lots of tourist dough, so we thought that, if the government felt their cash cow was being milked dry by Nicos or Colombians, they'd hurry their little selves right up. And look. Here they come now."

Over the crest of the mountain, two helicopters flew just above the canopy of the forest. Megan watched through the binoculars as the Colombians retreated back into the forest. "But what about Josh and Carducci? Won't the Costa Ricans think they're Nicaraguans?"

Logan shook his head. "Just watch Josh. He knows what to do."

As Megan focused on the two men, she watched in silent amazement as Josh covered Carducci with sand before burrowing in it himself.

"Josh is one helluva soldier, " Logan said, with pride.

Suddenly, the radio jumped to life, and Logan picked up the mike and rattled something in Spanish. "I told the authorities we're the tour group who called and will be headed into port shortly."

"Did they say if they saw the Colombians?" Gina asked

Logan shook his head. "It's just a recon for now. They aren't likely to share military info with a bunch of tourists. The only problem is we have to get this baby to port before either the Panamanians or the Costa Ricans send someone after us. Trust me, we don't want to spend a single second in a Latin American jail. We have a hell of a lot of explaining to do as it is."

Megan turned to Gina and searched her face for some sign of reassurance. Surely they weren't thinking of leaving the five of them out there.

"Gene?"

Gina sighed and looked at Logan. "What about the others?"

Logan's eyes narrowed. He wasn't used to dealing with so many emotions during a battle. In Nam, you did what you had to save as many of your unit as you could before going back for the others. It wasn't an emotional decision. It was a practical one. "We'll have to come back."

Megan shook her head. "That's not acceptable."

"Neither is being detained. I'm sorry, Megan, but there's no other way."

Everyone fell silent as the realization of what they must do began sinking in. Logan looked from Megan to Gina and back again before shaking his head sadly. It didn't appear as if practical was going to win out.

"Wait a minute," Sal said as she peered into the open ocean with her binoculars. "I think I see the answer to our prayers."

"Start saying your prayers, bitch."

Delta gulped loudly. She'd felt this way only once before in her life, and the same gripping fear seized her heart as she looked at the barrel pointing not twelve inches from her face. It appeared, for all intents and purposes, that the game was over.

"What a nice surprise," the soldier said in perfect English, not moving the rifle from Delta's face. "Look what we found, Carlos. The puta responsible for fucking up the general's operation."

From behind the first soldier came Carlos, also pointing a rifle at them. The odds were nearly impossible now, so Delta turned from the rifle and took Taylor's hands. "I am so sorry."

Taylor grinned, her pasty color now less apparent. "What? You're not gonna kick his ass? I'm disappointed in you, love."

Delta's eye grew wide. Maybe the fever made Taylor incapable of comprehending their hopeless situation.

"Um, Taylor..."

Taylor waved her off with the flick of a wrist. "You know, for being the black belt champ of your department, you sure don't act like a champion." Taylor looked away from Delta, disgusted.

Delta cocked her head in confusion. "I'm not..."

"The only way this guy can beat you is with that rifle. We already kicked their sorry asses once. Guess he's gotta make sure you don't do it again. Oh, I'm impressed, big macho man."

Looking in Taylor's eyes, Delta realized she was trying to buy time. Raising up, Delta turned to face the guard and started laughing. "Go ahead, Paco, shoot us, so you can go home and pretend to be a hero." Delta watched as the soldier barely lowered the rifle.

"Cowardly cocksucker," Taylor grumbled, pushing herself against the tree until she was standing on her good leg. Sweat dripped down both sides of her face. "Afraid she'll take you, asshole?" Taylor's words were spit out like staples from a staple gun.

"You're a stupid bitch," the soldier growled, handing Carlos his rifle. Carlos barely managed to keep his gun trained on Delta as he placed the other rifle over his shoulder.

"Yeah?" Delta mocked, crossing her arms. "Well, this 'stupid bitch' is gonna kick your sorry ass so hard, you'll look like a hunchback when I'm through with you."

With that, the soldier lunged for Delta, who sidestepped his wildly errant punch and rammed his left shoulder into a tree, forcing a loud grunt from him.

"Get him, Del," Taylor cheered, smiling and waving to Carlos, who kept his rifle on Delta.

The angry bull wheeled around, rage painted on his face.

"Come on, burro breath. I'm just getting warmed up, you pansy-ass piece of shit." Delta knew about using rage against an opponent. Connie had taught her well, but at what point would Carlos take her out because she was winning? And how long could they go before her opponent decided he was through being embarrassed?

"You're going to hurt, bitch," he said, pushing his sleeves up. Glaring angrily at Delta, he swung his right fist, missing but connecting with his left on her shoulder. With a quick leg motion, Delta swept his legs out from under him, and he landed on his back with a thud. Delta decided to make her move. With her back to Carlos, she did a spin move she'd only seen Connie do in exhibitions.

Straightening up, whirling her left leg like a rotor, she kicked the rifle to the side before landing squarely in front of a shocked Carlos.

Grabbing the rifle in her left hand, Delta and Carlos wrestled with it, until Delta head-butted him with the top of her forehead, hitting him squarely on the bridge of his nose. Hearing the crunch of cartilage against bone, Delta waited to feel the other soldier's grasp on her. If she had looked over her shoulder, she would have seen Taylor throw her body on the other soldier and claw at his face. As tough as Taylor was, she was no match for the Colombian, who roughly shoved Taylor off him and pulled his boot knife out all in one smooth motion.

When Taylor landed, she screamed in anguish, causing Delta to turn her head. When she did, she watched in helpless horror as the soldier raised the knife above his head. Taylor, holding her broken leg, could only close her eyes and wait for the knife to plunge deeply into her chest.

It never arrived.

Before he could bring the knife down, a screaming Connie Rivera came out of nowhere, and double-kicked the soldier, both feet landing on his chest. She hit him so hard; she dislocated one of his shoulders. Instead of the knife being thrust into Taylor's heart, it fell harmlessly to the ground, as his arm flopped helplessly to his side.

Returning her attention to Carlos, Delta smashed the heel of her hand deep into his bleeding nose, causing him to release the rifle. A second punch to his Adam's apple, and Carlos crumpled to the ground.

Delta flipped the rifle off the ground with her foot, catching it in the air, and blowing Carlos's head off before he knew what hit him. As she did, the soldier with the dislocated shoulder reached for the knife with his good hand, and Connie delivered a blow with her heel that snapped his collarbone with a resounding crack.

Whirling around, Delta aimed at the grimacing Colombian, who was growling as he rose to his feet, both arms dangling from unusable shoulders.

"You fucking bitches," he grunted through clenched teeth. He stood unsteadily on his legs and swayed back and forth, looking very much like one of the capuchin monkeys.

Delta tightened her finger on the trigger, but Connie held her hand up. "Don't."

Lowering the rifle, Delta looked questioningly at her best friend.

"This pig deserves a more painful death, Storm. One where he has time to think about what they've done here." Connie's face was taut and unemotional as she spun once and shattered his left kneecap, crumpling him to the forest floor as he screamed from the pain.

"Goddamn it, fucking bitch."

Connie stood in front of him, her hands jammed on her hips. "I'm getting really tired of your foul mouth, you scumbag." Leaning over him, she grabbed his ear. "You're gonna be worm food in a day or so, you asshole, but until then, I want you to remember that you were bested by three women." Releasing his ear, Connie took two steps away and winked at Delta.

"Cunt," he said. The word hung in the air like Los Angeles smog.

Connie stopped walking. "He didn't say the c word, did he?"

Taylor and Delta nodded. In the blink of an eye, Connie did the backwards spin kick, connecting with a precise blow to the hinge of his jaw. This crunch was the loudest of them all, and the soldier screamed as his face hit the leaves. When he rolled over, his jaw hung limply. His eyes burned with hatred.

Looking down at the suffering man, Connie felt Delta's presence by her side, as Delta slipped her hand into Connie's.

"We hate that word," Connie said quietly, watching as he passed out. The sounds of the rain forest replaced those of the battlefield, as Connie turned and hugged Delta tightly. "You finally believe, don't you?"

Delta nodded. "It was the earth, wasn't it? You've been waiting for me to understand the lessons from my journey."

Connie nodded, wiping the sweat from her forehead. "You're slow to catch on, Storm, but thank the spirits you finally figured it out." Connie threw her arms around Delta and hugged her tightly. "I knew you made it. You always do."

Squeezing Connie tightly, Delta lifted her off the ground.

"Damn it's good to see you!" Lowering Connie back to the soft floor of the forest, Delta smiled warmly into Connie's eyes. "I knew you'd come. I knew you knew we were alive."

Grinning back, Connie's eyes filled with tears. "You really think I'd let you have all the fun?"

Delta laughed, "Of course not."

"Besides, finding another best friend this late in the game isn't really on my agenda."

Messing up Connie's hair, Delta sighed. "Glad to hear it."

Groaning behind them caused them both to turn. Taylor pushed herself onto her elbows; sweat streaming down her pain-etched face. "Remind me never to get on your bad side, Connie," Taylor said, her eyes lingering on the battered body of the broken soldier. "I'm glad we're on the same team. You guys play for keeps."

As Connie and Delta moved over to help Taylor, they froze as a helicopter flew over.

"Ours or theirs?" Delta asked Connie.

"Can't tell."

Taylor wiped the sweat off the side of her face and breathed heavily. "Does anyone here have a plan?"

Connie nodded. "Yep. As-a-matter-of-fact, I do."

"And?"

As Connie knelt beside Taylor, Connie looked up at Delta and grinned. "To stay alive, Taylor."

"That's it? That's your answer?"

Connie shrugged. "For now, it's the best I can do."

Pointing toward the horizon, Sal handed Megan the binoculars. "There's our answer."

Taking the binoculars, Megan scanned the ocean until her eyes settled on what appeared to be another old fishing boat. "That?"

Logan, who was also peering through binoculars grinned and nodded. "I can hear what you're thinking, Salamander."

Gina, who didn't have binoculars, demanded, "What? What?"

As Megan and Logan both lowered their binoculars, Sal explained, "It's an old fishing boat."

"And?"

Logan finished Sal's explanation. "We need to get these women to medical help, right? But we don't want to leave them to fend for themselves. So, we pay the skipper of the boat to let us board and keep it out here until nightfall."

"That way, " Sal continued, "Logan can take this boat in and get these people help, while the rest of us lay low until nightfall, when we go in and get Josh and Carducci. We'll just be giving up one boat for another." Sal lifted the binoculars up when she finished.

Megan glanced at the shore before stepping closer to Logan. "Surely, we can't afford to sit around in an old fishing boat all day. What about Josh and Tony?"

Logan shook his head. "If those choppers scare the Colombians back into the jungle, Josh and Tony oughtta be safe until we can swing around to get 'em. But, going in before dark would be suicide."

Megan sighed and reached for Gina's hand. "So that's it? We get these people out of here and spend the rest of the day in a smelly fishing boat, hoping that the Panamanians and whoever else are threatening enough to keep Zahn at bay?"

Gina took Megan's hand and squeezed it. "It's better than leaving them."

Megan looked at the beach and sighed. "Okay. But the moment it's dark, we're getting those guys off that beach."

"At least those choppers kept those bastards from coming on the beach," Carducci said, spitting sand out of his mouth.

When the firing stopped and the helicopter's rotors faded in the distance, Josh lifted his head from the sand and looked over at Carducci. "Yeah. For the moment. You okay?"

Carducci nodded. "What in the hell was that all about?"

"Logan musta seen we were pinned and called in the forces. If it had of been theirs, they woulda pressed forward instead of returning like they did. That chopper belonged to someone our nasty Colombian buddies want no part of."

Carducci nodded but made no attempt to remove the sand. "Good. What now?"

"Now?" Josh laid his head back in the sand. "Nothing. As long as those choppers are in the air, these bastards won't come out of the jungle."

"So, how long do we act like sand crabs?"

"Til nightfall."

"What then?"

"Then, we get the hell outta here. We don't have enough ammo left to do much damage."

"We're kinda running low on plans, don't you think?"

Josh shook his head. "In a war, Carducci, you never run outta plans, you never stop thinkin', and you never give up. I learned that from Sal's old man. I learned a lot from her old man."

"Does that mean you haven't given up on Delta, Connie, and Taylor?" Carducci was dying to scratch his nose.

Josh nodded. "Givin' up ain't in my dictionary. Know why?"

Carducci whispered, "Sure." This Josh was a man full of surprises. Who would have thought he would want to tell a story when, only a hundred yards away, soldiers were waiting to blow their brains out. It made Carducci wonder what horrors Josh had been through in Viet Nam that enabled him to remain so calm now.

"We were on this mission about twenty clicks outside Da Nang. I was with eight other guys when we were ambushed. We fought like hell, but six of us went down. Sal's old man was about a mile away when the sarge told 'em to retreat. The sarge thought there was no way we coulda lived through the ambush, the choppers, the strafing. He was taking his best guess and wasn't gonna risk anyone else comin' after us. Well, Mac wouldn't have none of that. He didn't believe a guy was dead until he saw the corpse, so he and Logan came after us anyway."

"No shit?"

Josh shook his head. "No shit. He wasn't gonna give up on us just 'cause it didn't look good. Hell, in that fuckin' place, nothin' ever looked good, so ya just took chances and prayed."

"So what happened?"

"Mac and Logan crept through their lines and pulled our fat outta the fire.

We were lookin' at a painful, possibly torturous death if they hadn't come after us. The Cong knew how to inflict pain on a POW without killing him. That's why a lotta guys killed themselves before gettin' caught. Our history books don't talk about it, but believe it when I tell ya, death was better than being captured. Those fuckers have been torturing people since before the Roman Empire. And that mighta happened to us if Mac and Logan hadn't come back."

"So, they got you out?"

Josh nodded. "Against the odds, man, all four of us made it outta there alive. You learned who your friends were and that you didn't abandon them."

Carducci nodded as he laid his head back in the warm sand. "Police work's the same way. You gotta know who you can and can't depend on."

"Well, from what I hear and see, Delta can depend on you."

Carducci nodded as he gazed up at the sky. "I just hope like hell I haven't let her down now."

⊕

"Let's set her down here," Delta whispered.

Carrying Taylor between them, Connie and Delta put Taylor in a soft patch of shade, beneath a large palm tree.

"I think we should wait until nightfall to continue," Connie suggested, wiping her brow. "We're too slow as it is, and it would be harder for them to pick us off at night."

Nodding, Delta pushed her wet bangs off her forehead. "How far are we from the coast?"

"At this rate? A couple of hours. But they know that's where we need to go, so it'll be like crossing a minefield. They're in between us and the beach."

"What about the choppers?"

Connie glanced up at the sky and shook her head. "No way to tell whose side they're on until we get to the beach. If they're Zahn's, we're in for it."

"We can't just stay out here in the open." Looking around, Delta saw just what they needed to get out of the day's heat and keep them from being visible. "Over here."

Picking Taylor up, Delta made her way over a fallen tree about six feet in diameter and set Taylor in the shade beneath the trunk, which was suspended, leaning on the tree it had fallen on. It was slightly rotten on one side but provided good cover.

"Good idea," Connie said softly.

Nodding, Delta felt Taylor's forehead. She had passed out right after Connie redid the tourniquet and hadn't woken up since. "She's burning up."

"Infection. If we don't get her to a hospital soon, she may lose that leg. Or worse."

Taking Taylor's hand, Delta held it in her lap as she leaned against the tree. "She'll make it. She's tougher than she looks."

Sitting on the other side of Taylor, Connie sighed heavily. "Feisty little thing, isn't she?"

Delta nodded. "She saved our lives back there, Con. Quick thinking on her part bought me just enough time."

Connie rested her palm on Taylor's cheek. It was very warm. "She's in love with you, you know."

Releasing Taylor's hand, Delta lightly stroked Taylor's face. "I know."

Connie watched this gentle movement and grinned warmly at Delta. "Nothing ever happened between you two?"

Delta started to shake her head, and then stopped, remembering the kisses that had burned Taylor's lips into her soul. "We've...uh...kissed."

Cocking her head, Connie's eyes twinkled. "I knew it! Is that all? Be straight with me, Del."

Delta ran her hands through Taylor's short, wet hair and nodded. "That's all. Honest."

Looking away, Connie was still grinning. "I knew it. I can't believe you didn't tell me. I can't believe you, of all people, were able to keep that a secret."

Delta slowly turned to Connie. "Tell you? You? Hell no. Not after the ration of trash you gave me the night you thought I'd slept with Alexandria! No way. I'd rather be dipped in hot oil than be forced to listen to another one of your ravings. No thanks."

This made Connie chuckle. "Okay, I forgive you. Was it a good kiss?"

Delta looked away to hide her smirk. "That's none of your business."

Connie turned to Delta. "Oh, it most certainly is. I've risked my life to come back for you. You owe me."

This made Delta chuckle. "Fine then. They were great kisses. There. Feel better now?"

Connie stared hard at Delta. "Kisses? Plural?"

Delta held her hand up. "Don't make me try to explain, Connie. In the Harley world, there's a saying: If I have to explain it to you, you wouldn't understand."

"Oh, that's rich. Pithy. Brilliant even. Don't think this is over with, Delta Stevens. When this is all said and done, I want to hear the whole, sordid story."

"There's nothing sordid about it, Consuela. We kissed. End of story."

Connie tilted her head at Delta. "End? As in, it won't happen again?"

Delta nodded. "As in Megan is my heart, Con. You know that. She hung my moon. Taylor and I are just friends. I think we might even wind up being good friends."

Connie heaved a sigh. "Thank god. For a minute there...oh, never mind. I might have had to hurt you if did anything unseemly. Or didn't you see the kind of damage I am capable of inflicting on a human being who crosses me?"

Delta reached over and took Connie's hand. "It's sure good to be with you again, Connie."

Connie smiled. "Same here, Storm."

For the next hour, they sat in silence, listening to the birds, looking out at the leaves, and reflecting on the paths their lives had taken. Delta hated relying on others to pull her out of a scrape, but this time, she knew she and Connie couldn't do it alone.

"Think they made it?" Delta asked Connie in a whisper.

Connie nodded. "All they had to do was get in the boat and go."

"Easier said than done, don't you think? You really believe Gina and Megan would leave us here?"

Slowly turning, Connie shrugged. "My head thinks they would recognize the danger of waiting for us, and they would take the others to port."

"And your gut?"

"My gut says they ignored the danger of waiting and are going for the whole enchilada."

Delta nodded. She had to agree. There was no way Megan and Gina were leaving without them. Despite the risks, they had stayed.

TWELVE

Megan knew it was risky to stay and attempt to commandeer a boat they knew nothing about, but anything was better than leaving the guys on the beach to face certain death. That, she reasoned, she could not allow. Delta might be dead, and Connie might be wandering through the jungle trying to get to her, but Josh and Carducci were still very much alive and present. She would not leave them. Not now. Not ever. If they were going to go down, they would go down together.

Looking over at Logan as he set the radio mike down, Megan sighed. The fishing boat had not responded to their radio attempts, so they had finally decided to pull alongside it. As they neared the boat, Megan shaded her eyes and peered in at the bow. She was surprised to see a young woman at the wheel.

Logan joined Megan, and spoke rapid Spanish to the woman, who smiled and nodded before speaking back. Her hands flew wildly about her as she pointed at the coast and in the air. All the while, Logan nodded. When she finished, Logan shouted gracias to her and he returned his attention to the small band of weary travelers waiting for his explanation.

"She says there's a small town about two or three hours down the coast which has good medical facilities."

"What about our borrowing her boat?" Gina asked.

Logan nodded. "I offered her money, but she refused."

Megan was crestfallen. Their hopes of getting the rest of their family out of the rain forest hinged on having two boats.

"Then offer her more!" Gina ordered.

Logan shook his head. "I can't. She refused to take any money. Said she would be more than happy to assist us."

"Is she alone?" Sal asked suspiciously.

Logan nodded. "It's her father's boat, but he's too sick to fish today, so she came out herself."

"Excellent!" Sal exclaimed, rubbing his hands together. "Gina, get the raft. Megan, go and tell your friends that we're taking them to a hospital."

Sal raised an eyebrow at the old boat. It was actually larger than the one they were on, about thirty to forty feet in length, and it looked as if it had seen the better side of its life in the sea. "Umm, you think that thing can handle the weight?"

Logan laughed. "Always the optimist, eh, Sal?"

"Who's gonna be able to tell her where to go?"

"She says she speaks a little English," Logan said as he studied a map he'd laid out on the deck.

Sal peered at the fishing boat. "You think we can trust her? I mean, what the hell is she doing out here?"

Megan put her arm around Sal. "Sal, we need help. She's offering, we're taking. Relax."

Sal turned hard to Megan, the stress of the day etched on her face. "You relax! Josh is lying under a pile of sand with the fucking enemy not a hundred yards away, and he's waiting for us to come get him. I won't have some fucking native screw this up for us because she's on Zahn's payroll!"

"Sal, we don't know..."

"Think about it, Megan! We're in the land of the macho man. Doesn't it strike you odd that there is a woman behind the wheel of that rickety raft? And we're just gonna buy her story about papa being sick? Come on, people, think, for Christ's sake!"

Logan listened carefully to Sal's argument. "What would you have us do, Salamander?"

Sal shrugged in frustration. "Get more information from her. Ask her what she's doing here. I don't fucking know, man, just make sure she's legit!"

Megan glanced over at Logan, who nodded before returning his attention to the woman. After several minutes of Spanish, Logan returned, shaking his head. "She knows Zahn, all right."

Sal slammed her fist into the palm of her hand. "See! I told you not to trust her."

Logan smiled as he continued. "No, Salamander, not because she's on his payroll. Seems Zahn's been forcing her father to make gold runs for him. She hates the guy as much as we do.

She said it is normal for the boat to be out here and that Zahn wouldn't suspect a thing. They fish by day and transport the gold from the coast by night."

Everyone looked at Sal, who sighed and finally consented. "Better safe than sorry."

Gina took Sal's hands in hers and pulled her closer. "Don't worry, Sal. We're not going to abandon those boys."

Sal fought to keep from crying, something she thought a soldier should never do. "He's my only family, Gina. I don't know what I'd do if I ever lost him. Ever since dad was killed, Josh is all I've known."

Gina pulled Sal to her and hugged her tightly. "You aren't going to lose him, Sal. We're going to get both him and Carducci out of there the first chance we get."

Megan turned from Gina and Sal, and opened the door to the cabin. Inside, the former hostages were huddled together, some sleeping, others sitting quietly. When Siobhan saw Megan, she jumped to her feet.

"Megan! Are we leaving soon?"

Taking Siobhan's hand, Megan smiled warmly. "Yes, Siobhan. By day after tomorrow, all of you will be heading for home."

"But what about you? Aren't you coming with us?"

"Not yet, Siobhan."

"But why not?"

Megan released Siobhan's hand. "There is still some unfinished business I must take care of."

Siobhan's eyes narrowed, and her pupils became small black dots. "You're going to kill him, aren't you Megan?"

As Megan started up the ladder, she nodded. "Yes, Siobhan. I am."

⊕

"Think Megan will really kill him?" Carducci asked Josh after several hours of silence.

Josh looked up at the darkening horizon and nodded. "Yep."

"You think she has it in her to kill in cold blood?"

"Tony, everyone has the ability to kill in cold blood, and anyone who thinks different is only deluding themselves."

"You serious?"

Josh nodded, watching the last of the sun set in the west. "When you strip away our clothes and cars and houses, there's one thing everyone of us is, a mammal. And mammals all have the same instincts for survival. We all have the capacity to kill. Those of us who don't have just managed to tame that part of us. Megan not only has the ability to kill, she also has the motivation. Put the two together and you can answer your own question."

When darkness had fully replaced the dusk, Josh and Carducci lifted themselves from the sand. It was darker along the coast, where the taller trees blocked the moonlight. Carducci found it difficult to count his remaining ammo.

"I have about twenty rounds left," he whispered as his fingers traveled along the stock.

"Hopefully, we won't need it."

"So, we wait for Logan to come get us?"

Josh nodded. "Trust me. Logan'd never leave us here. They'll be back."

"What about Delta? We can't just leave her."

Josh thought about this for a moment. "We'll be right back."

Carducci nodded. "I don't imagine dragging Megan and Gina from here, do you?"

"Nope. Those gals are as tight as any Marines I ever met. Leavin' ain't likely to happen."

Carducci sat quietly for a while, thinking back to the first time he'd met Megan. He had actually tried hitting on her, unaware that she was both a lesbian and his partner's lover. Megan and Delta had had some fun at his expense. And after that time, Connie and Delta had hounded him, worked on him, and gave him grief for being the kind of man he was. But then, he'd deserved most of it.

Man, how he had changed.

All of his buddies knew unflattering terms like "dyke," "pussy licker," and "lesbo," would no longer be tolerated in Carducci's presence.

The last two men who had referred to Delta as such, had ended up spitting out some teeth and nursing broken noses, so now, no one dared to make homophobic comments with Carducci around. She was his partner, damn it, and anyone who was stupid enough to talk shit about his partner, had to deal with him.

"I'm not leaving without Delta, Josh."

"Shhh."

"I mean it."

"Be quiet." Josh listened for a moment. "Do you hear that?"

Carducci cocked his head and listened. There was a slapping sound in the water that hadn't been there before. As Carducci reached for his rifle, Josh laid a hand on his shoulder to stop him.

"Don't move," Josh whispered, as he crawled so he was facing the sound.

For what felt like hours, they listened as the sound neared. Finally, one sound broke above the slapping of the waves.

"Josh?"

It was Sal.

Crawling on all fours, Josh entered the water and pulled the raft up to the shore. Leaping out into the water herself, Sal threw her arms around his neck and whispered, "Miss me, big guy?"

Carrying Sal on piggyback to where he'd left Carducci, Josh answered, "Like bad gas. Is everyone okay?"

Sal nodded as Josh released her, setting her down between the two large men. "Hi again, tall, dark, and handsome," she whispered to Carducci. "What's a nice guy like you doing in a place like this?"

Carducci put his arms around Sal and hugged her. "Waiting for you, cutie."

"Sorry it took so long, but we had to wait 'til sundown."

"What's the plan?" Josh asked, tapping Sal's shoulder.

"Well, there have been a few developments today."

"Like the choppers?"

"Yep. And we needed a second boat."

"A second boat? What's wrong with the one you're on?"

"Nothing, but we needed to get the hostages ashore and out of the way, so we kinda contracted a fishing boat. Megan, Gina, and Logan are on that boat. The others took our first boat to a city up the coast."

"Fishing boat?" Carducci asked.

"Yep. You really didn't expect Megan and Gina to leave here without them, did you?"

"No."

"Logan says we give Connie eight more hours. If she gets back by then, we'll go back to the boat and get the hell out of here."

"And if she doesn't?"

"Then we still have a couple more hours of darkness to escape undetected."

This brought Carducci to attention. "Don't tell me Megan and Gina have agreed to leave?"

"Leave?" Sal said a little too loudly. "Hell, no. But if we're gonna find Connie and get whatever's left of Delta and Taylor out of here, we're going to have to do it from the air. Logan's been trying to run down a chopper of his own, but that's hard to do in these parts, what with all the drug trafficking and helicopter tours. And anyone who even suspects the Colombians are in La Amistad won't give us the time of day."

Josh rubbed his chin as he nodded. "Smart thinking."

"So, either someone makes it out here in the next eight hours, or they're on their own?" His distaste of the situation could clearly be heard in Carducci's tone.

"As it stands now, Tony, we don't know if Delta and Taylor are alive. For all we know, Connie could be trying to dig them out; she could be captured or worse. There are just too many unknowns. Our best bet is to locate the caverns by air and see what needs to be done to excavate. It may take getting the government involved but tough shit."

Tony shook his head. The solution was still unsatisfactory for him. "Maybe I should stay here, then. Just in case."

"In case what? In case the Colombians decide to storm the beach? Think about it, Tony."

Sal scooted next to Carducci and put her hand in his. "You'd do her more good in the air than here, Tony. We're sitting ducks here."

Carducci looked at Sal and slowly nodded. "Okay. But we give Connie the full eight hours; not a minute less."

Sal grinned. "You got it."

Carducci looked at the black sheet of jungle before him and sighed. Eight hours. If she wasn't back by then, he wasn't sure what he was going to do.

If they didn't get to the shore before dawn, Delta wasn't sure what she was going to do. Taylor needed medical attention right away, yet to travel through the jungle during the day would become more and more treacherous the closer they got to the beach. Surely, Zahn knew that the coast was where the escape party would head. He would be prepared.

Carrying Taylor made the going slower than Delta would have liked, but she was grateful she didn't have to do it alone anymore. Looking at Connie, Delta warmed inside.

"Con?"

"Yeah?" Connie answered, not looking over at Delta.

"We gonna make it?"

Connie stopped, forcing Delta to stop as well. It was nearly impossible to see Connie's features. "Seriously?"

Deltas nodded. "Well...yeah, seriously."

"Hell, yeah, we're going to make it. I didn't come all the way back here just to lose. It's third and long, but I have faith in our quarterback."

"Still?"

Connie chuckled. "Always."

Delta grinned. "How much further?"

Connie sighed. "A few hours. It's hard to tell going so slowly."

"Think the Colombians are waiting for us?"

"Count on it."

"What will we do?"

Taylor moaned, and Connie readjusted her grip. "I don't really know. We'll have to play it by ear, see what the others have up their sleeve."

"By ear?"

"Got a better suggestion?"

Delta shook her head. "So, we're third and long and you want me to call an audible?"

Connie chuckled again. "Wouldn't be the first time."

Lifting Taylor up, Delta started ahead. "Nope. Let's just hope it's not the last."

Carducci looked at his watch and sighed. It was the last hour left. In less than an hour, they would have to leave Connie behind, a notion that still didn't sit well with him. At the very least, he figured, one of them should wait for her, just in case.

"One hour left," he said quietly. The last seven hours had been calm, and he wondered if the Colombians had retreated, or if they, too, were waiting for the light of dawn renew their attack. Surely, they cared more about their gold and their freedom than a scrappy bunch of people.

"You think the Colombians are still out there?" he asked Josh.

"Count on it," Josh replied.

"But why? They've got their gold."

Josh started to sit up, waking a sleeping Sal. "Do they? We cost them a shit load of gold when those caverns blew. We know where the caverns are. We know what's in them. We've seen too much, Tony. The general can't afford to let us escape."

Sal stretched and yawned. "No sign of her?"

"Not yet," Josh answered, patting her head.

"He can't let us go because of the gold or because he kidnapped people?"

"Neither. This guy's reputation will be in the dumper if word gets out about this botched scheme. He'll be a liability to the cartels. Believe it or not, they prefer things to be all neat and tidy. If he fails at this as badly as he will, that's the end of his life. He'd be better off shooting himself in the head out here."

Carducci shook his head. He still did not understand. "The cartel's that powerful?"

"It's just like your beat, Tony. What happens when a main pusher goes down?"

The light bulb beamed in Tony's head. "He becomes a liability to the supplier."

"Exactly. The dealer may get out and still deal, but that supplier won't be his connection any more because the risk is too great. If we live through this, and we will, everyone in the world will know of General Zahn and what the Colombian drug lords are capable of. He won't be able to get a job as a busboy, let alone maintain any sort of leadership role. More than likely, he'll be fish food."

This much Carducci understood. Many mobsters ended up dead or missing after incarceration or bungled drug deals because they posed a threat to a bigger kingpin.

"But his men..."

"Are soldiers, Carducci, and soldiers follow orders. That's one reason why the cartels rely so heavily on the military. Who better to do as they're told than military personnel?"

Carducci thought about this before nodding slowly. "And you think the general wants us bad enough to come chasing after us all the way out here?"

"I have no doubt on that score. His life is over if even one of us escapes. They're out there, Tony, just waiting."

"Jesus..."

Josh nodded. "After all, how can he explain to his boss that a bunch of female captives escaped and killed many of his men?"

"He can't."

"Exactly."

"He's close to desperation, and that's a dangerous foe to face. He'll use every man in his outfit to stop us."

"But if they're out there waiting, they're between Connie and us. How in the hell will she get around them?"

Josh patted Carducci's shoulder. "In the jungle, at night, a person can walk five feet away from you, and you'd never know it. I can't tell you how many times we crept right up to the Cong in Nam and vice versa. If Connie's careful enough, it's possible she can get past the Colombians."

"She's running out of time," Sal whispered. "Don't you think she should have been here by now?"

As the blackness started to give way to a dark gray, Josh shrugged. "Maybe, hard to tell. Connie moves well in the jungle. Must be that Native American in her." Sal grinned and also patted Carducci's shoulder.

"You're right about that one. Any
minute now, she's gonna come barreling through those bushes, like
the warrior woman she is."

Regripping his rifle, Carducci slung it over the rock and
checked his aim. That was definitely a sight worth waiting for.

As the blackness of night slowly ebbed, Delta and Connie
pushed themselves harder. Inside, they both knew that daylight was
too dangerous made them too visible on the beach, yet Taylor
might not live if they waited another day out in hiding. As they
stopped to rest, Delta stood directly in front of Connie and
whispered her concerns.

"It's almost dawn, Con, what should we do?"

"Keep moving," Connie whispered back. "Or Taylor
won't make it."

Delta looked at Taylor, whose head was flopped to the
side. She had been dead weight for the past six hours, and every
time they stopped to rest, Delta was terrified she wouldn't be able
to find a pulse.

"Yeah. We have to chance it," Delta acknowledged.

"Del, we have to agree that if one of us goes down, the
other has to leave the injured ones here."

"No way."

Connie grabbed Delta's face between her hands. The early
dusk was upon them, and the darkness was fading. "Listen to me!"
she hissed roughly. "There's no reason for all three of us to die in
here."

"But..."

"But nothing! Someone has to get back to Megan and
Gina and let them know what happened, or they'll spend the rest
of their lives looking for us. Is that what you want?"

"No."

"Good. Now swear to me if anything happens to me,
you'll leave me with Taylor."

"Con."

"Swear it."

Delta hesitated before finally responding with a very quiet.
"I swear."

"Good. You ready?"

"No. Wait." There were so many things Delta needed to say to her, so many words that had gone unexpressed.

Connie paused and looked up. A slight grin played on her face. "I know, Storm. All the words you want to say to me, I already know. Right back at you. Now, let's go."

About fifteen minutes from where they had rested, Connie stopped abruptly and motioned silently to Delta. Following Connie's gaze, Delta saw a rifle peeking out from behind a tree. One black army boot also protruded from behind the gnarled trunk.

Lowering Taylor to the ground, Delta pulled the machete out of Taylor's backpack and held up a finger to Connie, who nodded and motioned that she would go around the opposite side of the tree. Delta nodded once before carefully picking her way to the right side of the tree, which had a diameter about five feet.

From the position of the rifle, he was clearly standing, and Delta could only hope that Connie would get his attention so he'd never see it coming. Glancing over at Connie, Delta regripped the machete in her left hand. She'd have one chance. She'd have to go for his throat and take his head off. Looking over at Connie and then back at Taylor, Delta had no doubts that she could do this. Thinking about what these men had done to her lover made the task that much easier.

Three feet from the tree, Delta nodded once to Connie, who tossed a rock into a group of bushes. As the rock lifted into the air, Delta stepped around the tree and started the swing of her machete. Halfway to its intended target, she pulled up and embedded the machete into the tree above the Colombian's head. Of all the mental pictures Delta had processed prior to taking her fatal swing, what stood before her wasn't one of them.

Standing rigid, still holding a rifle, was a Colombian soldier impaled to the tree by three long arrows, one through his neck, one through his chest, and one through his abdomen. The force from the arrows was so powerful, that they had pierced his body and attached his upright corpse into the tree trunk, holding him like a butterfly in a collector's case. By the looks of it, he had just recently been killed.

Stepping out from behind the tree, Delta waved Connie over. Connie stopped short when she saw the body.

"The Bri," Delta whispered as Connie examined the arrow's feathers.

"Uh huh." Turning from the corpse, Connie grinned. "What a pleasant surprise."

Delta did not know what to say. The people who had honored and accepted her warrior spirit into their tribe were among them now, helping Delta and Connie to escape the clutches of the Colombians.

"Come on, Del, we have to hurry. Dawn's broken and if the Bri are out there..."

"No ifs, Con. The Bri are here. Somewhere."

"Then let's amscray."

Dislodging the rifle from the stiff fingers of the corpse, Delta hung it over her shoulder. "They knew," she said quietly, as they returned to Taylor. "And they came."

Connie hoisted Taylor's right arm over her shoulder. "Come on, Taylor. Time to go home."

Josh studied Carducci's profile for a second as the dawn broke. "That's it, Tony. Time to go."

Carducci hadn't taken his eyes off the forest for an hour and still didn't. "I can't go. I'm sorry."

Josh started to say something, but Sal's soft touch on his leg and the gentle look in her eyes quieted his words. "Tony, Delta would want you to be smart here. It isn't disloyal to save yourself first. We'll be back. I swear."

Still staring at the wall of jungle before him, Carducci shook his head. "I'm not doing it for her, Sal I'm doing it for me. I'd never be able to look in the mirror if I left when she needed me most. You two go. If you get a chopper, pick me up, but I can't stand the thought of leaving Connie out here by herself. She wouldn't do that to me."

"No can do, pal," Josh replied softly. "Stay here, Tony, and you're a dead guy."

"Tony, we can still help her, but not here. We have to go get help," Sal offered.

For the first time, Carducci looked at them both. "You're sure we can get a bird in the air?" His voice was cold and metallic.

Josh and Sal both nodded. "It's the only option we have now. But if we stay much longer, they'll pick us off in the raft. We have to go."

Pulling his rifle to him, Carducci bowed his head.

"It's what she'd want," Sal said gently. "And you know it."

Holding back his frustration and tears, Carducci looked at Sal and nodded. "I know."

"Let's go," Josh said, grabbing the raft and tossing it in the water. "As it is, we still may be sittin' ducks in this thing."

When Sal and Carducci hopped in, Josh started pushing the raft farther out, until the water was up to his armpits. After hopping in, he turned for one last look at the jungle.

"Don't worry, Tony, we'll be right..." Stopping in mid-sentence, Josh squinted once before putting his rifle's scope up to his eyes.

"What?" Sal asked, trying to follow his gaze.

"Nothing. I...wait a second...I think I saw...nah, it couldn't be."

"What?"

Josh lowered the scope and turned to Sal. "I could have sworn I saw a native."

Sal grabbed the rifle and looked through the scope. She couldn't see what years of jungle warfare had taught Josh to see. "I don't see them."

Josh took the rifle back and peered through the scope. "They're out there. I'm sure of it."

"They're out there, Con. I'm sure of it."

Once they could see the shore, Delta and Connie picked up their pace. They had already stepped over three more dead Colombians, all with long arrows embedded in them.

"Why aren't the Colombians shooting back?" Delta asked Connie, as they pushed through the foliage.

"They don't even see it coming," Connie answered, out of breath. She was having to take two steps to every one of Delta's four-foot strides.

"You think they got them all?" Delta asked.

"Sure looks like they might have."

Nodding, Delta took twenty more steps before her path was blocked by a grinning Colombian soldier with a rifle pointed at her chest.

"Say adios, amig..." His final sound was abruptly stifled by an arrow through the side of his throat. Like a dropped barbell, he thudded heavily to the ground, his hand clawing in vain at the arrow protruding from his neck.

"Let me have her," Delta ordered, pulling Taylor from Connie.

"But..."

"But nothing. Get your ass out of here. We'll move faster now if I sling her over my shoulder."

Hesitating just a moment, Connie nodded as she watched Delta toss Taylor over her shoulders like a sack of dog food. "Go, Connie, and don't stop until you're out to sea."

Connie took one step and turned back. "I love you, Storm."

Delta nodded. "I love you, too, Chief."

With that, Connie took off running, with Delta not far behind.

Her legs struggling beneath the weight, Delta watched Connie's back as she opened the distance between them. As Connie's feet finally hit the sand, Delta prayed that the absence of gunfire would continue until Connie was safely out to sea. Her prayers, however, went unheard. Connie wasn't ten yards onto the sand when the first rifle shot of the morning cracked through the air. Connie managed one more step before landing face first on the beach.

"No!" Delta's anguished cry erupted as she pushed herself through the final bushes. "Connie!" Trying to balance Taylor's weight, Delta stumbled and faltered. When she regained her footing, she was surprised to see Connie up and running again, feverishly trying to get to the water, where bullet impact would be greatly minimized. Movement in the distance caught her eye, and Delta saw two men get out of a raft and make their way toward Connie.

Several more shots were fired, but that was about all; and Delta knew why. Every rifle sound alerted the Bri to the location of the shooter, who would soon look like a human pincushion.

The thought put a smile on Delta's face, and when her feet finally hit sand, she ran as if she were free of any burden. Ahead of her by nearly seventy yards, Connie was suddenly embraced by Carducci. Delta had hoped that they had actually waited all night for Connie's return, and there they were, standing neck deep in water, pulling Connie into the surf before pushing her over the side and into the raft, where Sal pulled her in. Carducci and Connie remained in the raft while Josh crawled on his belly back to the rocks that had protected them through the night. With rifle in hand, Josh fired two rounds into the forest just to the right of where Delta emerged, carrying the lifeless form of Taylor across her shoulders like a yoke.

Legs slogging through the unforgiving sand, Delta reached the shore just as a burst of bullets sprayed water up on them.

"Take her!" Delta commanded Carducci and Sal, flopping Taylor's limp body into their arms. "Go! We'll cover you." Delta grabbed one of the rifles lying on the floor of the raft and swam back to the beach.

As more bullets peppered the sand, Delta dove behind the rocks next to Josh. Delta squeezed the trigger of her rifle, sending bullets high into the trees. She could not afford to shoot head level for fear of hitting any Bri. The best she could do was to appear to shoot back, allowing the small raft to get beyond harm's reach.

"The Bri are in there, Josh. Don't take any head shots. We'll have to take them low."

"Got it." Josh fired a round into the kneecap of a soldier who went down screaming and cursing. "Like that?"

Delta looked at him and saw him grinning. If she didn't know him better, she would have thought her was enjoying this. "Just like that."

"We have to give them enough time to get out of here," Josh said, firing and killing another Colombian, whose body fell from a fifteen-foot tree. "And I'm just about out of ammo."

Delta looked at her rifle. She didn't have much left either. How were they supposed to cover those sitting helpless in the raft?

When another round went off from the Colombians, Delta peppered the jungle with her bullets. And then, it was silent. When she looked through the trees, there was movement coming toward them. It was a calculated, measured move that felt like a check in chess.

What was emerging from the jungle drained the blood from Delta's face. She had not anticipated this, nor had she any idea of how to counterattack.

"Fuck! Do you see it?" Josh asked coolly.

Delta nodded.

Two Colombians stood behind a massive tree at the edge of the jungle with a four- foot long bazooka aimed right at the raft. Before Delta could raise her rifle, they fired their first volley toward the raft and missed. The explosion in the water sent fountains bursting thirty feet into the air.

Delta fired a dozen rounds at the men, but the tree was the perfect cover. All of her rounds missed their mark.

"It's no good," Josh said, pulling a foot-long Bowie knife from a strap on his leg. "One more volley like that, and they'll blow that raft to smithereens. Cover me."

"Josh, no!" Delta yelled, reaching out to try to stop him. But it was too late. Like a wild man, Josh shrieked a warpath scream that reached into the marrow of Delta's bones. With the Bowie knife raised above his head, his big, burly body was the perfect distraction. The loader of the bazooka frantically reached for his pistol as Josh neared, and the best Delta could do was lay some ground cover for him.

The bazooka men weren't the only ones with their eyes trained on the lunatic advancing on them. Several others turned their weapons on Josh, but when the first bullet smashed into him, it didn't even slow him down.

"No!" Delta cried, standing up from behind the rock to draw some of the fire. Taking careful aim, she located the shooter and fired one round through his chest just as several bullets pinged off the rocks surrounding her. She knew, all too well, what Josh was doing, and in committing himself to saving Sal's and everyone else's life, he was forfeiting his own.

When the second and third rounds hit him, they spun him around like a rag doll, but he still did not go down. Delta squeezed off a few more rounds, taking out another shooter, but she still couldn't hit either of the bazooka men. When she saw the soldier withdraw his pistol and take aim, Delta turned her face away and looked back at the raft, expecting to see that it had gotten well under way, but, to her dismay, it was heading back to shore.

"Go back!" Delta yelled, waving them off. But Sal would have none of it. Jumping out of the raft, she and Carducci scrambled across the sand, while Connie held Taylor close to her in the raft.

Turning her attention back to Josh, Delta watched helplessly as he was hit two more times, once in the shoulder and once in the thigh. Still, he did not go down. Instead, he made his way closer to the stunned men standing behind the tree, who were readjusting their sights on the raft, which had, inexplicably, returned to shore; a move they had not anticipated; a move that just may have saved the life of everyone on board.

As Delta raised her rifle to provide more cover, Carducci landed next to her, his rifle poised. "Stop her," he ordered, and Delta whirled, just in time to grab Sal around the waist and pull her back down behind the rock.

"No, goddamn it! Let me go!"

"I won't let you kill yourself, too, Sal." Delta struggled with the little waif, trying to keep her from the same fate awaiting Josh. When Caducei's rifle kicked, Delta looked over the rock and saw that he had shot one of the bazooka men. The second one, the one holding the bazooka, suddenly turned the muzzle toward them.

"Oh shit," Carducci muttered, taking aim. But Josh, who was still moving toward the man, was in the way of a clean shot.

"Shoot!" Delta yelled.

"I can't. I'll hit Josh!" Carducci waited what seemed a lifetime, and as he watched, incredulous, Josh raised his Bowie holding the point and, with a flick of his wrist, sent it hurling toward the bazooka man, where it embedded itself in his leg. Falling to the ground with a scream, the soldier reached for his compadre's pistol, leveled it at Josh, who had slowed down considerably, and proceeded to empty the remaining rounds into Josh's body. He took three shots in the abdomen, two in his shoulders, two in his legs, and one in his cheek before the ammunition ran out.

That finally stopped him.

Swaying like a disoriented drunk, Josh dropped to his knees before collapsing face first into the sand, more than a dozen rounds of bullet holes draining the rest of his life from his body.

"Damn you, Delta, let me go!"

Holding tight to Sal, Delta stroked the back of her head. "He's gone, Sal. He's gone. You won't do him any good getting yourself killed."

"I don't care!" Sal struggled harder, making it difficult for Delta to hold her. Sal was small, but the man in her life had just given his life for hers, and her anguish made her strong.

Carducci turned to Delta and her wiggling bundle. "Sal," he said calmly.

Sal turned her angry eyes on him and glared, still fighting in Delta's arms. "Help me, Tony! I have to get to Josh!"

Carducci looked at Sal warmly. "I'm sorry." Pulling his big fist back, Carducci punched Sal so hard, that her army cap flew off her head. She now lolled unconscious against Delta's shoulder. Delta stared at Carducci in silent understanding and nodded.

"Sal wasn't going to go back to that raft without him," Delta said wearily.

Carducci nodded. "Neither are we."

"What? Carducci, don't be dumb."

Handing Delta his rifle, Carducci looked hard into Delta's face. "I was out here all night buried in sand with the guy. You learn a lot about someone under those conditions. You learn even more about yourself."

"Tony, wait."

Carducci hesitated a moment and then squatted next to Delta, who still held Sal in her arms. "If we leave him here, he alone will take all the heat from the international press for what's gone on down here. Can you see it? Berserk Vet Runs Amok in Central America? He deserves better than that, Delta. He deserves better from us."

Delta nodded. "I agree. That's not why I stopped you."

Carducci tilted his head in question. "Why, then?"

Delta pointed to the jungle with her rifle. "Listen."

Carducci looked up and realized there hadn't been any shots fired for several minutes. "Reloading?"

A slow grin spread on Delta's face. "Uh uh." Tenderly touching the jaguar tooth necklace around her neck, Delta knew why there would be no more shots today. "The Bri took them out. All of them."

Carducci looked surprised. "How do you know?"

Shrugging, Delta peered into the forest. "I just know. Don't ask me to explain."

As she and Carducci gazed into the jungle for a sign that the battle was over, Delta caught sight of a small, wrinkled old man, holding a bow in one hand and a walking stick in the other. When he saw Delta looking at him, he raised his staff in the air and pointed to a capuchin monkey hanging from its tail just feet above the old man's head. Turning around, the old man motioned to the monkey, who followed him, and they both disappeared silently into the rain forest.

"Itka," Delta murmured, suddenly seeing all of the warriors melt back into the forest. "And Kiki."

"Kiki, Bianca's monkey?"

Grinning, Delta nodded, knowing now who was responsible for sending the cavalry to them.

"I don't see a damn thing," Carducci said, squinting.

Delta slowly rose, cradling Sal in her arms. "It's okay, Carducci. Go get Josh."

Carducci looked over at Delta, his eyes brimming with tears. "You sure?"

Delta nodded. "The Bri have taken care of our enemies."

Carducci wiped his eyes and set his rifle against the rocks. "If only he'd waited just thirty seconds more. I should have..."

Delta reached out and touched Carducci's shoulder. "Should have what, Tony? Tackled him? Shot him in the leg? The man was a solider. He died a soldier's death. You couldn't have stopped him, nor should you have. He saved our lives. It's how he wanted it."

Carducci stared at Delta for a moment before shaking his head sadly. "I've never seen anything like that in my life."

Delta stared out at the jungle and back at Josh's body lying in the sand. "And I doubt you ever will again. That kind of courage, that kind of a man is one in a billion. Come on. Let's go get him." Setting Sal gently in the sand, Delta rose from behind their rocky cover.

Carducci followed Delta, half expecting the Colombians to shoot them where they stood. But there were no rifle remarks or pistol shots, only the eerie silence you hear when great beings leaves this world, the sound of a space that can never be filled.

"What in the hell are we gonna do about Sal?" Carducci asked when they knelt next to Josh's bullet-ridden body.

Delta reached out and brushed some sand from off Josh's temple. If it was possible, Josh actually looked peaceful, as if he was glad to have forfeited his own life for theirs. "I don't know, Carducci. I really don't know."

Chapter Thirteen

"How's Taylor doing?" Delta asked Connie as they loaded Josh's body onto the raft.

Connie shrugged helplessly as the weight from Josh's body sank the raft six inches deeper in the water. Her brown eyes held a mixture of sadness and anger. "Not good. She's shocky." Connie reached out and touched Delta's arm. "How are you? You okay?"

Delta shrugged, staring down at the man who had given his life to help save his new family. Her heart hurt, and she wondered if Sal's heart would ever mend from this loss. "I'm ready for this to be over."

Connie nodded. "You did well, Del. And so did you, Tony."

Carducci started the small engine on the raft and sat wearily next to it. "Then how come I feel like a failure?"

Connie placed her hand on his shoulder and gave it a quick squeeze. "You did your best. That's all anyone has the right to ask."

Carducci covered his face with his hands and shook his head. It sounded like he was crying. "If only he'd waited. If only..."

Connie sat next to him and held him. "Delta and I have never lived by if onlys, Tony. Every decision we make in our lives has several if onlys attached to it. If only Josh hadn't come down here. If only we kept the cave from being blown to bits. Josh knew what he was doing. He knew he wouldn't make it. He gave his life for us, for Sal. And if onlys minimize his courageous intentions."

Carducci looked up from his hands, his eyes filled with tears. "How can you be so calm about this, Connie? We lost him. He's dead."

Connie looked back at the jungle and sighed. "Not to me, he isn't. What Josh did will live in my heart forever."

Carducci sniffed once and stared at the jungle in silence, only turning his head to see what Delta was doing.

Delta had reached across to touch Taylor's face when Sal started to surface. "She's not going to be very happy with you, I'm afraid," Delta said to Carducci, gently stroking Sal's hair.

Carducci shrugged. "I couldn't think of anything else to do. It didn't look like you could hold her much longer."

Delta nodded, resting her tired head in her hands. At her feet lay a man who was the embodiment of a warrior. He had acted with courage and valor, and Delta vowed he would get the burial a warrior deserved. It was hard to believe he had sacrificed himself, but she knew why. He had made an oath a lifetime ago to protect Sal and keep her from harm. It was an oath he never took lightly, and when the moment came for him to make the sacrifice, she was sure he made it in the blink of an eye. She knew if he hadn't kept the bazooka from firing, the Colombians would have eventually blown up the raft, as well as the rocks they had used for cover. He had seen to it that neither of those things happened. His was the purest form of love she had ever seen, and she knew his death was a loss from which Sal might never recover. It would take everything in their power to see Sal through.

Life seemed so unfair.

"Josh," Sal muttered, slowly opening her eyes. Her left cheek was swollen and red from where Carducci had punched her. Seeing Josh lying still at her feet, Sal slid down to the bottom of the raft and lay on top of him, weeping quietly. "No...not you. Please, God, not him."

"Sal..."

"Leave her be, Tony," Delta said gently.

As the small raft cut its way through the water, Delta stroked Sal's head, which heaved and jerked from her sobbing. Sal was not a big woman, but against the chest of the man who saved her life, she appeared smaller than ever, and she seemed to shrink with every sob.

In the distance, out of firing range, was a small fishing boat. Turning to Connie, Delta asked, "Is that the boat?"

Connie shrugged. "I guess so. Sal was sketchy on the details. She said some girl in a fishing boat."

"Wait. What? A girl was on the boat?"

Connie nodded. "That's what Sal said." Connie looked at Sal, hoping she would answer Delta's questions, but Sal was in no shape to do anything except grieve.

"A fishing boat?"

Connie nodded again. "Uh huh. Why?"

"Did Sal say anything else?"

"Like I said, she was sketchy on the details. She did say the girl seemed okay."

"And does she speak English?"

"I don't know. Why all the questions?"

"Do you remember if Sal told you her name?" Delta also looked at Sal now, wishing she could interrupt her weeping for just a moment to see if the boat they were heading toward was the boat she thought it was.

Connie thought for a moment. "I don't think so."

Delta peered at the horizon, trying to catch a better look at the boat. If her suspicions were correct, Flora would be on that boat.

"If we're going to that boat, then where's Logan's boat?"

"Sal said the plan was to put the hostages on the newer boat and get them to the coast, where they could receive medical attention and stay out of harm's way. I suppose they've already made it."

"And so, now, our guys are on that fishing boat?"

Connie nodded. "Sal did mention something about the Colombians using that boat to transport gold."

Delta's eyes grew wide with anxiety. "Shit! It is Flora."

"What? Who in the hell is Flora?"

Delta ignored Connie's question and whirled around to Carducci. "Tony, stop the engine."

Carducci looked at her sideways. "Why?"

"Something's not right. Stop the goddamned engine."

Carducci did as she said, and, immediately, the little raft slowed to a near stop.

Connie leaned over and lightly rubbed Delta's back. "What is it, Del?"

Delta stared at the old wooden boat in the distance, every fiber in her body shouting at her. She had learned long ago to listen carefully to that part of her, and she couldn't help but heed the warning within her now as lit up inside her.

"It's Zahn."

Carducci shook his head. "Come on, Del, that guy's long gone. Josh said he's not going to stay around when all his men are dead."

Delta was quiet for a moment, listening to her inner voice, the voice that she had not listened to the night Miles Brookman was killed. From that moment on, Delta Stevens had listened to her instincts, and her instincts now were telling her that something was off. "If everything is okay, why haven't Megan and Gina come back for us?"

Carducci's mouth opened, but nothing came out. He and Connie looked at each other.

Delta studied the fishing boat thoughtfully. If she was Megan, and she knew the danger was past, she would have started the fishing boat and come to pick them up. "If nothing's wrong, Megan and Gina would be bringing that boat to get us."

Sal looked up from her crying, tears streaking her face. "They have binoculars," she said softly. "They shoulda known by now that they can come get us."

Delta closed her eyes and centered herself. Her gut raged at her, telling her all the things she didn't want to know. "He's on that boat."

"You don't know that," Connie said, slight panic in her voice. "It's an old boat. Maybe it had engine trouble or something."

"I've been on that boat, Con, and it purrs like a Ferrari. Trust me on this. Zahn's not leaving here without his gold and without taking us out."

Connie shielded her eyes from the sun and looked at the fishing boat. "It does seem odd that they haven't made an effort to come and get us. Surely they've seen that there is no more gunfire."

Sal rose from the bottom of the raft and pulled a Bowie knife similar to Josh's from the same type of belt. "I say we hop on board and gut the fucker."

Connie, Carducci, and Delta all looked at each other. Grief or not, she was right. If he were on board, this would be the last play of the game. "Sal's right. If it's us he wants, it's us he'll get."

"Oh man, I don't like the sound of that," Carducci said, sighing. "I've seen that look before, Delta, and no good ever comes of it."

Delta turned to the trio, fighting the rising fear that Megan, Gina, and the others on board might already be dead. "Let's give him what he thinks he wants. Right between the eyes."

Sal cheered. "Now, that's my kind of plan."

Delta inhaled a deep breath. "It's risky, but I think I have a plan that'll work. Here's what we're going to do."

Delta, Connie, and Sal floated the raft up to the side of the boat, waiting for the inevitable rifle to be pointed in their faces. Since Zahn hadn't picked them off when they were in the raft, Delta figured there was more on his agenda than just their deaths.

Before sending Carducci over the side of the raft, Delta had rubbed some of Josh's blood over Taylor's arms and face and positioned her so she appeared as dead as he was. Leaving Taylor in the raft was the only option, and though it could put Taylor at risk, Delta could think of no other way to keep her safe.

Docking their raft next to the one Zahn must have come in during the night, Delta looked over at Connie, whose face registered the most menacing look Delta had ever seen her wear.

"If they're dead, Del, stay the hell out of my way, because I'll gut the son of a bitch myself."

Delta barely nodded, wondering if Connie and Sal had it together enough to do what needed to be done. The desire for revenge was a poor replacement for a good, rational plan and common sense. If they were going to get out of this alive, they would need plenty of both.

"They're not dead," Delta said defiantly. "If Zahn did board this boat last night, you can bet Megan and Gina both figured out a way to make themselves less expendable."

Connie said nothing with her mouth, but her eyes burned with an intensity that scared Delta.

The expected rifle showed up immediately after they tied their raft to the dinghy bobbing next to the fishing boat. Delta checked Connie and Sal, and hoped they were solid enough not to go off half-cocked. She needed them all to stay clearheaded, in spite of all the horror Zahn had brought upon them.

The hands that lifted them roughly to the deck were not the loving ones of Megan or Gina.

Instead, four men, along with General Zahn, stood guard over Megan, Gina, Flora, and Logan, who was slumped against the side of the boat. Dead or unconscious, Delta couldn't be sure which.

Zahn stared down into the boat at Josh and Taylor. "Where is the other?" Zahn barked, standing toe to toe with Delta. His was the coldest, cruelest gaze she had ever locked eyes with, and she knew it took everything he had not to kill her right where she stood.

Looking over his shoulder at Megan, Delta winked. "Your men shot him in the back like the cowards they are." Delta waited for Zahn to slap her. Instead, a hate-filled grin spread across his face.

"You have proven to be much more trouble than you're worth."

Delta looked away from Zahn and over to Connie, who was stone-faced and trying not to look at Gina, whose eyes were wide with fear.

"Wondering why you and your friends are still alive?" Zahn asked.

Delta shrugged. She had to buy as much time as she could. "Nope. I find it useless to second-guess egocentric lunatics."

General Zahn slammed his fist into Delta's stomach, doubling her over. "Do you still not realize who you're dealing with, you filthy American whore?"

"I just ...told you." Holding her aching stomach, Delta straightened back up and cut her eyes to Megan, who instantly read them and gave her a slight nod. The soldier holding his gun on her looked suspiciously at Delta before stepping closer to Megan.

"I could snuff you out like that!" General Zahn roared at Delta, snapping his fingers.

"Then do it, and stop all the yammering." Delta pushed past him and reached out to hug Megan. The soldier stepped in front of Megan and glowered at Delta, but Delta pushed past him as well and embraced Megan.

If Delta could have seen the look on Zahn's face, she would have laughed out loud. He had probably never suffered such insolence as this. "You can't possibly be this brazen!"

Pulling away from Megan, Delta quickly whispered, "Tony's under the raft." Turning from her, Delta grinned at Zahn.

"As a matter of fact, I am. But you see, I know that you're a businessman, and I believe I have something you want."

Zahn's eyes narrowed, contempt etched across his tanned face. "What could you have that I would possibly want, besides your blood on my hands?"

Stepping across the boat, Delta pushed past Zahn's gun and leaned her hip against the side, her arms crossed casually in front of her. "Aren't you just the teeniest bit curious how I got out of that cavern?"

"Your luck is of no concern to me." But Delta could tell he was intrigued.

"No? You mean you're willing to leave behind the huge chunks of gold back there?" Delta saw a flash in Zahn's eyes, which betrayed his interest. The hook was baited. "Okay, fine then. Pull the trigger and be done with it. You're beginning to bore me."

General Zahn looked at his four men, their rifles trained on the women. It was more than simply losing face now, and Delta knew it. She had one card to play, and she had to play it to perfection. "I assume you're keeping us alive to help transport the gold your men have yet to deliver. You may want us dead, but if you don't deliver to your boss, you'll have more than just my blood on your hands. Capische?"

Zahn flinched. Another hit. Delta grinned. He needed them, and that shifted the balance of power. Zahn may have the upper hand for the moment, but pretty soon, this whole ugly ordeal would be over.

"Perhaps. And perhaps I am simply waiting for my men to signal me that all is well. Then, I shall fill your pathetic American bodies with holes and send you to the bottom of the ocean."

Delta shook her head. They'd all be dead already if Zahn was intending to kill them right away. He definitely needed them alive. Something was troubling Zahn. He had a boatload of hostages but didn't seem to quite know what to do with them. He was waiting for something.

"Well?"

"Shut up!" Turning to Flora, he instructed her in Spanish, and she started the engines. Delta persisted. "You wait much longer to go back after that gold, General, and you're busted. Caught. Nailed.

There'll be Panamanian police and who knows who else swarming all over the place. Don'tt tell me you didn't see those helicopters."

Nodding, Connie said something to him in Spanish, which caught his attention, but he didn't like it. He was a man cornered, looking desperately for a way out. As he conferred with his men, Delta spied Carducci's hand as he pulled himself up on the starboard side.

"Hey, General?"

"Shut up!" Zahn barked as he paced across the deck. His calm exterior was cracking. He approached Delta and sneered into her face. "You have given me a headache for the last time, you insulting bitch!" As Zahn raised his pistol, a loud crack reverberated through the air, causing him and the three living soldiers to turn in the direction of the shot. Zahn looked in stunned silence at Carducci, who was perched on the side of the boat. He started to swing his pistol around to aim at Carducci, but Delta grabbed it. As she did, Carducci fired two more fatal shots into the heads of the other soldiers before taking a round in his shoulder from the third soldier. He plunged backwards into the water.

"Tony!" Sal cried, running over to the side of the boat. Attracted by her movement, the soldier turned his rifle on Sal and would have shot her in the back, if Connie hadn't leveled the Colombian with a blow to the back of his knee. Buckled, but not out of commission, the soldier rolled to his back and fired a round at Delta that nicked her forehead, knocking her backwards against the side of the boat. Without releasing her hold on Zahn's gun, Delta fought to regain her balance as blood streamed down the right side of her face.

The lone surviving soldier, afraid of hitting Zahn, panicked as he tried to find another victim to shoot. Before he could, Connie's heel smashed into the side of his head. As she connected with his temple, his finger squeezed off one final round before he succumbed to the massive hemorrhaging in his brain.

Landing from her kick, Connie turned just in time to see Zahn's gun erupt and Delta and Zahn tumble over the side of the boat. When Megan saw them go over, she snatched the Bowie knife from Sal's hand just as Sal jumped into the water after Carducci.

Running across the deck, Megan looked at Connie and shouted, "Come on!" before following Delta and Zahn over the side of the boat.

Megan landed in the warm Caribbean water, a short distance from Delta and Zahn, who were still struggling for the pistol. Delta was determined not to let go and would have gladly sunk to the bottom with him to prevent him from hurting them any more. She knew why Josh made his sacrifice, and she was prepared to do the same. As Zahn clawed at her, Delta head-butted him in the face, sending more blood spurting around them. Still, he would not let go. With her left hand, she held the wrist of his gun hand, while, with her right, she repeatedly bashed his already broken nose. For Zahn's part, he had never fought a foe so vicious, so intent on inflicting his death, and it was all he could do to stay afloat.

Blood was pooling on the surface of the water as Megan swam over to the two of them, the bowie knife in her mouth like Tarzan in some old movie. Megan's eyes held the same hatred and bloodlust Delta had seen in Sal and Connie's eyes.

Suddenly, the pistol went off again, and, without hesitation, without thinking, Megan did something she never would have believed herself capable of a few weeks ago. In one swift motion, Megan climbed onto Zahn's back, plunging them both deeper into the water and forcing Delta to release her grip on his hand. The pistol went off one more time before Megan grabbed him by the hair and, as efficiently as any commando, silently slit his throat to the back of his spine, nearly decapitating him. A burst of red surrounded Megan as she regripped the knife and wheeled Zahn back around so that he was now facing her.

If Megan hadn't been so possessed, so bloodthirsty for his death, she might have laughed at the look of amazement forever stamped on his face. But she turned him around and furiously plunged the Bowie into his shoulders and chest. Blood gurgled from his neck wound as the knife hit home again and again, sending more clouds of red fluid into the salt water. She struck repeatedly, each blow a payback for the abuse she had endured. So intent was Megan on making sure he was dead, she did not notice that they were sinking like two stones, deeper and deeper into the sea.

Finally, when a hand reached down and stopped her from plunging the knife in once more, she emerged from her frenzy long enough to understand the danger she was in if she didn't surface soon.

Guided by a pair of hands that pulled her closer and closer to the air, Megan kicked her feet and looked at the clear blue sky above the water. She could not tell who it was that was bringing her to safety and could only hope that the shots had not found their intended target.

When Megan reached the surface, she gulped down lungfuls of air and looked over at Delta, who had a steady stream of blood flowing down the side of her face. "I think I'm hit," Delta said, reaching for Megan, who stuffed the bowie in her belt before wrapping her arms around her lover.

"I've got you, sweetheart. Hang on." Megan slowly sidestroked both of them to the side of the boat, careful not to touch Delta's torn forehead.

Flora leaned over and helped Megan get Delta over the side. When Megan climbed in herself, she stopped abruptly, staring at the mayhem strewn about the deck. Sal had managed to bring Carducci up from the water and was putting direct pressure on his shoulder to keep him from bleeding to death. He looked pale and weak, but it appeared Sal had everything under control. But the sight that caught Megan's breath in her throat was Connie kneeling next to Gina, who was bleeding profusely from her femoral artery. Connie was trying unsuccessfully to slow the blood pouring from Gina's largest artery by applying direct pressure with both hands, but like a broken water pipe, the artery continued to pump a steady stream onto the deck of the boat.

"Delta!" Connie cried, wild-eyed and panic-stricken. "Help me!"

Delta coughed and sputtered, spitting salt water from her mouth. "Con?" When she focused enough to see Connie's bloody hands trying to prevent the pulsing blood from escaping, Delta ignored the pain in her head and scrambled over to them.

From years of experience, Delta knew a fatal gunshot wound when she saw one. Although Gina's eyes were still open and she was conscious, it was only a matter of time before the loss of blood meant the loss of her life.

Her life, and the life of the baby still inside her.

"Delta?" Gina said, reaching with her bloody hand.

Delta took Gina's hand and put it against her cheek. "I'm here, honey. You just hold on, now, you hear me." Delta felt Megan at her side, and also felt the tears and panic she knew were consuming Connie, who looked at Delta with an expression that nearly ripped her heart out.

"Help me, Delta," Connie pleaded weakly. "I can't stop the blood."

Delta turned from Connie and searched Gina's eyes. They had been friends for nearly ten years, and Delta loved Gina more than she could ever love a sister. Gina had been there for them, always understanding, always supportive, always courageous, even when she questioned Connie and Delta's motives.

And in that one instant, Delta loved Gina enough and understood her friend well enough to know exactly what Gina wanted from her.

Gina squeezed Delta's hand, her eyes pleading for Delta to do what Gina knew Connie would never be able to do. Turning from Delta, Gina focused on Connie, her blood continuing to pour from underneath Connie's hands.

"Honey," came Gina's soothing voice to Connie, who stared, glassy-eyed, at her lover and partner of twelve years. "Consuela, you have to listen to me."

Connie nodded like a little girl who didn't know what else to do.

"Are you listening to me?" Gina asked, reaching a bloody hand out to stroke Connie's cheek. "I need you right now. I need you to be my genius, to be Delta's common sense. Do you understand me?"

Delta and Megan looked at each other, both with tears in their eyes. Megan squatted next to Gina and held her other hand. She, too, knew what Gina was about to ask.

Connie shot Delta a frantic expression that pleaded for her to create a miracle, any miracle. But, Delta was out of miracles, and Gina was just about out of time. "Storm? Oh god, Delta, please...do something."

Delta brushed Connie's hair off her shoulders. "She's not going to make it, honey, and she needs you to listen to her right now."

Connie's eyes blinked hard, as if her mind just wouldn't register this.

"Gina needs you to hear her. Do you understand? There isn't much time." Delta looked at the amount of blood on the deck and wondered how Gina had stayed conscious this long.

Connie shook her head and turned to Gina. "Hang in there, sweetheart. You're going to make it. We're going..."

"No, Consuela, I'm not. Listen to me."

"But..."

Gina shook her head. "No buts, sweetheart." Grimacing from the pain, Gina squeezed Connie's hand hard. "Are you listening to me?"

Connie looked hard at her lover before nodding. "Okay."

Gina inhaled deeply and pulled Connie close enough to kiss her. "I love you. I have always loved you. You and no one else."

"Gina, don't...please..."

Delta touched Connie's shoulder lightly. "Listen to her, Chief."

Connie's face was inches from Gina's. "I love you, too," Connie whispered, her tears falling onto Gina's face.

Gina smiled. "You're the best part of my whole life, but my life's ending, sweetheart."

"No!"

Gina squeezed Connie's hand again. "Have I ever, even once, lied to you?"

Connie shook her head as tears ran down her face. "Never."

"I'm dying, sweetheart. You know as well as I do that you can't get me to a hospital fast enough to save me."

Connie was crying freely now, tears dripping down her cheeks. "Don't go. Please."

"You can't save me, sweetheart, but you can save our baby."

This rocked Connie, and it was the look in Gina's eyes that Delta had read and understood. Gina wanted them to deliver the baby before she died.

"Save the baby?" Connie asked, as if she didn't get that there were two lives at stake.

Gina nodded. "You have to deliver the baby before I go, or she'll die with me. Please, don't let her die."

The tears continued running off Connie's face as she began to comprehend the severity of the wound she was holding beneath her hands. Connie looked at Gina's bulging body and then back into her eyes. "I...I can't."

Gina wiped Connie's face. "Yes, you can. You have to, sweetheart. For me. For us. She's all you'll have of me after today." Gina's face had lost all color, her voice was slower and her eyelids heavier.

Delta looked over at Megan, who was also crying. When Megan saw Delta's expression, she nodded and pulled the Bowie from her belt.

"Honey, there isn't much time."

Connie stared at the knife as if she'd never seen one before. "I...can't, Megan. She's my lover, for Christ's sake!"

Gina's darkening eyes moved from Connie's face to Delta's. "Delta? Please. For me. For Connie. Save our baby."

Delta stared into Gina's face and slowly nodded. Turning to Megan, Delta took the Bowie from her in trembling hands. "You're sure this is what you want." It wasn't a question.

Gina nodded, her voice becoming even slower as her blood continued flowing through Connie's fingers. She gestured weakly." If you cut from here to here...about this deep...it will open like...a suitcase and you can... lift the baby right out." Gina was struggling for the strength to talk and breathe. "When you lift her out, tie off the umbilical."

Delta nodded, feeling her head begin to spin. Her own blood still dripped from her head wound, mixing with Gina's blood beneath her feet. Steadying the knife, Delta switched places with Megan, who knelt next to Connie and held Gina's other hand.

Gina was weakening, but she grasped Connie and Megan's hands with whatever strength she had left, inhaled a brave breath, and nodded to Delta, who lifted Gina's shirt and placed the shaking tip of the knife against her belly. Delta could kill a man in cold blood, she could have torn Zahn apart with her bare hands, but cutting open one of her best friends was the hardest thing she had ever had to do.

"Pretend... you're drawing with a red...felt-tipped pen, Delta," Gina instructed, smiling up at her friend. "And don't stop when I flinch. It will hurt less if you make... one swift cut."

Delta pressed the knife into Gina's belly and imagined exactly what Gina had told her to. As the knife slid through Gina's skin, Delta concentrated on not cutting too deeply. Sweat, tears, and blood blended and slid down Delta's face and arms as she finished cutting the last inch. Pulling the Bowie out, Delta glanced at Gina, who was chalky white now, her jaw clenched tightly.

"The...baby..."

Setting the knife down, Delta put her hands on either side of the incision and opened it up much like Gina had described, causing Gina to wince. "Sorry," Delta muttered, gently pushing the sides of the womb apart. When she did, there was a perfectly formed little girl, lying in Gina's womb, waiting for someone to get her.

"It's a girl," Delta whispered, reaching in and plucking the baby from Gina's body. "She's beautiful."

"Pre...mature," Gina said softly.

"But still beautiful, honey."

Connie, who hadn't taken her eyes off Gina's face, did not look at the baby until Delta placed her in Gina's arms. Megan's eyes beamed with a combination of intense pride and sadness at Delta, as one life gave way to another.

"She's...beautiful," Gina said, kissing the top of her baby's head. Connie wrapped her arms around mother and baby and kissed Gina's cold cheek. "I love you so much. Please don't go. I need you."

Gina swallowed hard, barely able to stay conscious now. The loss of blood was overwhelming. Only a love that deep could keep someone alive long enough to say their goodbyes. Delta and Megan rose and started to back away, but Gina's raised hand stopped them. "No...I need you...to hear...this."

Returning to the trio, Delta and Megan placed their hands on Connie, Gina, and the baby.

"Consuela, this...child needs you now. You have to...pull yourself together."

Connie heaved with sobs, unable to say anything.

Touching Delta's cheek, Gina smiled her last smile. "Keep taking...care of her, Delta...she needs you."

Tears running into the blood from her head wound, Delta nodded. "I promise."

Gina ran her fingers across Connie's mouth. "Take care of our child, sweetheart. She is our love."

"I will. I swear." Connie laid her head on Gina's chest, her arms wrapped tightly around her family.

As the last of Gina's life bled from her body, she looked up at Delta, kissed the top of the baby's forehead, mouthed, "Thank you." and died.

THIRTEEN

"Thanks for patching me up," Carducci said gazing down at the makeshift bandage on his shoulder. Carducci's wound was clean, as the bullet had gone straight through, and Flora had managed to bind his wound so it no longer bled.

After making sure Carducci's shoulder, Taylor's leg, and Delta's head were patched up for the moment, Megan's exhaustion hit her hard, and she sat propped on the deck next to Connie, who had not left Gina's side. Taylor, who had been carried by Megan up from the raft, had regained consciousness a half hour earlier and was surprised at the events she had missed. She immediately fell in love with the baby girl and had volunteered to hold her while Connie said her final good-byes to Gina's spirit.

Logan, unfortunately, was dead, killed by a shot to the back of his head. Apparently, Zahn felt he could control a boat full of women, but felt safer with the lone man dead. Megan placed his body next to Josh's on the deck of the boat and covered them both with a blue tarp.

Sal sat with Josh's body, alternating between tears and words, as she said her goodbyes to the man who had repaid her father by saving his daughter's life. With all of the death around them, the survivors were still thankful to be alive.

Delta had cleaned up the baby and wrapped her in one of the blankets in the boat before handing her to Taylor who, it seemed, had maternal instincts no one had guessed. After checking on the injured, Delta walked over to Flora and took both her hands. "It appears I owe you twice for saving my life, my friend."

Everyone on board stopped their goodbyes, their cooing, their prayers, and stared at Delta.

"You know each other?" Megan asked.

Grinning, Delta put her arm around Flora's shoulders. "If it wasn't for Flora, her grandmother, and her father, I'd be dead. Flora nursed me back to health after fishing me out of the water.

"Then, it isn't a coincidence that she showed up here?" Sal asked.

Lowering her eyes, Flora shook her head.

Megan rose and pulled Flora to her. "Thank you so much, Flora. You are a very courageous woman."

Blushing, Flora shook her head. "No, Delta is brave. She saved my family from..." Struggling to find the words, Flora blushed. "From bad men."

"Your father will be worried, no?" Delta asked, casting a glance at Connie, wishing Connie would interpret for her. But Connie would not leave Gina's side, and Delta would never ask her to.

"Thank you, Flora, for all of your help. If there is ever anything I can do for you and your family, just name it."

A huge smile spread across Flora's face. "Can you...help me to American school?"

Delta looked over at Megan, who nodded.

"I remember you telling me that's what you really wanted."

Flora nodded hopefully. "Si."

Delta wrapped her arms around her and squeezed her tightly. "Then American college it is."

After dropping Taylor, Carducci, and Connie and her child off at the emergency hospital where Siobhan and the other hostages had been left, Delta had her head quickly sewn up before joining Megan in the waiting room. Taking Megan's hand in hers, Delta just sat there quietly, and being thankful they were both alive. It was a long time before either of them spoke, and when they did, it was Megan who spoke first.

"Well, we made it."

Delta nodded, not looking at Megan. "Sort of. It's the shallowest victory I've ever felt."

Megan gripped Delta's hand tightly. "Think we'll ever recover?"

Delta shrugged. "I don't really know. I know we'll never be the same."

Megan sighed loudly. "I should never have left you. Should never have come down here."

Delta finally turned and looked at Megan. "Now isn't the time for second-guessing. Every one of us could be blaming ourselves for the choices we made, but in the end, though we're left with two of our best friends dead and the rest of us wearing physical and emotional scars for the rest of our lives, we are alive. This isn't your fault, Meg. This isn't anyone's fault."

Megan sighed again. "I feel so empty."

"I know. I feel it, too."

More time went by before Megan asked, "How's Connie?"

Delta shrugged. "I have no idea. I can't imagine the pain she's in."

Megan squeezed Delta's hand again. "I'm really proud of the way you delivered that baby. It was an incredibly brave thing to do."

Delta didn't respond to the compliment but sat and stared at the traffic outside. She had delivered a baby from the jaws of death but had been incapable of saving one of her best friends. She didn't know whether to laugh or cry, she felt so confused.

When the doctor came out, he wasn't wearing a white lab coat but sported a t-shirt and khaki pants. His dark hair was cut short, and his caramel skin had a hint of golfer's tan. Delta wondered if even Central American doctors played golf on Wednesdays.

"Your friend and the baby are fine," he said in slightly accented English. "But, did I understand her correctly? One of you delivered the baby by cesarean using a Bowie knife?"

Delta and Megan exchanged glances as they rose in unison. "Stranger things have happened, Doctor. Can we see them now?"

The doctor, appearing perplexed, nodded and pointed in the direction of the room they'd left Connie and the baby in.

"I've sedated your friend. She's suffering from emotional duress, so I thought that might calm her. The baby will have to stay with us for awhile, but your friend can sleep on the cot next to her."

Delta started for the door and then turned to the doctor. "Can you set up two more cots in there?"

Again the look of puzzlement. "I suppose so. Can I ask why?"

Delta nodded. "That's my god daughter in there."

"That's our family," Megan said, threading her arm through Delta's. And with heavy hearts and exhausted bodies, Delta and Megan joined a slumbering infant and Connie in the only place where Gina Tarabini existed for them now.

The next morning, after showering and eating the first real meal they'd had in days, Delta, Megan, and Sal talked Connie into leaving the baby for a short while so they could visit the others. As reluctant as Connie was to leave, Delta found it equally as hard. The baby, now all cleaned up and cared for, had a shock of jet-black hair covering her rosy skin. Connie had wanted a baby of Native American descent, and this one was a dandy. Her tiny fingers moved as if she was trying to play the piano, and she kept wriggling her way out of the blanket. For a preemie, this little girl was ready for life.

The night before, Delta had watched Connie watch the baby until her eyes could no longer stay open, and then Delta had put Connie to bed and watched the infant for her. This precious bundle of joy was her goddaughter. This was the little girl she would watch in school plays, listen to in school choirs, yell for during ball games, and cry for when seeing her off to the prom with some boy. This was a child brought into the world by two women who loved each other so much, that they had created a life with which to share that love. She was a wonderful joy to behold, and Delta made a promise to her that she would never let anything happen to her or her mother.

Never.

Shortly after the doctor had taken the baby for some tests, the four women entered Taylor's hospital room. Taylor was sitting up reading, a magazine and talking on the phone. When she saw them come in, she said her goodbyes to the person on the other end and hung up. Less than twenty-four hours had passed since they'd left her, and already she was looking 80 percent better.

"Where is that precious baby?"

"Sleeping, like you should be," Delta answered, walking over to Taylor and planting a kiss on the top of her head. "How're you feeling? You sure look better than last night."

Taylor grinned at her. "You're such a sweet talker. They pinned it, pumped some shit into me, and here I am. Only a little worse for wear. Doesn't look like I'll be leaping any tall buildings at a single bound any more."

"No? So you're retired for good?"

Taylor shrugged. "Unless you get yourself into another jam that I have to bail you out of."

"You can come stay with us," Megan offered.

The others exploded. "What?"

"Meg, she's wanted by just about every industrialized nation," Delta explained. "As much fun as it would be to have her around, she can't return to the States."

Taylor shook her head sadly. "I wish I could. I could sure use some friends like you guys to make my life more interesting." Taylor reached over and took Connie's hand, her cheery demeanor replaced by a more serious one. "I am so sorry for your loss."

Connie, who was still sedated, nodded before lifting the covers to look at Taylor's leg. Denial was now part of her grieving process, and Connie couldn't, she wouldn't talk about Gina. "I was afraid you might lose it."

Taylor shot a questioning glance over to Delta, who nodded that it was okay to have what appeared to be a normal conversation. One doesn't lose a lover and handle the onslaught of emotions within the first forty-eight hours. Connie would need time. Until then, she would act as if nothing bad had really happened.

"I would have lost it, but the doctors said whatever magic potion our new warrior woman put on the wound kept infection out."

Delta stroked Taylor's hair. "Ancient Bribri secret."

Taylor reached for Sal's hand and repeated her condolences. Sal's eyes welled up and she nodded, but that was all she could do.

"So, did everyone else sleep like a rock?" Taylor asked. "And how is that hunk named Carducci?"

Sal found her voice long enough to answer. "He's fine. The bullet went clean through. He'll be out this afternoon."

Taylor suddenly realized what this meant. She would not be getting out that quickly. Her leg was fractured in several places, and she wouldn't be leaving the hospital any time soon.

"I see. Well, I suppose you guys need to be heading back," she said in a voice of forced cheer.

Delta took her hand and gave it a quick squeeze. "After all we've been through, you still don't get it, do you?"

Taylor looked over at Megan, who grinned warmly. "What? Don't get what?"

"We're not leaving until all of us are okay to leave."

"But..."

"But nothing. We can't go home until the baby is ready, and even then, we're going to have to take a ship. So, don't you worry your little head, Taylor. You're stuck with us."

Taylor glanced over at Megan, who nodded. "You're part of our family now, Taylor."

Taylor's eyes teared up, and she impatiently wiped at them. "I'd really like that."

Megan grinned. "So would we."

As Sal and Connie approached the bed, they all looked at each other and saw the faces of strangers, women who would forever be changed by what had transpired in the middle of a jungle. Life would never be the same for any of them, and as an uneasy quiet filled the hospital room, Delta wondered if the baby down the hall would ever experience friendships like the one binding everyone in this room.

She certainly hoped so.

More books to Stir the Imagination
From Rising Tide Press

FEATHERING YOUR NEST: An Interactive Workbook& Guide to a
Loving Lesbian Relationship
Gwen Leonhard, M.ED./Jennie Mast, MSW $14.99
This fresh, insightful guide and workbook for lesbian couples provides
effective ways to build and nourish your relationships. Includes fun
exercises & creative ways to spark romance, solve conflict, fight fair,
conquer boredom, spice up your sex lives.

TROPICAL STORM $11.99
Linda Kay Silva
Another winning, action-packed adventure featuring smart and sassy
heroines, an exotic jungle setting, and a plot with more twists and turns
than a coiled cobra. Megan has disappeared into the Costa Rican rain
forest and it's up to Delta and Connie to find her. Can they reach
Meagan before it's too late? Will Storm risk everything to save the
woman she loves? Fast-paced, full of wonderful characters and
surprises. Not to be missed.

STORM RISING $12.00
Linda Kay Silva
The excitement continues in this wonderful continuation of *TROPICAL
STORM*. Another incredible adventure through the magnificent rain
forest leaves the reader breathless! The bond that connects Storm and
Connie, shines through the most difficult challenges. This story gives
the reader an incredible ride of adventures in the physical and spiritual
dimensions.

AGENDA FOR MURDER $11.99
Joan Albarella
A compelling mystery about the legacies of love and war, set on a
sleepy college campus. Though haunted by memories of her tour of
duty in Vietnam, Nikki Barnes is finally putting back the pieces of her
life, only to collide with murder and betrayal.

CALLED TO KILL $12.00
Joan Albarella
Nikki Barnes, Reverend, teacher and Vietnam Vet is once again
entangled in a complex web of murder and drugs when her past
collides with the present. Set in the rainy spring of Buffalo, Dr. Ginni
Clayton and her friend Magpie add spice and romance as Nikki tries to
solve the mystery that puts her own life in danger. A fun and exciting
read.

SIDE DISH $11.99
Kim Taylor
She's funny, she's attractive, she's lovable – and she doesn't know it.
Meet Muriel, aka Mutt, a twenty- something wayward waitress with a
college degree, who has resigned herself to low standards, simple
pleasures, and erotic fantasies. Though seeming to get by on margaritas
and old movies, in her heart, Mutt is actually searching for true love.
While Mutt chases the bars with her best friend, Jeff, she is, in turn,
chased by Diane, a former college classmate with a decidedly romantic
agenda. When rich, seductive Beverly Hills lawyer named Allison
steals Mutt's heart, she is in for trouble, and like the glamorous façade
of Sunset Boulevard, things are not quite as they seem. A delightfully
funny read.

COMING ATTRACTIONS $11.99
Bobbi D. Marolt
It's been three years since she's made love to a woman; three years that
she's buried herself in work as a successful columnist for one of New
York's top newspapers. Helen Townsend admits, at last, she's tired of
being lonely…and of being closeted. Enter Princess Charming in the
shapely form of Cory Chamberlain, a gifted concert pianist. And Helen
embraces joy once again. But can two lovers find happiness when one
yearns to break out of the closet and breathe free, while the other fears it
will destroy her career? A sunny blend of humor, heart and passion. A
novel which captures the bliss and blundering of love.

AND LOVE CAME CALLING $11.99
Beverly Shearer
The rough and ready days of the Old West come alive with the timeless
story of love between two women: Kenny Smith, a stage coach driver in
Jackson, Colorado and Sophie McLaren, a young woman forced to
marry, then widowed. The women meet after Kenny is shot by bandits
during a stage coach holdup. And love blooms when Sophie finds
herself the unexpected rescuer of the good-looking wounded driver.

HOW TO ORDER

TITLE	AUTHOR	PRICE
☐ Agenda for Murder	Joan Albarella	11.99
☐ And Love Came Calling	Beverly Shearer	11.99
☐ Called to Kill	Joan Albarella	12.00
☐ Coming Attractions	Katherine Kreuter	11.99
☐ Danger! Cross Currents	Sharon Gilligan	9.99
☐ Danger in High Places	Sharon Gilligan	9.95
☐ Deadly Gamble	Diane Davidson	11.99
☐ Deadly Rendezvous	Diane Davidson	9.99
☐ Dreamcatcher	Lori Byrd	9.99
☐ Emerald City Blues	Jean Stewart	11.99
☐ Feathering Your Nest	Leonhard/Mast	14.99
☐ Heartstone and Saber	Jaqui Singleton	10.99
☐ Isis Rising	Jean Stewart	11.99
☐ Love Spell	Karen Williams	9.95
☐ Nightshade	Karen Williams	11.99
☐ No Escape	Nancy Sanra	11.99
☐ No Witness	Nancy Sanra	11.99
☐ Playing for Keeps	Stevie Rios	10.99
☐ Return to Isis	Jean Stewart	9.99
☐ Rough Justice	Claire Youmans	10.99
☐ Shadows After Dark	Ouida Crozier	9.95
☐ Side Dish	Kim Taylor	11.99
☐ Storm Rising	Linda Kay Silva	12.00
☐ Sweet Bitter Love	Rita Schiano	10.99
☐ Tropical Storm	Linda Kay Silva	11.99
☐ Warriors of Isis	Jean Stewart	11.99
☐ You Light the Fire	Kristen Garrett	9.95

Please send me the books I have checked. I have enclosed a check or money order (not cash], plus $4 for the first book and $1 for each additional book to cover shipping and handling. Or bill my Visa/Mastercard

Card #_____Exp.

Date_____

Name (please
print)_____Signature_____

Address_____

City _____State_____Zip_____

AZ residents, please add 7% tax to total.

RISING TIDE PRESS, 3831 N. ORACLE RD., TUCSON AZ 85705

Or visit our website, www.risingtidepress.com